The Witches
of
Hibbard Corners

Book I in The Saga of The Ice Bear

By

Douglas Ewan Cameron

W&B Publishers
USA

W & B Publishers

For information:
W & B Publishers
Post Office Box 193
Colfax, NC 27235
www.a-argusbooks.com

ISBN: 978-0-6159641-1-9
ISBN: 0-6159641-1-7

Book Cover designed by Diane Evans

Printed in the United States of America

Acknowledgements

Authors are often asked where their inspiration comes from. In the case of this story, it was a February 2013 local author booking signing at the Barnes & Noble in Montrose, Ohio. There were at least twelve authors there and we were seated at long tables, three authors to a table. I was seated next to a very interesting lady name Sherri Brake (www.HauntedHistory.net) who had recently married and was now living in West Virginia. She writes historic books about haunted mansions, prisons, etc. and often leads tour groups, sometimes staying overnight in the place of interest. I was telling her about my yet to be published third book entitled *Muddy Waters,* which I hoped would find fans in the young adult population. Her response was that if I wanted young adult readers I needed to write about vampires or werewolves. Not to put down those genres, but I had no interest in either but her idea kept reactivating itself in my head. Finally I thought 'Witches, now there is an interesting idea'. That thought continued to ferment in my mind and suddenly, 'Four witches having a summoning out on an ice covered lake in the middle of the night when suddenly …' You'll have to read the book to find out the rest. As you read this, please remember that the Legend of the Ice Bear is my creation and is not a true Chippewa Legend.

I didn't know much about witches and so read several books, most notably three: *The Witches' Book of the Dead* by Christian Day, Red Wheel/Weiser, LLC, San Francisco CA, 2011 (Kindle Edition) which was invaluable in preparing Ingrid Swartz's altar; *The Book of Witches (The Paranormal)* by Oliver Madox Hueffer, F+W Media, Inc., (Kindle Edition); and *The Witches Book of Spells* - (Revised Edition) by Roc Marten, PDP Publications, 2012 (Kindle Edition), from which I used both of the protection spells used by Ingrid Schwartz. *The Mide'wiwin or "Grand Medicine Society" of the Ojibwa / Seventh Annual Report of the Bureau of Ethnology to the / Secretary of the Smithsonian Institution* by Walter James Hoffman, Government Printing Office, Washington, 1891 (Kindle Version) from which I took the story of the Mide'wiwin as told by Rachel Whitehorse to Jennifer Wilson. The details of the birth of Feebee's fawn were gathered from *The Deer of North America* By Leonard Lee Rue III. This source I found on the web thanks to Jennifer Kleitch, Wildlife Biologist with the Michigan Department of Natural Resources.

At the end of the book when the coven of witches is assembled, several of those are women I know from Hubbard Lake whom I asked to use their names and they agreed.

There are several individuals I want to thank:

❖ George Roy of the Saginaw Chippewa Tribal College (http://sagchip.edu) for bringing my Ice Bear Ritual Chant to life in Ojibwemowin, the language of the Chippewa (the Anglicized version of Ojibwe). The Chippewa/Ojibwe call themselves "Anishinaabe" (singular form) or "Anishinaabeg" (plural form).

❖ Diane Evans of Alpena MI for the cover. She is a

wizard with CGI.

❖ Chris Wright, a diver with the Hammond Bay Bio-
logical Center for help with the recovery of the
body and meteor from the depths of Hibbard Pond.
He was previously an Alcona County Deputy Sheriff and a founding member of the Alcona County
Dive Rescue team.

❖ Irene Herrmann of Hubbard Lake, MI, for helping
Ingrid do sewing machine embroidery correctly.

❖ Andy Durkee of Hubbard Lake, MI, for his ren-
derings of the buildings (which also appear on
the cover of the book) in Spruce MI for the map
of Hibbard Corners. The funeral home is the
Spruce Presbyterian Church, the post office is the
Spruce Post Office, the Hibbard Corners General
Store is the Spruce General Store (now out of
business) and the front of Helen's Hair Quarters
is Heather's House of Hair in Lincoln MI, the library is the former Thompson's Sales & Service
currently located in Alpena (thanks to Helen
Timm of Spruce for that piece of information.)

❖ My wife Nancy Calhoun Cameron and my Up
North neighbor Mary von Zittwitz for their
proofreading.

❖ Most especially David Buchthal, former colleague
at The University of Akron and long time friend,
for the final editing of the manuscript.

And as I will do in all my books (you can skip it if
you've read it before) I must acknowledge two writers who
have influenced my work. First (and only chronologically)

is Mary Higgins Clark whom I heard speak at a Book and Author Luncheon sponsored by *The Plain Dealer* of Cleveland OH. She said that many of her works got their genesis with the words "What if."

The other writer is the late Philip R. Craig, author of the Martha's Vineyard based J.W. Jackson mysteries. My wife and I met he and his wife Shirley on a riverboat trip from Constanta, Romania to Amsterdam, Netherlands in 2005 and shared many a happy meal together including my wife's birthday dinner. He told me that in his writing, while he knew the story line, he often didn't know how it was going to come out and let the characters lead him. Often that is what I do, and I did in this book.

To Sherri Brake
www.HauntedHistory.net
who inspired this story

TO THE READER

If you are new to my books, welcome.

If you are a reader of my Up North books you might find it a little strange and I introduce witches and their magic into a "normal" setting. First, the main characters in this book do not and will not (at least to any great extent) appear in my other books centered around Hibbard Pond. Second, if it bothers you, then please just consider this is another time continuum and be content with that. I think you will enjoy this book.

Also, I must reiterate that *The Legend of the Ice Bear* is my creation. It is not a Chippewa legend and to my knowledge there is none like it.

The Legend of the Ice Bear

The old bear had been awakened from his winter's hibernation by hunger more than by the early thaw. The slowness that comes with advanced age had prevented him from adequately preparing for his long winter nap. Now with his stomach aching for food, he was searching the ice-covered stream, looking for an opening through which he might be able to find food. Several hours of searching had brought him out of the deep woods where he had made his cave at the base of a huge white pine to within sight of the ice-covered lake. There he found the opening he sought and sat watching. Before long a huge fish appeared and paused in the opening seeming to be enjoying the sun. With a quick flick of his paw, the old bear scooped the fish out of the water and onto the ice where it flopped, struggling to find its watery home, until the bear put his paw on it.

The old bear picked the fish up in his mouth and was about to crush it when he heard a sound that made him stop and look. About ten feet away on the bank sat a young bear barely a year old. It, too, was thin from hunger and the old bear sensed that its mother, who should have been caring for it, was probably with the Great Spirit. Knowing that the young bear would soon die without having a chance for a full life like the one he had lived, the old bear crushed the fish's head and then tossed it toward the young bear. The young bear watched the fish land on the ice and slide toward him, stopping at his feet. Looking at the old bear, the young bear seized the fish, raised itself on his hind feet, took hold of the fish's body with both front paws and tore the head off the fish. The old bear watched as the young bear devoured the fish and then turned from the fishing hole and headed down the stream toward the ice of the big lake. Reaching the lake, the old bear turned and looked back. The young bear was sitting at the hole and suddenly stuck its paw into the water and flipped another fish onto the ice, eagerly chasing after it and stopping it with a paw. The old bear seemed to nod in satisfaction knowing that the young bear was going to survive and headed out onto the lake's ice intending to cross to the other side.

It was a big lake and the old bear was desperately in need of food. Halfway across, over the deepest part of the lake, its energy waned and the bear stopped to rest. It curled up trying to stay warm and fell asleep. The daylight passed into darkness and the bear slumbered, its energy sapped by the cold of the wind and the ice. Gichi-Manidoo (Gih-chee-Muh-nih-doh), the Great Spirit, had been watching the bear all day and in the early morning hours knew that the bear was going to die and its spirit would join him in the sky. But he was impressed by the bear's thoughtfulness to help the young bear survive.

"Wake up, old bear," Gichi-Manidoo said.

The old bear awoke and stood up, looking at the Gichi-Manidoo who had assumed the form of a white bear.

"Is it time for me to join you?" the old bear asked.

"No," replied the Gichi-Manidoo. "It will be a long time before you join me. You have others to help in their time of need. I want you to stay here in this lake and when someone in need calls, you will help them."

"But how can I stay here in this lake?" the old bear said. "I am old and cannot last in the water very long."

The Gichi-Manidoo waved its paw and the old bear shivered and felt strange. He raised a paw in front of him and saw that it was ice. He turned his head and looked at his body and saw that it was ice. Then he looked at the Gichi-Manidoo who smiled knowingly.

"The water here is deep and cold," Gichi-Manidoo said. "You can live in the depths during the summer and come up on the ice when summoned."

"But I could melt in the sun," the Ice Bear said.

"You will only come up in the middle of the night when it is cold and the ice is thin as it is tonight," said the Great Spirit, striking the ice in front of him and making a hole in the ice. "Now go."

The Ice Bear bowed in recognition of the power and wisdom of the Gichi-Manidoo, but when he rose, Gichi-Manidoo was gone. One last look around and the Ice Bear slipped into the icy water and swam to the bottom of the lake where he made his home in the depths.

THE ICE BEAR RITUAL SUMMONING CHANT

Je•jii•baan O•jib•we a•kiing nda nji•baa•mi, bgo•se•ndi•mi•go•yin wii wii•doo•koo•yaang.

From all over the Ojibwe land we are from, asking your help.

Mko•mii-ma•kwa, kiin ge•chi-pii•te•ndaa•go•zi•yin, bi-di•shi•shnaang, mii•nzhi•naang nbwaa•kaa•win.

Ice Bear, you of greatness, come visit us, give us your wisdom.

ANISHINAABEMOWIN SOUNDS[1]
Ojibwe Vowel Sounds Equivalent to the Boldface English Sounds

ENGLISH WORD	SAMPLE OJIBWE WORD
"**a**" as in n**u**t	s**a**b – net
"**aa**" as in c**au**ght	n**aa** –nan – five
"**i**" as in p**i**n	nz**i**d – my foot
"**ii**" as in b**ee**t	g**ii**n – you
"**o**" as in l**oo**k	ni m**o**sh – dog
"**oo**´as in m**oo**n	g**oo**n – snow
"**e**" as in g**e**t	kw**e** - woman

Consonants: The following English consonants are used. (ch, sh, and zh) are considered as consonants in the Ojibwe language.

B D G J Z ZH P T K CH S SH M N W Y

Letters of the alphabet not used include: X, L, R, F, & Q (K can be used for Q)

---

[1] George Roy of the Saginaw Chippewa Tribal College told me "Anishinaabemowin is 'The Language Of The People' the people being the 'Anishinaabe.' The Anishshinaabeg (plural for Anishinaabe) comprising of many different Tribes, ex. the: Ojibwe; Odaawa; Potwaatomii... around the Great Lakes area/region. These three major Tribes and other sub-tribes identified themselves as the 'Anishinaabe/Anishinaabeg' and shared a common language called 'Anishinaabemowin' with tribal derivations. Therefore the Ojibwes call their particular language 'Ojibwemowin.' Thus we identify the common language as Anishinaabemowin or Ojibwemowin."

Chapter 1

Just after two o'clock in the morning, the Witch of the North and the Witch of the East came onto the ice just south of the Loon Creek Inn. It was closed for the winter, so their cars could be parked there with no problem and not be seen. At approximately the same time, the Witch of the West and the Witch of the South came onto the ice from Timber Point. Basically closed for the season, there was a caretaking couple who lived there year round, but they were away on a well-deserved two-week cruise. If they had been in residence, the two witches would have parked their cars off the entry road and walked through the property to the lake. Instead they had parked very close to the lake. Like the witches of the North and East, they were tied together with a thirty-foot nylon rope, an end knotted around the waist of each one. The Michigan DNR (Department of Natural Resources) had issued its "Ice Unsafe" warning two weeks ago and all the fishing shanties had been pulled. The four witches knew the ice was unsafe, but it was the proper time and they had no choice. The day and hour was decreed by the Legend of the Ice Bear.

Despite the fact that the sky was partly cloudy and the moon was in its wane, the two groups showed no lights other than the dim blue screens of their smart phones used in GPS mode to be guided to their goal. The coordinates of their target had been set in the middle of the summer on a boat ride by the Witch of the East. It was over the hole that was the deepest part of Hibbard Pond: 110 feet. They moved slowly with the lead witch of each group poking the ice in front of her with the handle of a broom. And it was no ordinary broom because, of course, these were not ordinary witches. These were Besoms with handles of oak limbs cut live and bark removed. The bristles were thin branches of Birch trees that abound on the shores of Hibbard Pond and tied to the oak handle with ropes made from natural materials. Each group's path was not straight because weak ice was constantly encountered. Accordingly the journeys took close to an hour, giving them an hour to prepare and the preparations were numerous. While the lead witch carried a broom in one hand and smart phone in the other, the trailing witches carried the burden of necessary accessories. Following The Witch of the North, The Witch of the East carried metal buckets. In her left hand, she had two buckets nested together with the top one containing a two-gallon zipper freezer bag with four cloths soaked in kerosene. In her right hand, she carried two nested buckets with the top one containing six spray paint cans: two large red and four small gold. The Witch of the South, who followed the Witch of the West, carried a gas-powered ice auger and that required her to use both hands. To see them crossing the lake you would have believed they were witches because they wore black robes with bell sleeves and hoods that they had pulled up over their heads for warmth. Yet except for the color of the robes they could easily have been monks because of the similarity of the robes. They were two strange looking pairs: in both cases the lead witch was tall, the Witch of the North being five foot ten inches and the Witch of the West five foot eight. However, the Witch of the East was five foot two and weighed only a hundred pounds, yet she bore her load like a trooper. The Witch of the South was taller by four inches but weighed a good one hundred fifty pounds more.

Finally reaching their goal, they put down their burdens and three of them unfastened the safety ropes that had connected them. Then the Witch of the North stood on the ice above the deep hole of Hibbard Pond holding in her hand one end of a thirty-foot rope. The Witch of the East had kept the other end tied around her waist and she swept the ice clear of snow and debris as she walked counterclockwise in the circle dictated by the rope. When the first circuit had been completed, the broom was replaced by a spray can of red paint and a second circuit completed, moving clockwise this time, marking the circle. Once this was done, the other two witches used the brooms to clear the ice and snow from the inside of the circle just marked.

The area cleared, guided by her GPS, the Witch of the North moved to the exact northeast point of the circle and moving southwest marked her path with red spray paint while the Witch of the East did the same southeast to northwest. Then a small circle with a five-foot radius was made at the center, and two diameters made in the small circle, one north to south and the other west to east. Then the northeast point on the big circle was connected to the east on the small circle and the east on the small circle to southeast on the large and continuing until a four point star had been made.

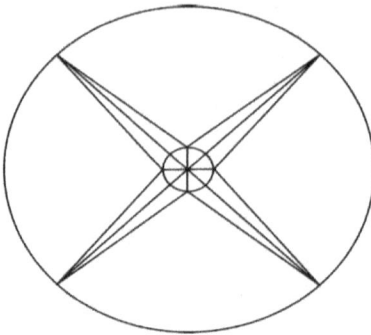

Then each of the witches used a spray can of gold paint to make strange rune-like words in the four open areas of the large circle outside the star. This work was all completed in a half hour. Then the Witch of the South used an ice auger to drill holes in the center of the circle and at the northeast, southeast, southwest and northwest points of the large circle. Each of the witches put a metal bucket containing a kerosene soaked rag into an outer circle hole. In this entire process, no areas of thin ice had been encountered but this was expected. After all, this rite had been preordained.

With ten minutes to go before the anointed time, the four witches gathered outside the circle to drink from bottles of water they had carried with them in pockets under the cloaks and to share tokes of a spliff (a marijuana cigarette rolled with some tobacco in it for better burning). Then feeling sufficiently fortified (although the South Witch would have traded the spliff for a pint of vodka), each witch took her place just outside the circle and watched her smart-phone. The North Witch was at the northeast point, East Witch at the southeast, and so on. Precisely at 3:20 an alarm sounded on each phone and the witches each used a butane charcoal lighter to ignite the kerosene rags in her bucket. At 3:23 they began to chant the words that appeared on the screens of the smart phones:

Je•jii•baan O•jib•we a•kiing nda nji•baa•mi,

bgo•se•ndi•mi•go•yin wii wii•doo•koo•yaang.

Mko•mii-ma•kwa, kiin ge•chi-pii•te•ndaa•go•zi•yin,

bi-di•shi•shnaang, mii•nzhi•naang nbwaa•kaa•win.

While these were words most people could not understand, they were not the kind of words that people would expect witches to say – rather they were Ojibwe, an Algonquian language spoken by the Chippewa Indians of Upper Michigan. They were words of an ancient ritual derived from the Chippewa Legend of the Ice Bear.

Each of them was so intent on the recitation that the Witch of the North almost didn't hear the faint boom that emanated from the darkness above them. For her the ritualistic chant had been memorized and she was able to move her eyes from the smart-phone to the skies above her without ever missing a beat. What she saw there brought terror to her heart. She had expected an emanation coming as a result of the ritual, but through the hole in the center of the circle, the one not filled with a metal bucket containing a burning kerosene soaked rag. But she had not expected to see a fiery ball plummeting earthward from the dark night sky and heading straight for them.

Chapter 2

"Run for your lives," the North Witch shouted pointing skyward as she turned away from the circle and took off running toward the distant shore. The other three did the same without even bothering to look skyward. None of them had taken more than five steps when the meteor struck the ice. Had the center hole drilled a foot further to the north-northeast, it was possible that the meteor would have hit water and possibly not had the impact that it did. But that was not the case and the meteor, smaller than a basketball but larger than a softball, hit the ice traveling over two hundred miles a minute. The impact caused an explosion of the ice that propelled the four witches skyward and outward in the directions of their flights. Perhaps by some spiritual intervention, they would think later, three of them hit solid ice and, though momentarily stunned, were able to get up, orient themselves, and continue their wild dashes away from disaster and toward the nearest solid land. The Witch of the East was not as fortunate, hitting thin ice head first knocking her unconscious as her body crashed through the ice and traveled many feet underwater. The shock of the icy cold near thirty-two degrees water shocked her heart to stillness and her lifeless body, weighted down by her quickly water-soaked clothes, sank to the bottom of Hibbard Pond.

West Witch found herself behind the plodding South Witch, who was following their earlier tracks. Scared to death by the explosion, West Witch wanted nothing more than to get off the ice, so she took a detour around South Witch. As she ran across untested ice, she heard it crack from three consecutive steps but dared not stop because she knew she would go under. Passing South Witch, she got back on their trail knowing that it was safe because of South Witch's size. Reaching shore, she turned around to be certain that South Witch was okay and surprisingly found her only ten feet from shore. Casting a quick glance across the landscape from which they had come, she saw that the area where they had been chanting was covered with mist. She turned and continued her flight to her car. When South Witch reached shore she didn't stop her head-long flight, but continued her steady plodding run to the warmth and safety of her van.

North Witch followed her prior track easily and reached shore several minutes after West Witch and South Witch who had a shorter distance to travel. On solid ground she, like West Witch, turned and looked back and also saw just a white mist covering the area of their ritual. She scanned the lake's icy surface but could see no trace of the East Witch. She tried calling the East Witch on her smart-phone but it went immediately to voice mail. After a last look out at the lake desperately hoping to see East Witch running toward her, she left the shore and went to the parking lot of the Loon Creek Inn.

Neither North Witch nor West Witch was close enough to the ritual site to be able to discern the form that appeared to pull itself up out of the water. Once on the ice floes, the beast shook itself and fragments of ice flew everywhere. The animal appeared to be a white bear smaller than a polar bear, but a closer look would have revealed that it was, in fact, clear ice with red flashing eyes. In its mouth was a huge fish of undeterminable species. The Ice Bear, for it was indeed that bear of Chippewa legend, looked around for whosoever had summoned it from its icy depths. Seeing no one, it tossed the fish into the air, adroitly catching it by the head as it fell back to earth. Two huge bites and the fish was gone. The mist, caused by combination of the extreme heat of the meteor and the icy cold of the air and water, was starting to dissipate. Looking around once more and seeing no summoners, the Ice Bear shook itself again and then silently slipped back into the water and disappeared.

Mentally crossing her fingers, the North Witch reached for the door of East Witch's car and then stopped herself. *Fingerprints,* she thought. She used her cape as a glove and tried the handle. The door opened. *Halfway home*, she thought breathing a sigh of relief. Picking up the floor mat and seeing nothing on the carpet under it, her good feelings plummeted. They had agreed to leave their vehicles unlocked and the keys under the floor mat just in case something like this happened. They hadn't expected an attack from the heavens, but more likely the ice giving way and, despite their being roped together, one of them drowning. *Certainly that was most likely what happened to East Witch anyway*. Then, North Witch reached up and pulled down the visor forgetting all about fingerprints. Something brushed past her hand, hit the seat with a soft plop and a jingle. The keys!

North Witch pulled out her smart-phone she had thrust into a pants pocket during her flight and called West Witch.

"You both make it?" she asked.

"Yes, South Witch just got into her van. What about East Witch?"

"She didn't make it!"

"What happened?"

"I DON'T KNOW," North Witch screamed and then got hold of herself.

"Sorry. I need your help. I'll drive East Witch's car home and you pick me up and bring me back."

"Certainly," and West Witch broke the connection.

North Witch went to her car and took off her cape and put it inside. She put on a winter jacket she had left on the back seat and a pair of work gloves she had in case she needed to change a tire or something. Returning to East Witch's van, she started it and drove out of the parking lot and onto the road leading to North Hibbard Pond Path, driving without lights until she neared The Path as the locals called it. All the way halfway around the lake, she thankfully didn't encounter another vehicle, but not many people were out at four in the morning. Turning down East Witch's street, she turned the lights off again and only activated East Witch's garage door when she turned into the short driveway. She was thankful that the garage was not attached and nobody in the house would hear it. The house across the street was dark so nobody was probably up to notice, but she hit the opener button as soon as the car was passed the garage door sensors. Putting the keys back behind the visor thinking East Witch might keep them there, she got out of the car and closed its door. She turned the garage door opener light off on the pad by the access door before opening it and left the garage, quickly and quietly closing the door behind her. Walking quickly she was back at East Hibbard Pond Path just as West Witch arrived. She got into the car and West Witch made a U-turn and headed back toward Loon Creek Inn.

"What happened?" West Witch asked.

"A meteor, I think," North Witch said. "All I saw was a fiery ball."

"Did we cause that?"

North Witch looked at her incredulously and laughed.

"Maybe real witches could," North Witch replied.

West Witch looked at her with distain. *Maybe real witches could?* she thought.

Chapter 3

She was cold. Colder than she had ever been in her life. She reached to pull a blanket up but there weren't any. *Was the furnace broken? It hadn't supposed to be that cold. What a night for her father to be away! What time was it?* Through half opened eyes she looked at the clock. 4:12. She closed her eyes to go back to sleep but her sleepy brain nudged her. *What?* she thought. Then the light dawned – literally, as a soft light from somewhere had lit the bedroom. And there was a voice. A soft, yet almost chilling, voice. A voice that was vaguely familiar. *Jennifer. Jennifer,* the voice was calling. She sat up and looked at the foot of her bed and became instantly awake.

What she had seen was a glowing white mist rising beyond the foot of the bed. A slowly swirling white mist from which that voice emanated – *Jennifer*. She was frightened yet intrigued. She watched as the mist seemed to coalesce into a truly ghostly shape. It was a person. A woman. Dressed in a long robe. The robe had big sleeves and a hood that was pulled up over the head and concealed the face of … the woman. She was certain that it was a woman.

"Who are you?" Jennifer asked in a quaking voice as she tried to hide her fear.

In answer to that question, the figure raised her hands to the hood and pushed it back.

"Mother!" Jennifer screamed and started scrambling to get out of the bed.

"No, my dear Jennifer," her mother's spirit said. "Stay there. You cannot touch me for I am not here."

Jennifer sat back, pulling the covers up around her.

"You are not here?"

"No, I am … dead."

"NO," Jennifer screamed. "YOU CAN'T BE DEAD!"

"It was an accident."

"Where? When?"

"Tonight on Hibbard Pond."

"On the lake? But there's ice!"

"Calm yourself, my daughter," her mother's spirit said. "I don't have much time. The Ice Bear has granted me this final wish, but I only have a moment."

"The Ice Bear?"

Tears began flowing and Jennifer couldn't stop them but she listened to her mother. Gladys's spirit told her of the events of the night.

"But the others?" Jennifer said. "Were you the only one who died?"

"Yes, the others were lucky."

"They should be dead, too," Jennifer said that in a way that one could sense she wanted them dead in retribution for her mother's death.

"No, Jennifer, there is no reason for them to die. But you need to watch for one of them because I don't trust her."

"Who?"

"The West Witch."

"Who's she?"

"Ingrid Swartz."

"She's a witch?"

"As much as I am."

"A witch? You're not a witch."

"Yes, I am. I have been all my life and so are you."

"Me. I have no powers."

"Until tonight your powers have been latent, but with my passing they have been unlocked sooner than ordinarily expected."

"What powers?"

"You will learn all in good time. For now you must heed my warning. Beware the West Witch for she will try to kill you."

"Kill me? But she's your friend."

"Yes, but she has evil inside her. I have sensed it recently."

"But the other two?"

"They are harmless. They have no powers."

"But you and she do?"

"Yes. Mine are only used for good, hers I am afraid are going to be used for evil unless she is careful. That is why you need to watch. I need you to protect North Witch and South Witch."

"Me? I have no powers." Jennifer could not believe what her mother was saying.

"Yes, you do. I have watched these powers develop as you have grown but they are hidden within and you have not learned how to use them."

"Powers, inside me? How do I …"?

"That will come with time, my child. My time grows short, so listen carefully. You will be granted some limited powers to use until my friends are safe from the West Witch. When you need them, you will know what they are and how to use them."

"But who are the other witches?"

The question was not to be answered that night as the mist was beginning to swirl again and her mother's image to disintegrate. Jennifer felt her eyelids start to droop.

"But for now you need to sleep. You will not remember this conversation until you know that I am dead."

"But …"

"Sleep, my darling daughter."

And the room went black. Suddenly at peace and very sleepy, Jennifer laid down pulled the cover up, and once pleasantly warm drifted off into sleep again.

Chapter 4

The West Witch was so mad when she got home, she knew that she couldn't sleep and needed to talk to someone. The only problem was that the person she wanted to talk to was dead! So she went downstairs to the family room that had a glass wall almost across its entire width permitting a beautiful view of the ice-covered Hibbard Pond. This was not the view she particularly wanted tonight but there wasn't much she could do about it. Wanting privacy for what she was about to do, she pulled the curtains across the door wall blocking the view of the ice-covered lake.

The nerve of the North Witch to say that they weren't real witches, she thought. *Well, maybe the North and South Witches weren't but she and East Witch were.* That thought made her pause and collect her thoughts. *The East Witch had been a real witch. Not as powerful as I am, but she had the power.*

With that thought in her mind, she pushed the glass-topped coffee table off the braided rug. Ordinarily she might have found this difficult, but the energy she felt made it easy. Then she rolled up the large braided rug starting at the lake end of the room. As it rolled back, a stunning inlaid pattern was seen in the oak flooring that her husband Karl had done before his passing over the veil last spring. He had been a true craftsman and had done the re-modeling of the family room himself. Unlike so many others whose remodeling projects seem to take forever, Karl never wasted any time. He had begun the project a year before his death, six months before they had discovered the cancer in his pancreas. They had both known when they heard the news that there was nothing to be done. Survival rates for this form of cancer were low and his was far-gone when it was discovered. A year before that time, treatments might have prolonged Karl's life at least two years but at his stage there wasn't much hope. He had continued his work; at that point he was getting ready to do the inlay of her symbols. He thought it was silly but he was always willing to humor her and it was the kind of challenge in which he reveled. *If he had only known,* she thought. *Well, he does now and had from the first time she had tried to summon his spirit after his death.*

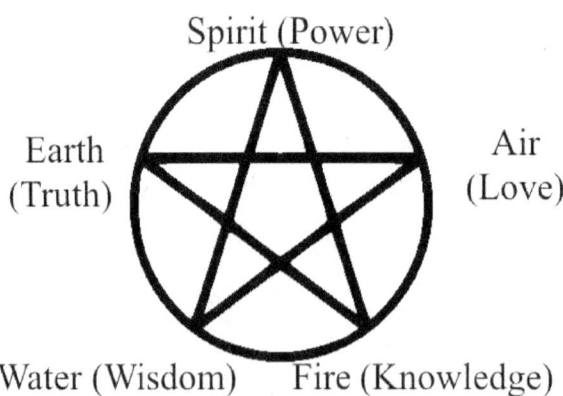

He had known about the pentagram, the five-pointed star whose points represent the five Wiccan elements:

Wind, Water, Earth, Fire, and Spirit. He had laughed about those as being so similar to the old Greek ideas: Air, Water, Earth, Fire, and Ether. What he hadn't known (and she hadn't bothered to tell him) was that each of them had a meaning. The twelve o'clock or top point was Spirit and represented power. Clockwise from there were Air representing Love, Fire representing Knowledge, Water representing Wisdom and Earth representing Truth. She had asked him to inlay the pentagram in a circle, thus making it a Pentacle. It hadn't been easy but he had done it, inlaying all the images in ebony. She had explained to him that the Pentacle was known as the "Endless Knot" and should always be drawn with one continuous motion. So with great pains (and at that point the pain was also physical but keep mostly in check by drugs and her magic, she liked to think) he had made the pieces and then inlaid them in the grooves he had routed in one continuous motion. It had taken a lot of planning and the routing had not been done all at once but had been done as though in one continual motion as he had promised. Then the pieces had been inlaid without use of glue and as much as he could do it following the order of that one continuous motion. After he had inlaid the pieces, he covered the floor with five coats of polyurethane with the final coat polished to a high sheen. He hadn't questioned the fact that the pentagram was inverted when one looked at it from the stairway entrance to the room but that was what she had wanted.

He didn't know that done this way, it is associated with evil by many people but to her it was more than just evil. To her it was not just good versus evil but signified a different outlook on life. Whereas an upright pentagram is more about becoming, the inverted pentagram is more about being and that is where she felt she was. She had become a witch and it was time to be a witch.

With the carpet rolled up, she stopped and looked at the main part of her altar, which was the mantle above the fireplace. Karl had found a big timber from an old barn that was being torn down and had used it for the mantle. He had left the front and the part of the bottom that you could see rough, but had planed the other parts smooth and applied the protective polyurethane. Above the mantle hung the fifty-inch high definition flat screen television he used to watch sports but which had no part in the altar. On the left side of the altar was a picture of them on their wedding day with a white candle in a silver candleholder beside it. At the other end was the urn with Karl's ashes and beside it a black candle in a silver candleholder.

In the center of the mantle, was a pewter cup kept full of mead with an ebony carving of a mare on one side and an ebony carving of a hound on the other. She had read in *The Witches Book of the Dead* by Christian Day that in order to communicate with the dead, you needed a god or goddess to whom you paid homage. She had chosen the Norse goddess Hel because of her Norwegian background. Not that Hel was at all attractive because, while half of her body is alive, half of her body is dead and decaying. Her demeanor is sullen and downcast. *Of course,* thought Ingrid when first learning about her, *if half of your body is dead and decaying, how can you be happy?* She was said to be the daughter of Loki (who is often characterized as an impish god) and a giantess witch – Ingrid liked that latter part. It is said that the "hell" of the Christian faith was named after Hel and Helheim, the underworld where she dwells. Helheim is filled with spirits of the dead who were not fortunate enough to die in battle or at sea. *Well,* Ingrid thought, *Helheim must be a pretty full place.* Hel required offerings among which were the mead and black figurines. She also required burnt offerings of personal sacrifices. To satisfy this requirement, there was a brass dish in which Ingrid had burned her marriage license, something that was extremely dear to her, especially with Karl gone.

There was one thing missing in this altar setting – a skull. That was said to be, at least in *The Witches Book of the Dead*, an absolute necessity for communicating with the dead. If you wanted to hear the dead talk, the skull needed a lower jaw. It didn't have to be a real skull but if not, it needed to be a skull made in a spiritual manner. Above all, the skull must be obtained legally – no grave robbing. Ingrid didn't have a skull, didn't want to buy one because – if she truly had to have one – it had to be one that had meaning to her personally.

In the fireplace under the mantel was the required brass caldron in case a burnt offering was needed. If a fire was needed in the fireplace, the cauldron was easily removed and also, if needed, could be set in the pentagon in the middle of the Pentacle. That space was not wood but was an inlaid ceramic tile that had cost Karl a small fortune, but he hadn't questioned the need at all.

After replenishing the mead, which had a strange way of disappearing, she lit the two candles on the mantle and then set a candle on each of the pentagram's vertices and then lit them in counterclockwise order starting with Earth and ending with Spirit, for tonight she was going to summon Karl's spirit. As she lit them she chanted a short spirit message. With all the candles lit, she took off all her clothes and put on her white gown and her silver chain with the inverted pentagram. She had made her gown as well as the cloaks the four witches had worn out onto the lake. Inwardly she laughed at the fact that she needed almost twice as much material for the cloak of the South Witch because of her bulk. The other three were basically svelte but not the South Witch. It was a wonder she hadn't broken through the ice on the run back to shore. In each of the gowns, she had used her sewing machine to embroider an inverted pentagram as she had on her white gown. In all cases, the thread used was the same color as the material on which it was sewn so that it was basically invisible unless you did a careful examination.

After donning her gown, she stood in the center of the Pentacle facing the Spirit vertex, which aptly was pointed at the lake. Then she started her summoning chant and tried to pull herself deep within her subconscious.

She didn't know how long she had been meditating when she felt the room suddenly grow extremely cold as though something had risen from the grave and entered the room. She sensed rather than saw that the candles had gone out. She opened her eyes and saw a whitish blue light emanating from a white mist coalescing at the Spirit point. That blue light provided the only illumination in the room. This had never happened before in her attempts to communicate with Karl, but she was neither surprised nor afraid. Her calm didn't last long and she became not only surprised but also extremely frightened. She wanted to run but she couldn't. She was frozen in place as the mist thickened and swirled and assumed the shape of a huge white bear – no, not white, but almost crystalline as ice. The bear seemed to have come up through the floor and stood on two rear paws facing her, its forepaws held in the air.

"You called me once already tonight," the Ice Bear said. "But when I came on the ice you weren't there. What is it you want now?"

"I … I…" the West Witch stammered. "I didn't call you this time. At least I didn't mean to. I was calling to my husband Karl."

The bear looked at her. "Tonight I am all that you can summon," the Ice Bear said.

"BUT I NEED TO TALK TO KARL," screamed Ingrid. She was beginning to fall apart. She and Karl were what are referred to as kindred souls and with his death she had lost the stabilizing influence in her life. Though she had been unable to make a spiritual connection, she had felt she was close and kept trying. Tonight she needed some reassurance that all would be well.

"I am sorry but things are twisted tonight," explained the Ice Bear, sensing her dilemma. "The connections are fragile. The fireball from the Great Spirit has disassembled what is normal. I know of your husband Karl. He is with the Great Spirit and is happy. Tonight he is welcoming a new spirit from the lake."

The West Witch stared at the Ice Bear not comprehending. "A new spirit from the lake?"

"Yes. The Great Spirit sent a fireball to bring a new spirit to him. She was with you on the ice when you summoned me the first time."

"Gla... Gladys is with you?"

"No. She is with the Great Spirit and he is very pleased with her."

It was at this point that the West Witch lost consciousness.

Chapter 5

"This better be good," Nathanial snapped. "At …" he glanced at the clock, "3:45 in the middle of the night!"

"Sorry, Sheriff," responded Gail Hennessy, the late night dispatcher, apologetically. "There are never any good calls at 3:45 a.m."

"Well, get on with it, I losing sleep."

"There's been an explosion on Hibbard Pond," Gail explained. "We've gotten lots of calls."

Nathanial sat upright and swung his legs over the side of the bed and started moving toward the bathroom.

"An explosion?"

"Yes, sir. Apparently happened about 3:25."

"Where?"

"Off Timber Point according to the majority of the callers."

"You mean on the West Path?" Nathanial asked, using the shortened name the locals used for West Hibbard Pond Path as he closed the door to the bathroom.

"No, sir. Off Timber Point in the middle of the lake."

"But nobody's out there!" Nathanial exclaimed.

"At least not supposed to be," Gail agreed. "But every-one says there was an explosion. Two callers said they think it was a UFO …"

"UFO? At Hibbard Pond?"

"Well, they report a light in the sky descending rapidly before the explosion."

"Like airplane navigation lights?"

"No, sir. Like a burning fire."

"A fire?"

"Yes, sir. One caller, a Zebulah Pyke – that's with a "y" – says he thinks it was a meteor."

Zebulah Pyke, thought Nathanial. *A reliable source.*

"Anyone on the scene?" he asked.

"Yes, Officer Dempsey. The North End Fire Department responded with an engine. When I talked to Chief Henson, he said there were twenty volunteers there."

All wanting to get paid, Nathanial thought.

"But he sent most of them home after twenty minutes. One of them had binoculars and says there is rubble out in the middle of the lake"

"Rubble? What kind of rubble?"

"Blocks of ice. Zebulah Pyke showed up and has gone home to get cross-country skis to go out on the ice. Chief Henson won't let any of his volunteers out what with the ice danger. He and two others are waiting for Mr. Pyke to get back."

"Tell them not to let him out on the ice. Call Roberts and Walker."

"Next on my list, Sheriff. You, of course, were first."

"Right. I'll be there in thirty minutes. Keep me in touch in case anything else happens."

"Right …," Nathanial heard as he shut off his phone.

Opening the door, he headed for the chair where he kept his clothes for just such an emergency when a light snapped on.

"What's happening?" his wife Dawn asked sleepily.

"Some kind of explosion over on Hibbard Pond," Nathanial said as he stepped into his pants.

That comment brought Dawn upright in bed.

"Explosion?"

"Yeah," Nathanial said, pulling on a tee shirt with his legs spread to hold his pants up. "Reports of something in the sky."

"A plane?" Dawn's voice quivered at the thought.

"UFO," was the response as Nathanial slipped arms into his shirt and pulled a pre-tied tie over his head.

"You've got to be kidding," Dawn said as she slipped into her robe.

"Nope, something in the night sky is always a UFO." Nathanial finished buttoning his shirt and started fastening his trousers.

"But it could have been a plane?"

"Doubtful but possible. There are several reports of flames." His belt fastened, Nathanial started adjusting his tie.

"Maybe a comet?"

"Well, could be," Nathanial said. "Although comets become meteors when they hit the atmosphere I think." Nathanial reached for his leather jacket on the back of the chair.

"Want some coffee?" Dawn said as she started for the door.

"No time, we'll find some somewhere." He kissed her on the forehead and headed for the front door with Dawn trailing. He took his anorak off the hook and slipped it on. Reaching for his keys he realized they weren't on the hook and heard a jingle beside him. Turning he saw Dawn standing there with the keys in her hand.

"If you think you are going to get out of here in the middle of the night with only a kiss on the forehead, you are sadly mistaken."

Nathanial corrected his mistake soundly and received his keys in exchange.

"Don't call until noon," Dawn said opening the door.

Twenty-seven minutes later Nathanial turned onto the Timber Point entry road following Bob Roberts' cruiser, which had come from the north, and preceding Rich Walker's that had fallen in behind him as he turned onto South Path (South Hibbard Pond Path).

"Martians?" Rich Walker quipped as he and Nathanial exited their cruisers simultaneously. Roberts was already walking toward the shore where the fire department had set up some generator-powered floodlights. Across the frozen expanse of the West Bay of Hibbard Pond, Nathanial could see lights on in many of the house across the way. Even in the middle of the night there were gawkers.

Before Nathanial could answer Walker with *probably Venusians,* his cell phone rang.

"Morning, Sherriff," came the ever cheerful voice of Barbara Ann, the daytime dispatcher and office manager. "There are no reports of missing aircraft in the area and no reports of UFOs."

"What are you doing there?" was Nathanial's reply. "Shouldn't you be keeping Henry warm?"

"What and miss all the fun?"

"You know there's no overtime." This comment came because it had been recently discovered that Karen Nelson, the county treasurer, had embezzled several million dollars from the county's already meager coffers and fled the country to her native Canada.

"Who cares? This is exciting."

"Keep me informed," Nathanial said.

"Likewise," Barbara Ann said as she rang off.

When Nathanial and Walker reached the shoreline, they were greeted by Jay Henson who was standing with Zeb Pyke, the latter holding a pair of cross-country skis.

"Morning, Sheriff," Zeb Pyke said. "We should send out no more than four onto the ice. It's dangerously thin."

"Who put you in charge?" Nathanial asked, slightly shocked at Zeb's authoritative statement.

"Are you an ice fisherman?" Zeb Pyke responded.

"No, if I want frozen fish, I'll buy them at the super-market," replied Nathanial.

"Then, as the only ice fisherman here and therefore the person with the most knowledge about being on the ice, I'm in charge," was Zeb's factual reply.

Chapter 6

Nathanial had no problem with Zeb's reasoning and fifteen minutes later three people headed out on the ice. First was Zeb on his cross-country skis tethered by a twenty-foot length of rope to Bob Roberts and he by an equal length to Rich Walker. Bob Roberts and Rich Walker had eagerly volunteered and had been chosen because of their size: Bob Roberts was five foot seven inches and weighed one hundred fifty pounds and Rich Walker was five feet six inches and weighed one hundred forty pounds. Bob Roberts had on snowshoes to help distribute his weight but Walker was just in his boots.

Zeb had cautioned them about the ice. "Even without the explosion the ice is treacherous. The DNR ordered all shelters off the lake ten days ago. There are thin spots everywhere. The explosion, whatever it was, has spread cracks throughout the area. It's definitely not safe to be out there and, if it weren't for figuring out what happened, we wouldn't be going. Take it slowly and listen – if you hear a crack or think you hear a crack, sing out."

Naturally Bob Roberts had responded in a deep bass voice belying his size, "Out." Normally it would have produced laugher from Rich Walker but not this morning.

They had covered a little over two thirds of the distance when Zeb held up a hand, ski pole in the air.

"Hold it," Zeb said. "I'm backing up."

He moved slowly back about ten feet and then tried to his right but ten feet further on pulled back again. Twice more it happened until he found solid footing and thus they approached the area from the southwest. What they saw was riveting. Huge slabs of ice projecting from a hole that was virtually filled with big pieces of ice and there were small pieces scattered across the area. At a distance of twenty feet from the hole, the ice creaked and groaned and Zeb moved back quickly until it ceased. He called to his two companions.

"If you want pictures come up here slowly."

Rich Walker was the one who usually took pictures and he edged by Bob Roberts walking carefully, sliding a boot forward a foot or two, then testing and slowly moving his weight on to it. When he was finally beside Zeb, he took out his camera.

"This has an infrared flash," he explained. "The pictures won't be in color but at least we'll get the effect."

After some twenty pictures he put the camera away.

"Let's get off this deathtrap," he said.

Both he and Zeb backed up to where Bob Roberts was standing. Then Zeb took the lead and found the going back just as tedious. What tracks they had left were covered because a light snow had begun to fall when they were less than halfway to the hole. Zeb was constantly backing up and sidestepping to find firm ground. They had covered about a third of the distance to the shore when the inevitable happened. Bob Roberts took a step and heard a sharp crack. He stopped and felt the ice moving under him. Before he could move or shout, the ice gave way and he dropped into icy water.

Rich Walker saw it happen and yelled to Zeb. Both grabbed the tether rope and pulled it toward them pulling Bob Roberts up as he struggled to gain the surface. With the rope held taut by Rich Walker but letting it slide slowly through his hands, Zeb pulled the rope and Bob Roberts out of the water and onto the ice. One of his snowshoes had come off in the process and he released the other, leaving it on the ice. Once he was safely away from the hole and on his feet, Rich Walker start moving to the right side of the hole. When he was beside the hole but ten feet away, he heard the ice crack.

"Lie down spread eagled," Zeb called, moving forward to stand with Bob Roberts who was so cold he could barely walk. Rich Walker got down on the ice and spread his legs but held onto the rope. The Zeb reeled him in like a huge fish on a hand line. As he moved across the ice, Rich Walker heard it creak and groan but with his weight distributed it didn't give. Finally he reached his comrades and got to his feet.

"Let's get the hell off this ice," he and Bob Roberts said simultaneously.

Fortunately from then on, the ice was firm and they made it to shore quickly. Bob Roberts got into the squad, which a couple of the first responder volunteers had brought, shucked his wet clothes, and was wrapped in thermal blankets. Then at Nathanial's insistence, the squad headed for the Alpena Regional Hospital emergency room to get him checked out.

"It's nasty out there," Zeb explained to Nathanial. "The ice all around the explosion site is cracked and extremely treacherous. I don't think you can do any searching until the ice melts and you can get a boat out there. Knowing the equipment the divers required from when we pulled that body from under the ice, I don't think they can do it now. If there was anyone out there, which I doubt because I saw the meteor fall, they're dead and down. It's deep there – right near the deepest part of the lake."

Rich Walker had been looking at the images on his camera.

"All you can see is ice," he said showing Nathanial on the small screen. "We can blow them up back at headquarters, but all you will see is ice. You take the camera back with you. I'm going to Alpena to see what's happening with Bob. He'll probably be released and need a ride back here to get his cruiser."

"Right, nothing else to do here. Shouldn't be anyone coming here but I'll get Dempsey to stay. See you back at the office."

He turned to Zeb.

"And thanks for your help again."

"Glad to do it. Just don't find a body when you get someone to go down."

"Why not? It would make you two and Dugal one. You'd be the king."

Zeb laughed. Dugal McBruce had discovered the skeletal remains of a young girl in a farmer's earthen dam that the Hibbard Pond Sportsman were renovating for raising perch in the pond the dam made. This was the start of a mystery that including finding another young girl's body and the rescuing of a third girl from a mentally ill kidnapper. Zeb had been ice fishing a few weeks ago and hooked a corpse hiding on the bottom of the lake.

"You're right. Maybe you should find a body," and Zeb waved as he carried his skis to his truck.

Chapter 7

"My mom's not home."

"Okay, sweetheart," said Barbara Ann, Alcona County Sheriff's daytime dispatcher. "Who are you?"

"Jenny … Jennifer Wilson. We live at 4997 East Hibbard Pond Path."

"How old are you, Jennifer?"

"Fifteen. Until next month."

"Who's your mother?"

"Gladys Wilson."

"So tell me about your mother."

"I don't know. I got up and she wasn't home."

"Was she home last night?"

"Yes, she was reading when I went to bed. She's always reading."

"Did she tell you she was going out?"

"No. She told me she'd see me in the morning. Just like always."

"Does she work?"

"No."

"Is your father home?"

"No, he's away. He drives long-distance trucks."

"Maybe…"

"I called him. He doesn't know. He says he talked to mother last night before she went to bed. She didn't say anything."

"Do you have a car?"

"No ... I mean, I don't ... we have a car."

"Is it there?"

"Yes, in the garage. The keys are in it."

"You mean in the ignition?"

"No, behind the visor. Mom always puts them there in the garage."

"Is the car warm?"

"I don't know. I can check."

"Okay, do that."

There was a pause. Barbara Ann heard a door slam, a long silence, then the door slammed again."

"No, it's cold. I checked the hood and put the key in the ignition. I'm taking Drivers Ed. I know how to do that."

"Good girl. Did your mother leave a note?"

"No, I looked."

"What about her bed?"

"What?"

"Has it been slept in?"

"No ... I don't know. It's made up but mom always makes the bed right when she gets up. I do too. I think it's anal retentive but she likes it that way and it's easy. Otherwise I might forget."

"Yes. Any clothes missing?"

"I don't know. She has lots."

"What about her coat? It's cold."

"Wait ... Oh, I remember. It's in the car! I saw it when I looked at the heat thing."

"Does she always leave it there?"

"No. We don't have an attached garage. She'd freeze getting to the car."

"Okay. Have you talked to the neighbors?"

"It's too early. It's 6:15. I am only up because I have to go to school. "

"What's going on, Barbara Ann?"

The deep voice from behind her scared her because she hadn't heard him come up. He was always quiet. Like a ghost. Amazing for a man so large.

"Hold on a minute, Jennifer."

"Okay."

Barbara Ann turned to face Sheriff Jefferson.

"You're amazing," she said.

"Yes, I am," he said, "But the call?"

"Oh, yes. It's Jennifer Wilson, age fifteen. She lives on the East Path. Her mother isn't home. She was there last night when Jennifer went to bed but not this morning. Car's there, doesn't appear to have been driven."

"Bed ..."

"Made but she makes it as soon as she gets up."

"Maybe she's out walking."

"There was no note."

"Ask ... please"

"Jennifer, could your mom be taking a walk?"

There was silence on the phone.

"Jennifer ..."

Then louder, "Jennifer..."

"Oops, I'm sorry. I went to get a glass of milk."

Barbara Ann breathed a sign of relief.

"Does your mother take walks?"

"Not in the morning and her coat is in the car."

"That's right." Barbara Ann shook her head so the Sheriff would know.

"Who's near there?" Nathanial asked.

"Wait a minute, Jennifer."

Barbara Ann turned to the sheriff. "Warren Libka."

"Have him stop in and check," Nathanial turned and went back to his office.

"Jennifer."

"Yes, the bus is coming soon."

"No school today, dear."

"But I have perfect attendance."

"They'll understand."

"Are you certain?"

"I'll call them."

"Okay." Jennifer said, not wanting to go to school but knowing that her mother would have insisted.

"I am sending a deputy sheriff to stop in and help look for your mother. His name is Libka. He'll be in a sheriff's car."

"How long?"

"About ten minutes. Why don't you call some neighbors while you're waiting."

"Won't they be mad?"

"I don't think so dear. Tell them your mother is missing."

"Okay."

Chapter 8

"Who's there?" There was a tremor in Jennifer's voice.

"Alcona Deputy Sheriff Warren Libka."

"How do I know?"

"My cruiser's in the driveway."

"It could be stolen."

Officer Libka breathed deeply. Teenagers were always a problem.

"The sheriff sent me."

"Anyone could say that."

"Barbara Ann asked you to see if your mother's car had been driven."

A moment of silence and then Officer Libka heard the deadbolt unfastened and the door opened a crack.

"Step back so I can see you," Jennifer said.

Officer Libka complied, stepping back from the door into the full brightness of the outside light. Jennifer saw a tall man, over six feet she guessed, dressed in a uniform wearing a Smokey hat, the kids said. He was thin, not a bean pole but not big. He looked like a sheriff.

The door was shut, Warren heard the safety chain being removed and then the door opened again.

"Come in, Officer," Jennifer said. "Sorry but my mother was very safety conscious and she always insisted that I check and be certain who is at the door. Especially last year after that Williston killing young girls."

"That's a good idea," Warren Libka said as the stepped inside, closed the door behind him and took off his hat.

"Excuse me," Jennifer said, stepping by him to lock the door, turn the dead bolt and slide the safety chain in.

"Always pays to be safe," Warren said.

"Mom's anal retentive about it," Jennifer said as she move away from the door.

"Now tell me about this morning,"

Jennifer started to repeat her story but then stopped. "Would you like a cup of coffee, Officer ... ?"

"Libka. L•I•B-K•A, accent on the first syllable. And, yes, I would."

Normally he wouldn't because, going off duty soon, he would be heading home to sleep for a few hours, but he wanted to make the young girl feel at ease.

As she turned toward the coffee pot and the mug sitting beside it, "I thought you might, so I made some. I don't like coffee but mom taught me how to make it. She doesn't drink it any more, something about hot flashes, but daddy drinks it all day."

TMI, Warren thought but said nothing.

"Cream or sweetener?" Jennifer said before pouring the coffee.

"No, thank you, Jennifer. I drink it just like the Good Lord intended."

"Mom always says Mother Nature," Jennifer said as she poured the coffee. "Not that we're not religious or anything but she says that anyway." She handed the mug to Officer Libka.

"Thank you," Warren said and took a sip to be courteous. "That's good coffee."

"We grind the beans for every cup. Daddy insists," Jennifer offered.

"Good idea," Warren answered, making a mental note to follow the example. "Now tell me about this morning."

Jennifer did so adding at the end, "I called two neighbors but they haven't seen her for a few days. One was sort of mad when he answered but when I explained that my mother was missing, he apologized."

"So," Warren said, "Her bed was made."

"Yes, sir."

"What about the bathroom?"

"What do you mean?" asked a puzzled Jennifer.

"Any sign that your mother was in the bathroom this morning, washing, brushing her teeth?"

"I didn't look."

"Let's do that, shall we," Warren said, putting his hat on the kitchen table and the coffee mug beside it.

He followed Jennifer down a short hall.

"We only have one bathroom. Just two bedrooms. Sort of small," Jennifer explained almost apologetically.

In the bathroom, Warren noticed that the towels were all neatly folded on racks and three toothbrushes hung in a rack on the wall with a glass on top of it.

"Which towel is your mother's?"

"The yellow one," Jennifer said pointing to it. "Mine's pink and daddy's is blue."

Warren felt the yellow towel but felt no moisture.

"What about toothbrushes?" he asked but knew the answer in advance because they were yellow, blue and pink.

"The yellow one is hers."

It was dry.

"Does your mother brush her teeth?"

Jennifer looked at Warren as though to say, *That's a stupid question.*

"Religiously," Jennifer said. "And flosses, too."

Warren looked in the wastepaper basket beside the counter. Two tissues and one piece of floss.

"Do you floss?"

"Not in the morning, only at night."

"So the piece of floss in the wastepaper basket?"

"That's mine from last night."

"So your mother didn't floss?"

"Oh, she uses one of these plastic things," Jennifer said pointing to a plastic cup on the counter with a red flosser in it. "Her mouth is small."

"Okay, let's look at the bedroom and then the garage," Warren said.

The master bedroom—if one could call it that—was small, filled with a king-sized bed covered with a blue patchwork quilt. There were two dressers; one was tall with six drawers. The other was low with three drawers on each end and two doors in the middle. A mirror was hanging above the short one. The dressers didn't match. On the wall to the right of the mirror was an earring rack.

"Any earrings missing?" Warren asked.

Jennifer looked carefully.

"Don't think so. Mom's fastidious about her earrings. Won't even let me wear them, except once for a dance at school I got to wear the diamonds." She point to a pair sitting in a dish on the dresser.

There didn't appear to be anything out of place in the room. Not a clue as to whether the bed had been slept in.

"Can you show me the garage?"

Warren followed Jennifer down the hall and into the kitchen where he picked up his hat while Jennifer was unlocking the door. She waited for him to go out and then followed, turning the lock on the handle before closing the door.

Looks as though you are a bit anal retentive also, Warren thought.

As expected, Jennifer had to unlock the access door to the garage. She turned on the light as they went in. It was a two-car garage holding only one car, a white Ford Fusion. After pulling on a pair of latex gloves, Warren felt the hood and it was cold as expected. He opened the door and looked inside.

"The keys are behind the visor," Jennifer said.

Warren got the keys and put one in the ignition and turned it until the instrument cluster lit up. The temperature gauge showed cold. Warren put the keys back.

"Another car?" he asked.

"Daddy's got a pickup but he drives that to work."

Exiting the garage, Jennifer locked the door, started for the house and then stopped and turned around to look at the door.

"What's the problem?" Warren asked looking at her.

"The door," Jennifer said. "I just realized that when I went out to check this morning the door wasn't locked."

Chapter 9

She was cold. Opening her eyes all she could see was blackness. Putting her hand out, she felt only a cold hard floor. Where was she? She rolled over and got on her hands and knees and started crawling slowly, feeling in front of her. Her right hand encountered something – a glass jar. She felt in the jar and realized that it had held a candle. *Ooh,* she thought. *The Ice Bear*! Then she realized that the phone was ringing. Crawling slightly faster toward the sound of the phone, she encountered the rolled-up rug and scrambled, if that was the appropriate word, across it. Then she felt the bottom stair and stood up reaching for the light switch, which was a dimmer. She turned it and the lights came up. There was a phone on the wall, an old pay phone that Jim had refitted to work without money.

"Hello," she said groggily.

"Mrs. Swartz?"

"Yes ... umm ... Jennifer?"

"Yes, ma'am, have you seen my mother?"

She had known this would happen. Known and dreaded it. She and Gladys were best of friends. Certainly when her mother went missing, Jennifer would call her.

"Two days ago, I think. What time is it?"

"Six forty-five. I woke up and mom wasn't home. I couldn't find her. There was no note."

Of course not! We couldn't tell anyone what we were doing.

"So I called the police."

"THE POLICE," Ingrid almost shrieked the words out. "Sorry, Jennifer, that just came out."

"I understand. I was screaming for my mom when I couldn't find her."

"You called the sheriff?"

"Yes, ma'am. I was supposed to, wasn't I?"

"Yes, of course, Jennifer. I … I'm confused. I just woke up."

The sheriff! Did we leave any clues? DNA! I don't think so. I wore gloves. Did North Witch when she was driving Gladys's car?

"There is an officer here."

"Now?"

"Yes, ma'am. He wants to talk to you."

"Okay."

What do I say?

"Mrs. Swartz, this is Deputy Sheriff Warren Libka."

"Yes."

"Mrs. Wilson is missing. Her daughter says she is your best friend."

"Yes, I guess she is."

"Do you know where she might have gone?"

To the bottom of Hibbard Pond.

"No, she didn't say anything."

"Is there someone she might have gone to see?"

The Great Spirit.

"I don't …"

"I mean, anyone special."

"You mean a man?"

She's with my husband. At least, that is what the Ice Bear said.

"Yes, ma'am."

"That's insulting! Gladys would never …"

"Sorry, ma'am. I have to ask."

Covering all the bases, Ingrid thought. Then gathering her wits as much as she could at the moment – "No. But she might not have told me." *I wouldn't tell her.*

"Yes, ma'am. Well, if you think of anything would you please call the sheriff's office."

"Yes, of course." *Not likely.*

She hung up the phone. *They hadn't really done anything wrong. Going out on the ice was foolish – at least it would be in the eyes of some. Whether or not they had caused the fireball, or whatever it was, to appear is a matter of conjecture. But don't wave it off as impossible as the North Witch had. Yes, we had fled – initially to escape the fireball and the unexpected devastation that it wrought. But what could we have done to save Gladys? Undoubtedly she had gone under as a result of the gigantic upheaval of ice. Yes, of course, we could have called for help but it would have been too late and how much help could there have been? The ice was treacherously thin. Getting any kind of rescue team out there would have been questionable and then what could they have done? She – her body – was a hundred feet down. How could they have retrieved it? Is it a crime not to report an accident? None of us are going to say anything. Well, maybe the South Witch. Somewhat of a timid soul in my opinion. North Witch? No, let out the secret that they were witches would probably ruin her business.*

Her thoughts were not cohesive and offered no solution other than silence and that had been the plan even before they went out on the ice. She needed to sleep to get refreshed and then maybe she could sort through things. Turning on the lights on the stairs, she put her foot on the first step and reached to turn off the lights in the family room. Then she turned and saw what she was leaving: a rolled up braided rug; a witch's pentacle that anyone would recognize for what it was; and five candles that would alert anyone with any sense that there had been a witch ritual of some sort. She couldn't let anyone see that.

She put sleep on hold for a while. Collecting the candles or at least their containers as the candles had melted down, she stuck them in the bench where they had been before. The rug was easy to roll out, just kicking it with her foot, two, three, four times and it was flat. She opened the curtains on the door wall and was greeted with the dim blackness of a late winter's morning. Daylight savings time had kicked in a few weeks before and taken the early morning's light and shoved it into the late evening. Turning she went to the stairs, put her hand on the light switch and turned to look. Something was out of place! The glass-topped table! With some effort she moved the table into position and returned to the stairway. One last look – her clothes! She gathered her clothes and once again turned from the stairs to look. Yes, all was in order. She stumbled up the steps, turned the lights off and made her way through the house to her bedroom. The clothes she put into the hamper – who could argue with that? Her gown? She took it off, folded it and put it on the top shelf of the linen closet where it would be least likely to be noticed. Then pulling down the covers of the bed, she collapsed and was asleep before she could pull the covers over her.

Chapter 10

A rap at his door caused Nathanial to look up from the report concerning the explosion on Hibbard Pond. Standing in the doorway, hat in hand, was Officer Libka.

"Warren, what are you doing here?" Nathanial asked, waving him in to take a seat. "You're off duty and probably should be home in bed."

"Yes, on most days that would be the case but today's circumstances are different."

"Oh, you mean the Wilson woman's disappearance?"

"Yes, Sheriff, I do," Warren said. "I spent some time with Jennifer today and have grown to like her. She could be the daughter or granddaughter, I suppose, that we never had. She's a nice girl and well in grip with reality. She's not one of those text-messaging types who always have a cellphone in front of her face. She's got one, it's pay as you go, but she only uses its for emergencies."

"Different," Nathanial agreed.

"Yep, and when Roberts and Walker showed up to check for strange prints, she was very interested in what they were doing. I thought she might drive them nuts with questions but didn't seem to bother either of them a bit."

"No, they're fairly laid back."

"Anyway, they finished in the house and were headed for the garage to look at the car and she turned to me and said, 'Can you take me to school?'"

"She wanted to go to school!" Nathanial said flatly instead of questioning.

"Yep. She could have stayed at home, she's old enough but she didn't want to. Guess the house being all quiet would get her to thinking about her mother."

"Where's her father?"

"Kansas. Well, he was an hour ago. He's on the way back. He was getting ready to load up when his daughter called."

"He's a truck driver?"

"Yep. Long distance. Fortunately, his schedule had him headed back today. Got a load to take to Flint, then he'll be home. What with regulations and all that won't be until tomorrow but she says she'll be fine. Got frozen stuff in the freezer. She can cook, she says. Makes good coffee, I know that."

"So you just dropped her at the high school?"

"Well, not just. First I called the school and explained what was happening. I explained that Jennifer didn't want it to be public information but you know how things are. If she would tell her best friend and she would tell someone and bang, it would be all over the school."

"Yes, and soon after all over the county."

Warren laughed. "Yep, the Gert Grapevine."

Gert Pickard, who owned the Hibbard Corner's General Store with her husband Peter, was well known to be the center of gossip in the county. Let Gert know something and in thirty minutes it would be around the county.

"Yes, and thanks for reminding me, I need to stop in this morning. What's today?"

"Oatmeal cookies. It's Wednesday."

"Right, maybe she'll put nuts in them."

"Raisins," Warren said.

"Nuts," Nathanial countered.

"Betcha a quarter," Warren said. He wasn't a betting man but couldn't resist on a sure thing.

"A whole quarter? How about fifty cents to make it interesting."

"Hate to take your money but you're on," Warren said. "Now back to Jennifer. I asked the school to have a professional talk to her sometime today just to see how she's doing. I think she'll be fine but just in case."

"And legally that's the thing to do," Nathanial agreed. "Good job, Warren. I appreciate it."

It was a dismissal statement but Warren didn't budge. Nathanial looked at him questioning.

"Sheriff, I know this is unusual what with me being on the night shift and all. Most investigating gets done during the day. We just keep the riffraff from tearing the county apart."

"Warren," Nathanial was a bit condescending. "That doesn't mean you are not as good as the daytime people."

"Oh, I know that. I mean I asked for this shift because I don't sleep much anyway. Delores can sleep twelve hours a night and take a nap in the afternoon. I can't do that. But that's not the here or there."

"What is it then?"

Warren sat there as though collecting his thoughts.

"I'd like to see this through."

Nathanial was surprised.

"You mean the Gladys Wilson's disappearance?"

"Yes, sir. See, as I said, I am a bit taken with young Jennifer. I want to stay with this for her sake."

"You know it could have a bad ending?"

"Yes, I know."

"And you'd have to do it during your off time. Can't offer overtime, you know."

"I understand. The budget and all. But I'd do it for free even if you could pay me."

"What about Delores?"

"She takes in stray cats all the time. Me taking care of Jennifer is like that. T'won't be a problem."

"If that's what you want, it's okay with me. Tell Barbara Ann to keep you informed of any information we get."

Warren stood up. "Thanks, Sheriff," he said as turned and walked out the door almost bumping into Bob Roberts who entered Nathanial's office simultaneously rapping on the door's frame.

"Covered the Wilson's house but there's not much. Nothing out of place. Got lots of fingerprints. Take awhile to match them up. Got Mrs. Wilson's from her hairbrush. Couple of nice ones. Got Jennifer's prints. She was a hoot. Wanting to know about classifying prints, etc."

"Nothing strange then?" queried Nathanial.

"One thing. Jennifer said her mother is short. Five four or so. Jennifer is taller. Five six or seven. But whoever was driving the car was taller. Pushed the seat back. We had Jennifer sit in the seat and she agreed. She says when she drives she doesn't have to adjust the seat. Just the mirrors a little."

"That's not good."

"Maybe. Also whoever was driving last wore gloves or mittens. Not latex but winter gloves. Sort of wiped parts of the wheel where you'd hold it."

"So you think that someone drove the car into the garage and left it?"

"Yep. Goes along with Jennifer saying that the entry door was unlocked this morning. That's something her mother would never do. Also, there's one other thing. Might be important."

Nathanial knew by the slight smirk on Robert's face that it really was important.

"What's that?" he said playing along.

"Jennifer said her mother never wore gloves while driving. Didn't feel she could grip the wheel correctly."

He left me an opening, Nathanial thought.

"What about mittens?"

Chapter 11

No sooner had Bob Roberts left the office then the phone rang. Roberts was on his way to call Warren (if he had left the building) with the information he had just given the sheriff. Nathanial had told Roberts to inform the case officer about the information. Roberts asked, *"Who is that?"* and stared at Nathanial in disbelief when he had said *"Warren Libka. Just because he works nights doesn't mean he isn't capable,"* he had explained but knowing that the word would spread rapidly and there would be questions. In truth he did have his doubts and would keep a check on things.

"Sheriff Jefferson," Nathanial had answered the phone.

"John McCaulay," the local DNR officer had responded. "Been getting a lot of emails about an explosion, possible meteor, over on Hibbard Pond. Know anything about that?"

John was a kidder.

"Really," Nathanial said. "Hadn't heard a thing."

John laughed.

"Okay, what's the scoop?"

"The best I know is meteor. Many reports about an explosion and a meteor hitting the ice would make a noise. Several people reported seeing a ball of fire heading for the lake and two reports of it hitting. One very reliable. Three men went out and there is a big jumble of ice in the middle of the lake, just about the deepest spot interestingly enough. So my guess would be meteor."

"Anyone get a GPS on it."

"Bob Roberts and Zeb Pyke, the guy who saw it hit."

"How many people are up at 3:00 in the morning looking at the lake?"

"Don't know. Of course there was a boom before the explosion. Sound barrier or something, I guess."

"Anyone hurt?"

"Unknown but doubtful," Nathanial didn't even think about Gladys Wilson. "Only a fool would be out on the lake with its thin ice and especially at night. Plus it would take an act of God to hit someone on an expanse that big." If Nathanial had known what really happened he would have put *"or the devil"* after "God."

"So your department has no interest in the incident at all?"

Nathanial paused. "Not at this time. I'm only saying that because one never knows."

"Right," McCaulay said skeptically. "I'm going to contact the U.S. Geographical Service (USGS). They seem to have an interest in such things."

"Well, keep me informed so I can field any questions."

After talking to Nathanial, John McCaulay called a friend in the USGS.

"United States Geographical Service, Ryan Jirik. How can I help you?"

"Pay back the twenty you owe me."

That brought a hearty laugh from Ryan.

"John, that goby you caught could scarcely be called a fish."

"It is a fish. A nuisance fish, true. An invasive species, true. But it is a fish."

"We'll go double or nothing next time. I know that's not the reason for your call."

"No, we had a little incident last night. Meteor hit in the middle of Hibbard Pond."

"How big?"

"Oh, Hibbard Pond's pretty big. Got a twenty-two mile shoreline …"

John McCaulay could hear Ryan laughing.

"No, I meant how big was the meteor?"

"That's where you come in," John said. "You can send a team down to find it."

"Well, if it's the size of a pea, it would be a waste of time."

"According to all reports, … Just got an email from the sheriff, has a picture attached of the damage. I'd say good-sized. I see big chunks of ice covering a fairly wide area. Of course, the ice is thinning. We got all shelters off the lake about two weeks ago. Some of the pieces look to be a foot to foot and a half thick."

"Sounds like it would be big enough to make it worthwhile. You say the ice is unsafe at this point?"

"Yes. I think best to wait until the ice is off and we can get a pontoon out there. Borrow one from Hibbard Marine. It's more like a barge. Be easy to get on and off."

"When does the ice normally go out?"

"Mid-April. But it's been warm.""

"How deep is the water?"

"One hundred feet, give or take."

"Be cold too, that deep. We'll need winter gear. Want to get it out before the curious go after it."

"I'll be in contact. Email address still the same?"

"Yep."

"Okay, see you in April and have that twenty ready."

All John McCaulay heard was Ryan Jirik laughing as he hung up.

Chapter 12

Hibbard Corners is one of those nonentities in the state of Michigan. It has a name and there is a speed limit (35 miles an hour, but if you blink you'll miss it) but that is about all it has. With a population of 2, it is too small to be a village. According to the Census 2010, the smallest village in Michigan with a population of 114 is Turner, located in Turner Township, in Arenac County on Michigan's mitten just above where the thumb juts out. By contrast, the smallest city in Michigan with a population of 290 is Lake Angelus in northern Oakland County near Detroit. However, for years the city of Omer, also in Arenac County, has proclaimed itself on signage on US 23 as "Michigan's Smallest City."

Indeed Hibbard Corners is just about that: four buildings on four corners. The road from the south is East Hibbard Pond Path that continues on the north side of the intersection as Grouse Road, from the west is North Hibbard ond Path continuing on the east side of the intersection as Huron Road. The most imposing building in the town (we have to call it something) is the Hibbard Corners Funeral home on the northwest corner of the intersection. The building used to be the Hibbard Corners Lutheran Church of the Missouri Synod. The congregation split in a disagreement about the new pastor and formed two new congregations, both forsaking the church building. It stood vacant until claimed for back taxes by Steven Hibbs who turned it into the funeral home. His son Wallace currently runs it.

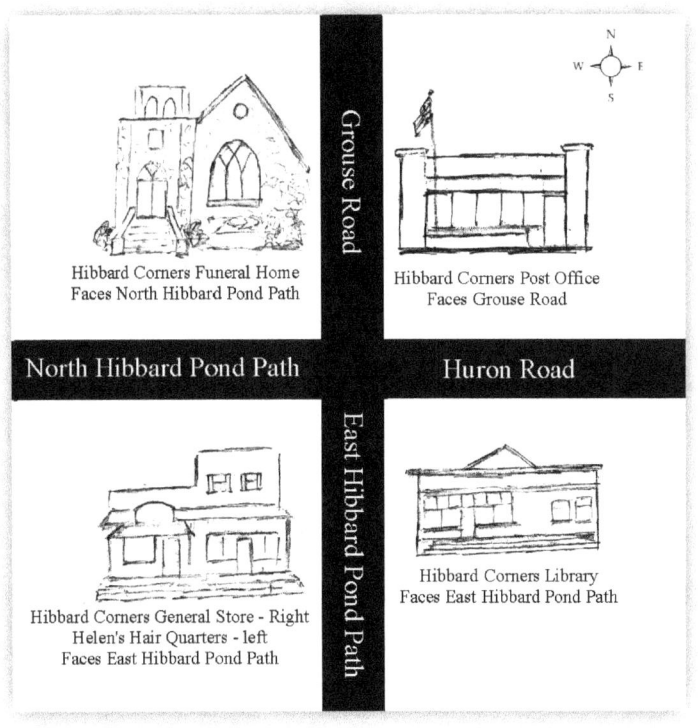

Across the street (the northeast corner) is a one-story brick building that is the home of the Hibbard Corners Post Office with its postmaster Owen Whitehawk, a full-blooded Chippewa. Until construction of the new building, the post office had been in the building on the southwest corner and is now occupied by the Hibbard Corners General Store. The store itself occupies the first floor of the two-story section of the building. The second floor is home to Gert and Peter Pickard who run the general store. Gert runs it actually. Peter stays in the background making certain that things function properly. There is a one-story addition on the south end of the store building that is home to Helen's Hair Quarters (run by Helen Trumball-Grant or Mrs. T-G) catering to women, children and the occasional man. Across the street in a one-story building is the Hibbard Corners Library, a division of the Alcona County Library. The librarian is George Haversack, a transplanted Ohio Buckeye who used to be a history professor in a small Ohio college. Upon retirement he had moved to Michigan with his wife who had grown up in the area but had died a few years before of ovarian cancer.

Nathanial pushed open the door of the store and was greeted by the tinkling of a small bell and the smell of oatmeal cookies with a hint of something else he couldn't place. There were always good smells in the store as Gert was a wonderful baker. You could tell the day of the week by the smell as you walked in: Blueberry muffins meant Monday, fudge brownies Tuesday, oatmeal cookies Wednesday, Lemon Crisps on Thursday (Nathanial never missed a Thursday), and cornbread on Friday (to go with the fish, Gert often explained). Saturday used to be whatever Gert felt like but lately almost always some sort of double chocolate fudge brownie with nuts.

"Get youse a cuppa coffee, Nathanial," came the cheery greeting from the kitchen separated from the store by a latticework wall of Peter's creation. "I'll be right out with the first batch."

"Smells delicious but different today," Nathanial said as he obeyed pouring a strong black cup of coffee into a Styrofoam cup.

"Yes, trying something new," came Gert's response.

Nathanial blew over the top of the cup in an effort to cool it and then took a tentative sip.

"Wow, this is great, Gert. Not your usual."

He took another drink.

"This is Dugal's mixture," he stated emphatically.

Gert's laughter rolled from behind the latticework.

"Can't fool you," she said as she appeared bearing a tray of cookies. "He offered to provide me with the mixture for a week to see what people thought."

"It's great. Did he tell you how he mixes it?"

"Nope. Just brought it in already mixed."

Nathanial reached out and snatched a cookie from the tray as Gert set it on the counter thus escaping a playful slap she often gave him.

"Youse could have asked," she said looking up at him. Gert was at most four eight (her husband perhaps two inches taller) and weighed not much more than 100 pounds. So she did have to look up at him standing six foot eight and weighing two hundred eighty pounds on a good day. He had been an All State offensive tackle in high school and had received a full ride scholarship from State. However in the fourth game of his freshman year, he got sandwiched by two Iowa Hawkeye defensive linemen and a knee was shattered. Unable to play again without risk of serious injury, after a long rehab he had left school and joined the Michigan State Police. When he retired he had taken a job with the Alcona County sheriff and been elected as sheriff after the previous one retired on disability because of a massive heart attack.

"I knows why you are here, Nathanial. Youse wants to be certain that what I hears about that explosion on the Pond last night is factual."

Nathanial, mouth full of an oatmeal cookie with bits of apple and flavored with cinnamon, nodded and waited.

"Do I have to tell youse before?"

He nodded again.

Gert sighed and began. "It was a meth lab run by them hoodlums Roger Harrison and Bert Weaver."

The idea was so ludicrous that Nathanial could not help but spew pieces of oatmeal cookie out of his mouth before he got a hand over it. He coughed like he was choking and Gert came from behind the counter to try to pat him on the back but couldn't reach.

"A meth lab?" Nathanial finally managed.

Gert nodded trying to figure out if she was right or not.

"But Harrison and Weaver are in jail." The two had been arrested and convicted of killing a farmer who had accused them of killing his sheep and Weaver had shot him with a crossbow bolt to prevent him talking.

"Well, I thought that but Martha ..." Gert quit while she was ahead.

Chapter 13

Having set Gert straight and carrying a bag of oatmeal cookies and a Styrofoam cup of the best coffee around the Pond, Nathanial headed for a chat with Owen Whitehawk, also a source of gossip but his was always more likely to be the truth. He sidetracked to the library and saw that George Haversack hadn't come in yet. He wanted to ask him about meteors, which was not George's specialty but he would use the Internet to get answers.

He stopped at the corner and watched a dirty pickup truck pass through headed east on Huron Road. Then he crossed the road and entered the post office lobby. A small room, maybe eight by eight, to the left was the door to the post office service area and next to it a copy machine with a sign announcing "10¢ a copy – black and white only." The wall across from the door held post office boxes and two mail slots, labeled "Local Only" and the other "Out of Town." A handwritten sign above stated, "We sort it anyway." This was Owen's continuing fight with patrons to read. Nathanial knew there were a couple of hardcore pranksters who intentionally put the mail in the wrong slots just to irritate Owen. The other wall contained a large bulletin board and a white board where people could leave messages and, of course, there were the usual wanted posters always adorned with pencil mustaches, beards, scars, glasses and anything else that might irritate Owen. Nathanial noticed that in the corner above the mailboxes and copier was a video camera with a red light showing. This was something new and Nathanial doubted that it worked but was just another ploy of Owen's to keep people on the up and up. Of course it was more likely to make people more mischievous just to see if Owen would catch them.

Holding the bag of cookies with his teeth, Nathanial opened the door with his free hand and entered the service area. Owen Whitehawk looked up from behind the counter.

"Behold. The fuzz bearing gifts."

"Good morning, Postmaster Whitehawk," Nathanial said removing the bag from his mouth and setting it on the counter. "Indeed, I do have gifts. Something tempting and delightful and I bet you can't guess what it is."

"How many guesses?"

"Let's pretend I'm a genie. I give you three guesses," Nathanial responded while waving his free hand above his head.

"Oatmeal cookies," Owen said emphatically. "It's Wednesday."

"That's true but incorrect."

"You mean Gert changed?"

"Is that one of your guesses?"

"No, that's a question. This is a guess 'with apples…'" Nathanial shook his head.

"… and cinnamon," Owen said as he opened the bag and removed three of the cookies.

"How?" Nathanial stared at him incredulously.

"ESP."

"Hogwash!"

"Superior Chippewa deductive techniques." Owen said with a mouthful of the first cookie.

"Gert called you!"

"Guilty as charged. Arrest me, Sheriff."

"For what?"

"Insider trading?"

The two men laughed. Nathanial got himself a cookie. "Best she's ever made."

"Nope, the double fudge walnut brownie delights are the best she ever made."

"True."

"So what's this about a meteor hitting Hibbard Pond?"

"Ah, you got the real story."

"Yep, Zeb was in here earlier. Said he went out there. It was downright scary, he said. Almost as scary as being there when it hit."

"I saw pictures. You didn't want to be there when it hit. Wouldn't have survived."

"Wouldn't have survived if it was a meth lab explosion either."

Nathanial laughed. "Gert tell you that too?"

"No, I don't reveal sources of erroneous information. Learned that before Zeb came in but didn't believe it. Both guys mentioned are under lock and key." Owen looked at the sheriff. "Aren't they?"

"Last I heard."

"So is that what brought you in this morning?"

Nathanial looked at him questioningly.

"To see if I had the correct scuttlebutt?"

"Yes, unless you happened to know a lot about meteors."

"Just that they come from the area where no man has gone before, boldly or not."

From outside they heard a car horn sound.

"However," Owen continued, "you could go and ask George. If you offer him one of your …" he peeped into the bag and pulled out another cookie "… four cookies, he might be willing to search the electronic netherworld."

"Just what I was planning on doing. However, I am going to offer him all three of my remaining cookies." Nathanial pulled a cookie from the bag and it disappeared into his mouth in two bites. Taking the bag in his right hand and the coffee still in his left, he turned the handle of the door with the right hand until it clicked and then he shouldered it open and held it as a tall lady in a long black coat with a bright red knit cap pulled down over her ears bustled into the service area past him.

"Thank you, Sheriff Jefferson," Helen Trumball-Grant said. "Morning, Owen."

"You're welcome, Mrs. T-G. Owen knows the true story," Nathanial said as he let the door close. Helen Trumball-Grant stared after him in shocked disbelief.

Nathanial exited the post office and hustled across Huron Road chasing the figure of George Haverstock disappearing into the library. He might not have been so quick to vacate the premises if he had known that the two people who got the witch ceremony started were together in the post office service center where it had all begun.

Chapter 14

On a mid-October Saturday morning of the previous year, two teenage boys paid an infrequent visit to Hibbard Corners. They arrived on a small bicycle, one pedaling and the other standing behind, balanced on a metal protrusion from the rear hub and hanging on to a metal support behind the peddler with one hand and his straw hat with the other. That hat was the first indication of the dissimilarity of the two boys. The bicycle stopped next to the library, the boys dismounted, and the peddler put the bike into the conveniently located rack. He was wearing blue jeans, a light tan jacket underneath which he wore a tee shirt. On his feet were white socks and sneakers. In addition to the straw hat, the other boy wore a black jacket that looked like a suit coat but had no lapels. The front was fastened together with snaps. Under the jacket he wore a white shirt held together with snaps. His pants were dark and baggy and help up with cloth suspenders made from the same material. His leather shoes were brown and his socks dark. He was an Amish boy named Joshua Beiler and the Englisher (that's Amish for "non-Amish") was Chris "Muddy" Waters. They had met early that summer through both an unfortunate and a fortunate event. The unfortunate part was that Joshua had been riding his scooter near his house and been blown off the road into a drainage ditch where his leg was severely cut on broken glass. The fortunate part was that Muddy was coming home from fishing on Hibbard Pond and arrived in time to use his tee shirt as a tourniquet and called 911 on his cellphone. That was the start of a friendship that had taken the boys through several unordinary adventures, but that is another story or two.

Their venture this day was to the library to use the Internet to check on a couple of things, visit the Hibbard Corners General Store for some of Saturday's brownies, and to chat with Owen Whitehawk, but not in that order. These three things had become standard in their visits (no need to visit the funeral home thankfully) and, as usual, the post office was number one on the list.

"Chris and Joshua, what a wonderful way to enliven my Saturday morning," the postmaster said as the boys entered.

"Hi, Mr. Whitehawk," Joshua said. "How was the war dance?"

On an earlier visit that fall, they had found Owen wearing a wig so that his normally close-cropped black hair looked like the Chippewa hair of old days. He had explained that his wife Rachel had bought the wig for him to wear when the Chippewa held a fundraiser including traditional tribal dances. As most people know, the Chippewa didn't have to hold a fundraiser dance because the Saginaw Chippewa tribe owned casinos in the Up North portion of the lower peninsula, as did the Sault Ste. Marie Chippewa tribe in the Upper Peninsula. But it was done to educate tourists in the history of the tribe with the money going to help various charities in the area.

"Didn't work," Owen said solemnly.

"What do you mean 'didn't work'?" Muddy asked.

"Well, have you heard about an Indian uprising?" Owen said as he reached under his counter where he had a rubber tomahawk waiting just for this occasion.

"No," the boys said simultaneously.

"That's because it starts today." As he said this, Owen pulled the tomahawk out, raised it high and did the familiar wha wha wha with his other hand patting his mouth. The boys jumped back and fled out the door. Owen was about to go after them and apologize when the boys peeked back in.

"Just checking," Muddy said as they reentered the service area.

"That's was pretty good, Mr. Whitehawk," Joshua said. "Had me going for a minute."

"He almost peed in his pants, Owen" Muddy said laughing and Joshua punched him in the shoulder.

Owen had tried to get Joshua to call him "Owen" but Joshua's Amish background was too strong although one time he had called him his true Indian name "Aart," which means "like an eagle." Truth be said, Owen never called him Muddy but always Chris. His explanation, from the point of view of the postmaster, was that nobody would send a letter addressed to Muddy Waters. The boys had thought once or twice about doing just that but that would ruin the explanation.

"So did you learn any new dances?" Muddy asked.

"No," Owen admitted. "But I did hear an interesting old legend about a bear from one of our elders."

The boys looked at each other wide-eyed. "A legend about a bear?" they whispered. At age thirteen they were still fascinated with such stories.

"Yes, it is *The Legend of the Ice Bear*," and Owen proceeded to tell them the story. The boys were so rapt in listening they didn't notice Mrs. T-G entering the service area and also becoming enthralled in the story.

"The Ice Bear bowed in recognition of the power and wisdom of the Great Spirit, but when he rose, the Great Spirit was gone. One last look around and the Ice Bear slipped into the icy water and swam to the bottom of the lake where it made its home in the depths," Owen concluded.

"Is that true?" Joshua asked.

"Like most legends, it probably has its basis on fact. Maybe long ago some Indians crossing a lake like Hibbard Pond in the middle of the winter found the remains of a bear frozen on the ice in the middle of the lake. From such things legends are born."

"Wow," Muddy said. "That's a great story." He looked at Joshua and as though a thought had passed between them, Joshua asked, "Is there a legend about a cougar?"

"Haven't heard of one but maybe? Why do you ask?"

Joshua didn't know what to say so Muddy hopped in, "Well, as 'legendary' as cougars are in Michigan, we just thought there might be."

"I don't know. Next time I'm in Mt. Pleasant, I'll ask."

"Why Mt. Pleasant?" asked Muddy.

"Because that's where the Saginaw Chippewa tribe has its headquarters."

"In a big teepee?" Joshua asked, a slight smirk showing he knew the answer.

"Fourteen stories," Owen said. Then the three of them laughed joined by Mrs. T-G. Muddy and Joshua stopped laughing and turned to look at her. "We didn't hear you come in," Muddy said.

"I was enjoying the story," Mrs. T-G explained.

"Got to go," Muddy said, pulling Joshua with him. "Thanks, Owen."

"Yes, thank you, Mr. Whitehawk," Joshua said as they disappeared through the lobby door.

"Owen, that is certainly an interesting story. Are there any dances or rituals associated with it?" Mrs. T-G asked, her mind spinning about a possible local supernatural event.

"Don't know. As I told the boys, just heard the story myself within the past couple of weeks."

"Who might know?" Mrs. T-G asked.

Chapter 15

"Morning, George," Nathanial said as he entered the library. It was still chilly inside and Nathanial could hear the furnace humming as it struggled to warm the building. There was no answer to Nathanial's greeting and so he guessed that George was in the lavatory as he often called it. "Rest room?" he said to Nathanial at one time. "That's an Americanism. Meaning a room where one 'refreshes oneself.' 'Refreshing oneself' usually means resting. I suppose some people do think of it as resting judging from the amount of time they spend in there. We don't have a 'bathroom' here, because there is no bath or shower in it. Could call it a 'toilet' I suppose. That's from the French 'toilette' meaning 'dressing room.' Think it might refer to people going to powder their wigs at one time. So to keep from calling it a 'pissoir,' a French term that literally means 'to piss' or a 'shithouse' – pardon my French" at which point he had laughed, it was the only joke that Nathanial could recall him telling, "I use the term 'lavatory' because when you're done you're supposed to wash your hands. 'Lavatorium' is Middle Latin for 'washbasin.' "

Nathanial had held his hands up admitting defeat. George had just smiled.

"TMI, huh? You know, I was on a tour in Egypt with my wife and we had a wonderful Egyptian tour guide whose children accused him of exactly that. You ask him the time, they would say, and he would expound on the history of timepieces but never tell you the time. He did expound and gave us much information that we both relished."

Sure enough in a few minutes, George emerged from the book stacks that concealed the entrance to the lavatory. At least it should have been George but not the George he knew. George Haversack always dressed in coat and tie that usually didn't match each other or the shirt and trousers. It was as though he threw on whatever was handy. This George was dressed in a dark blue blazer; powder blue shirt; red, white and blue striped tie; and gray slacks.

"George?" Nathanial said in disbelief. "Is that you?"

"Who else did you expect it to be?" George Haversack said sitting down at his desk and opening the bag that Nathanial had placed there. He looked inside and then at Nathanial. "Is this a bribe?"

"No, of course not," Nathanial stammered somewhat taken aback. "It's just that I couldn't eat them all … and thought you might like them."

"I was just joking anyway. I suppose that you want information on one of three things."

Three? Nathanial pondered.

"Meth labs," George continued, "although as a law enforcement officer you know more than I do so that can't be it. Nose cones from antiballistic missiles, probably ones with nuclear warheads? No, we'd be swarming in military by now. So it must be meteors."

"Yes, exactly," Nathanial said. "Nose cones from … you really heard that?"

"No, but I expect I will when I visit Gert after lunch."

"No, she had meth lab and now has the straight skinny. Whether she keeps it or not heaven only knows."

"Well, you know I'm a historian by training and a librarian for something to do. Didn't like physics. No, I can't say that. Never really had a chance. In college my advisor steered me into the wrong beginning physics course. It was for people who didn't want to do more than get a smattering and satisfy a science requirement. Terrible teacher, always spoke in a monotone. If his voice changed, he'd stop, clear his throat and then continue on and on and on monotonically.

"Oops, pardon the digression. People accuse me of that. Must be an old age thing. Meteors was it? Yes. I'll look into it. Might have to call someone. Exactly what do you want to know?"

"The ice where the meteor hit varies from a couple of inches to two feet, at least that is our guess looking at the pictures Rich Walker took." He took a picture out of his pocket and gave it to George.

"He was one of the three out on the ice?" George asked as he looked at the picture closely.

"Yep, he and Bob Roberts because they weighed the least. I sure as hell was not going out there. And Zeb Pyke."

"Figured Zeb might have been one. Wearing cross country skis?"

Nathanial nodded.

"I … we want to know how big the meteor was to cause that explosion. Figure they all must travel about the same speed but how big was it? Think the guys are starting a pool. Sizes from golf ball to beach ball."

"I'll take soccer ball," George said reaching into his pocket to get his money clip and taking a five-dollar bill out. "Put me in with this Lincoln."

Nathanial pocketed the money.

"Now about your clothes!"

"What's wrong with my clothes?"

"They … uh … well … they match."

"Are you saying my clothes usually don't match?"

"Well, not as a rule."

"I know, terrible taste in colors and plaids and such. My wife used to pick out my clothes."

He lapsed into silence. Nathanial let him be and walked out the door.

Chapter 16

It was a long day at school for Jennifer. Of course her friends wanted to know why she was late and she explained that she had overslept and was late for the bus.

Well, why did you arrive in a sheriff's car?

"Because when I got to where the bus picks me up and it had already gone, I was going to walk back home. He stopped and asked me if I was in trouble. I think that's because I was walking on the wrong side of the street, you know, with traffic instead of facing traffic. I told him I had missed the bus and he told me he was going off duty and headed for Harrisville so he brought me."

Well, why did he come in the building?

"To explain to the school why I was late."

Well, duh, you missed the bus.

"Yes, but he wanted them to know why I was in a sheriff's car."

That satisfied all but the one student who was in the office when Officer Libka had come in and talked to the principal for much longer than it took to explain why he had brought Jennifer in the police car.

Then there were more questions about why she wasn't in study hall. The reason there was that she was talking to a grief counselor the school had brought in. Fortunately nobody saw that person come in or he had looked more like he belonged there. Her response to questions was that she had to talk to her guidance counselor about some personal issues. That felt good to her. The white lies about being late, which were at the suggestion of Officer Libka, didn't sit well with her. She didn't like lying and in fact was not used to it at all. She tried not to lie.

She knew that this would all come back at her if her mother didn't show up today or at latest tomorrow. Her dad would be home then and he could help her. Sooner or later though, the truth would come out. She knew that and would accept what would happen then. Especially as long as her mother was safe.

Of course it got easier throughout the day to steer the conversation to the explosion on Hibbard Pond. Her friends thought she might have been awoken by it but she wasn't certain. She vaguely remembered being awake in the middle of the night but that was it. It could have been the explosion and she would have awoken but not known why. That's what she finally decided to say.

The explanations about the explosion went from meth lab (a popular answer) to alien spacecraft. The more scientific kids (the nerds) tended to say it was a meteor or space junk.

But wouldn't NASA know about either of those things?

Not if it was small. NASA doesn't know about all shooting stars and those are small meteors that never hit the ground.

The nerds explained that there were four classes of meteor showers that happen every year. The classes are based on the number of meteors per hour and are classified as major, minor, variable and weak.

There was a lot of kidding by her friends on the school bus of course. She heard one girl (who she despised) say that she was running away from home because her mother/father had beaten her. It was her poor luck and lack of lying skills that the cop had seen her and taken her to school.

On the bus home, she chose to sit by herself that day. Across the aisle was a younger boy she didn't know very well, also sitting by himself. She knew that his friends called him Muddy and knew about his saving an Amish boy that past summer, and then falling in a well and being rescued. The girl who was making the accusations about abuse was sitting right behind him with one of her friends. Muddy had turned around on the seat and said, "You don't know what you are talking about. So why don't you just put a lid on it." She had stared at this young upstart in disbelief but, she had indeed "put a lid on it."

When Muddy had sat back down, he had looked at her and smiled and she had mouthed "thank you." He had just nodded.

She had gotten off the bus at the drop-off spot across East Path from the pick-up spot and the bus driver Lucy had put on the lights and stop signs so that she could cross the road. Jimmy Lukas, the other student who got off there, lived on the other side of East Path and didn't have to cross. Each had a short walk in opposite directions to their homes. They had agreed in the fall that the school bus should stop in between the two houses rather than make two shops.

In nice weather Jennifer liked to walk home through the woods that separated her house and the other two on the long driveway from East Path. Today she decided to walk through the woods despite the thin layer of snow that lay on the ground. The snow crunched under her feet as she made her way around trees and over or around fallen trees and branches. She was watching where she was walking and didn't see the doe until she was almost upon it. She just happened to look up and there was this obviously pregnant doe just ten feet in front of her. Of course that brought Jennifer up short and she just stood and stared.

The two stood there for several minutes although to Jennifer it seemed like an hour. She could hardly breathe not wanting to spoil the moment. She had never seen a deer this close. She expected it to turn and bound away as they usually did even when she was walking the road to or from the house. After several minutes, the deer went back to nuzzling the snow and leaves on the ground in search of food and seemed to take no notice of Jennifer who stood there watching. Finally Jennifer chose a path around the front of the deer, not wanting to give the deer any reason to try to kick her with those sharp hooves. She moved extra cautiously and because of a fallen pine tree had to pass only three feet from the deer. When she was directly in front of the doe, it stopped searching for food and raised her head staring straight at her. But this was a quick look and then she was back to looking for food.

Jennifer moved past the deer and continued walking but stopped about ten feet away and looked back. The doe had raised her head and was looking at her, but then once again resumed her search for food to nourish both herself and her unborn.

When Jennifer reached her house, she turned back but the doe had gone. This was certainly something that she would have to tell her mother and her father. As expected, the door was locked, so she used her key to unlock it. Stepping into the house, she called out, "Mother, I'm home." But there was no answer.

Chapter 17

After getting herself a glass of milk and some Oreos, Jennifer sat at the kitchen table (the only dining table in the small house) and called her father using her cellphone.

"Hi, daddy," she said. "I just got home. Mom's not here." This verbalized realization almost brought her to tears but she fought through them.

"Hello, sweetheart, I'm sorry to hear that."

Jennifer started to tell him about the doe but he continued on.

"I'm in some heavy traffic here," her father explained, "and I need to concentrate."

Jennifer knew that her father had a blue tooth earpiece and so he didn't need to hold the cellphone.

"I'm taking a break at the next rest area in about half an hour. Did you get the mail?"

"No, I forgot," and she started to say, "Mother usually does" but didn't.

"Well, please get it and feed the birds. Your mother would appreciate that."

"Okay," she replied.

"Got to go. Love you."

"Me too."

Jennifer finished her snack and rinsed the glass, putting it in the dishwasher, the one modern convenience her mother had insisted upon in the small kitchen. Then she put on her jacket and went out to the patio where her mother had six bird feeders. Unfastening the chains that held the lid on the metal trash can in which her mother kept the birdseed, she filled the hanging bird feeders, put two ears of corn on the little seesaw feeder her father had made, and took down the suet holder. The suet block was almost gone and so she put a new one in. She had just hung it back up when there was a whirl of wings and something big brushed by and landed on the feeder. She took a startled step backwards and stared at the bird that was already pecking at the suet.

It was a large bird, about seventeen inches in length, mostly black with a red crest and a white face with the white continuing down the throat and then under the wings so that the bird shows white in flight overhead. There was a black line running from the rear of the red bill to the black of the throat. Jennifer knew that this black line that she and her mother called its mustache meant that the bird was a female pileated woodpecker because the males have a red mustache. Most likely this was the same female who always came because they are solitary birds with a territory of about twenty acres. The previous summer a female had brought its young (a male) to the feeders. She and her mother had enjoyed sitting in their chairs on the patio and watching the mother get suet or peanut butter from another feeder and then go to its young on a big white ash and feed it. But she had never seen a pileated this close. She and her mother could hear the woodpecker calls all the time and remembered last summer when they heard answering calls and later surmised that the responses came from the father of the young pileated.

Jennifer watched the woodpecker for about five minutes before it finished and took flight to a nearby tree where it burst forth in its cry that was used as the model for the cartoon bird Woody the Woodpecker. It was Jennifer's second favorite birdcall with those of the loon being her favorites. She had been so entranced with the pileated that she hadn't noticed the other birds that were flitting about the feeders. There were chickadees, tufted titmice, wrens, cardinals and blue jays. And a squirrel was on the seesaw eating at an ear of corn. The number of birds was not amazing, but the fact they were all there while she was standing there was.

She put the lid back on the trash can and fastened the chains. The sound of the lid going on and the clink of the chains startled the birds and they scattered but quickly came back. She felt as though she was invisible. Then she walked to the mailbox, going through the woods hoping to see the doe again, but she was gone. In the middle of the patch of woods were three evergreens. They were all full and even all around and would have made beautiful Christmas trees but none of them would fit in the small house. She knew that in the middle of the trees was a small clear space and she looked in and could see from the way that the ground had been disturbed that a deer, very possibly her doe, had been sleeping there. She hoped that the doe would return to this spot when she was going to birth her fawn and she and her mother could watch it as it grew for at least a couple of weeks until the mother would lead it into the deep woods across East Path.

Continuing on toward the mailbox, she passed a large oak and heard a squirrel chattering at her. She looked and there was a black squirrel head down on the tree just above her height and it was looking at her. She felt that she could reach out and touch it, but didn't try because it would run away or possibly try to bite her. As she neared the mailbox she picked up her pace, anxious to see if there was a note from her mother. She knew it was a ridiculous hope and she knew that her father was wishing the same thing and that is why he had asked her to go to the mailbox.

Theirs was the middle of three metal mailboxes sitting on wooden posts. The one belonging to the Herberts had its red flag up so she knew that they had gotten their mail and left outgoing. The mail was delivered like clockwork every morning between 11:00 and 11:30, Sundays excepted of course. The Gilmores' box on the other end didn't have a flag up. If it had been the Herberts' mailbox without the flag up she would have checked to see if there was any mail for them, but Mr. Gilmore was as a fanatic about his mail. "That mail belongs to the U.S. Post Office until removed from the mailbox and the only person who can legally do it is me." It had only taken once for Jennifer to learn this lesson. *Let the old coot drive his golf cart out here and get the mail where it would have been just as easy for her or her mother to take it to him.* She opened their mailbox which was bigger than the other two because her mother used to receive a lot of books from book clubs until she had gotten her eBook reader and she used that most of the time. *Where was that?* Jennifer thought. *I'll have to look for it.* The mail consisted of an advertising circular and two bills. Nothing from her mother.

Chapter 18

As Jennifer turned away from the mailbox to start for home, she heard the quick chirp of a police siren and turned around to see Officer Libka's cruiser roll to a stop just off the road ten feet from the mailboxes. She waved at him and started toward the cruiser as he got out, putting on his county mountie hat.

"Hi, Officer Libka." Jennifer was smiling at seeing her new friend.

"Hello, Jennifer. How did it go today?"

"Okay, I guess. The kids were curious and there were all sorts of rumors."

"Guess you'll be labeled a J.D., huh." Officer Libka was also smiling.

"What's a J.D.?"

"Juvenile Delinquent. Guess that's an old school terminology or maybe used in the big cities. Many folks nowadays say that he or she is 'incorrigible.'"

"Well, not so much that as maybe I was running away from home. One girl, that nasty Sarah Lindsey, said on the bus that my dad had beaten me and I was running away. Muddy set her straight though."

"Oh, Muddy rides your bus?"

All the deputies knew about Muddy and Joshua Beiler not only from Muddy's rescue from the well, but from the efforts to keep Joshua from testifying at the trial of the poachers.

"Yes, he's not in my class, still in middle school. I don't really know him except by sight."

"Well, from what I know of the lad, he is the kind to stand up to wrongs."

"Did you find anything out about my mother?"

A sad looked crossed Officer Libka's face and he shook his head.

"Nothing, I am sorry."

After he had reported to the sheriff and then received the information from Rich Walker about Gladys's car most probably having been driven by someone else, he had gone home. First he had called his wife Delores before he left Harrisville so she could have his breakfast ready. When he had gotten home he had recounted the events of the morning to her but not the part about the car having been driven, because that was the kind of information that the investigators always held back.

"Goodness gracious,' Delores said setting his breakfast plate down.

"Looks good, love," Warren said as he looked hungrily at a plate with two sausage patties, hash browns, two basted eggs and an English muffin with butter.

"Let me get youse some more coffee," she said picking up his mug. "So what do you think happened?"

"No idea," Warren said through a forkful of hash browns and sausage he had eagerly shoveled into his mouth. "Strange disappearing at night like that. She may have gone out with someone and something happened."

"But she didn't leave a note for her daughter … what's her name?"

"Jennifer."

"Yes, Jennifer, I'll remember."

"No note. But, say she was having a little tête-à-tête"– Warren used his hands to indicate parentheses around "tête-à-tête" – "with someone and didn't want anyone to know. She wouldn't have left a note."

"Tête-à-tête? Youse don't have to mince words with me, Warren. You mean, if she was having an affair?"

"Yep," Warren said, wiping up some egg yolk with part of a muffin and shoving it into his mouth. "Husband's away. Ideal time."

"So how do youse find out?"

"Ask questions. Soon as I finish my breakfast," and he was almost done, "I'm getting a shower, putting on a clean uniform shirt and heading out to ask around."

"Who's on the list?"

"Well, I'll stop at the Hibbard Corner's General Store. Gert's always up on the scoop."

"Especially the dirt," Delores said, being a receiver and contributor to the county gossip but never saying anything about the sheriff's department.

"Then I'm going to go talk to this Ingrid Swartz. Jennifer said she was her mother's best friend. Then I'll ask around her place. Actually, do that before Ingrid so that Jennifer won't be home from school."

"Do the neighbors know her mother's gone?"

"At least one of them does. They'll know sooner or later anyway. Better to learn it from me than hear it over the grapevine."

* * *

"Lands sakes, Warren," Gert greeted him, "Haven't seen youse in a coon's age."

"Wahl, when you work graveyards, what do you expect? That's a great smell. Oatmeal with apples and cinnamon?"

"Youse got a good nose, Warren. Second batch today. Peoples really loves 'em. The sheriff even came back for a second dozen." She scooped up a handful of cookies, not taking the time to put on a plastic glove, and dropped them in a bag.

"Here. On the house 'cause it's been so long."

"Thanks, Gert," Warren said discretely dropping a couple of one dollar bills on the floor. He had known what was going to happen and had been prepared.

"Iffen youse work nights, what's youse doing here in the middle of the day."

"Working on a case."

"No! 'Bout that explosion is it? Youse mean it really was a meth lab?"

"No meth lab. It was a meteor. Sheriff Jefferson is quite certain of that."

"Well, what is it then?"

"You hear of anyone sneaking around seeing someone she shouldn't?"

"Youse mean a woman?"

"Yep, guess I kinda gave that away, didn't I. But I'm interested in either sex. Maybe you heard of one half of a tryst and not the other."

"Tryst?"

"Fancy work for affair," Warren said half apologetically.

"Something recent youse wants?"

"Yep," Warren said, biting down on his first oatmeal cookie. Soft and sweet, the sensations titillated his taste buds.

"Nothing recent. Youse wants to tell me 'bout it?"

"I don't know anything. That's what I am trying to find out. And I don't know anything for a fact. Just trying to get some information."

"Youse not going to tell me anymore, are youse?" Gert seemed affronted not getting a live item for her verbal blog.

"No, but when things break, and they will, I'll give you the true story."

"Or what's youse wants me to think is true."

A hand on the doorknob, Warren said, "Gert, I'll tell you as much of the truth as I can."

Chapter 19

"Mr. Gilmore?" Warren said when the man opened the door in response to his knocking.

"Yes." Donald Gilmore was a short man. Well, shorter than Warren who was six one or had been until the shrinking of age had set in. Gilmore was between thin and fat, *stocky* Warren might report. He was dressed for staying inside on a cold day. Blue sweater with an emblazoned yellow M showing loyalty or favoritism to the Wolverines of The University of Michigan, but the green sweatpants with Spartans in white down the side dictated otherwise. *Maybe from his kids or just happened to be on sale*, Warren thought.

"I'd like to ask you some questions, sir."

"This about this Wilson woman? The one who's disappeared? Her bratty daughter called me this morning. "

"Yes, sir." *I wouldn't consider Jennifer bratty*, thought Warren.

"Always in trouble, that one," Don Gilmore continued. "Stole the mail out of my mailbox."

"What?" Warren said.

"Yes, well, okay. Not really stole it. She took it though. Brought it down to me like she's doing me a favor. I like the walk to the mailbox. Good exercise you know.

Well, used to walk. Now my knees are bad. Were really bad then I got replacements. Still don't work right. Have to use the golf cart to get to the mailbox. Course when it snows, I drive the car."

"Don, for heaven's sakes, invites the man in. You're standing there with the door open and letting all kinds of cold air in."

"That's my misses," Don said beckoning for Warren to do as his wife wanted. "She's blind as a bat so she can't be of much help."

Warren wiped his feet and entered the house as Don's wife responded, "If I had that sonar system like the bats have, I wouldn't be blind."

Warren entered a comfortable looking but crowded living room. Wilma Gilmore, as he was to learn her name, was sitting in a Lazy Boy type of chair that was partially reclined. There was another near it with a table covered with magazines and newspapers in between. The chairs were aimed at an old-style television set, big and bulky. Probably a 40-inch screen, Warren thought. Wasn't cheap when they bought it but it was still working. The sound had been muted.

"I'm Wilma in case Don didn't mention. He's like that."

Wonder if the squabbling goes on all the time?

"Please to meetcha, Mrs. Gilmore. Deputy Sheriff Warren Libka."

"You the one who was over there this morning," Don Gilmore said, settling himself in his recliner and tilting it back.

"There? Where?" Warren said being clueless intentionally.

"Over at the Wilsons."

"Yes, sir."

"So what's the scoop?"

"Don. Don't pry," Wilma snapped. "He'll tell us what he can."

Don glared at Wilma and then returned his attention to Warren.

"Well?"

"Not much to say," Warren said. "When Jennifer got up this morning, her mother wasn't home. There was no note. The car was in the garage."

"It was put there in the middle of the night," Wilma said.

Don looked at her. "And how would you know?"

"Because I was up getting a drink of milk. My stomach was bothering me."

"What time was that, Mrs. Gilmore?" Warren said as he jotted down the information in his notebook.

"Don't know. I didn't look."

"You couldn't have seen it anyway," Don snorted.

"Shut up." Then to Warren. "I've got macular degeneration, the dry kind. They can't do anything about it. I have no vision in front, just peripheral and that's not too clear. But I can see and get around just fine. Long as Mr. Clutter keeps his stuff picked up."

Don glared at her but knew better than to differ in Warren's opinion. Being married for 45 years, he was a pretty good judge of when to keep his mouth shut.

"Yes, ma'am," Warren injected into the bout, "could you tell me what you saw?"

"Well, I was at the sink getting ready to wash the glass out and set it in the rack. Milk is really hard to get off if it dries. I noticed a light, well a brightness really, and saw the Wilson's garage door going up. Then a car went it and the door came back down."

"What kind of car?" queried Warren.

"Have no idea. I can tell it was a car, not a big one. Not one of those SUVs. Just a car."

"Yes, ma'am."

"And I'll admit that I was curious so I watched for a minute. I mean, what's someone doing coming home in the middle of the night?"

"Tom does," Don interjected. "When he's been working and drives home from Flint." Then to Warren. "He's a long-distance truck driver. Works from Flint. Got a pickup he drives there and back. Not one of those who owns his own truck."

"Well, it wasn't a pickup. I may be blind, legally at least, but I can tell the different between a car, a pickup and an SUV."

"Yes, ma'am," Warren said in an attempt to mediate the bickering. "Did you see anything else?"

"Yes, I did," Wilma said glaring at Don. "I saw someone walk up the road to the East Path."

"From the garage?"

"I don't know but it was right after the car went in. About time for someone to get out of the car, leave the garage and walk to the street."

"Was it a man or woman?"

"She's lucky she didn't think it was a moose," Don said and chortled a bit, which drew another glare from Wilma.

Wonder if they have a guest bedroom, Warren thought. *That's where I'd be sleeping tonight. Wouldn't be safe in bed. Not with Delores's cold feet.*

"It wasn't a moose, you ninny," Wilma said. "Men!"

"Could you tell anything about the person? Warren asked.

"She wasn't short or really tall," Wilma said.

"It was a woman?"

"Did I say it was? Didn't mean to. I don't know. There's no lights out there and all I could really see was that it was somebody walking toward East Path. And I know it wasn't a moose or deer so keep your yap shut." This last comment she slung verbally at Don.

Warren took one of his business cards out of the pocket of his notebook and handed it to Don.

"If she thinks of anything else, would you give me a call? I'll let myself out."

As he sat in his cruiser, he felt happy to have escaped the battle unscathed. His experience from his days on the force in Ann Arbor had told him that he had learned all he was going to learn from the Gilmores. The Herberts, where he had stopped first, wanted to know what was going on but knew nothing. *Piece by piece,* Warren thought. *Cases come together piece by piece. At least we know that someone drove the car home. But where's the body?* He felt certain with the information from Wilma that there was foul play involved somewhere.

Chapter 20

After leaving the Gilmores, Warren drove to the south end of the lake where he parked on a pull-off near the old wooden bridge over the West Branch River, the main feeder other than rain runoff of Hibbard Pond. He spent about half an hour going back over the conversation to see if there was anything he missed. With the constant bantering it was difficult to keep things straight. What he ended up writing was an important piece of the puzzle: Wilma Gilmore saw a car enter the Wilson garage and someone walked to East Path. Sadly, Warren knew that if the case (whatever it turned out to be) went to trial, her credibility would be challenged. But a trial was a long way off.

After satisfying himself that he had all the knowledge he was going to gain from that visit, at least that mattered to the investigation, Warren settled back and ate the liverwurst and cream cheese sandwich Delores had packed. Ordinarily she would have put a slice of onion on it, but not when he was out questioning people. She did include two quarters of a dill pickle. He was careful not to drip any pickle juice on his uniform. His lunch complete, he started the cruiser, entered the Swartz's address in his GPS and started out.

The Swartz house was set back from West Path about a hundred feet and about a half mile south of Timber Point. The driveway was gravel up to the house and had one turn in it obviously made to preserve a big white pine that stood majestically, its green foliage in stark contrast to the bare grey, white and brown of the surrounding trees. The attached garage had a concrete apron where Warren parked.

He got out of the cruiser thinking how nice it was not to have to report to headquarters what he was doing because it was his own time. True he was in uniform but that was because it was an official investigation.

It was a minute after he rang the doorbell until Ingrid Swartz opened the door. Ordinarily he would have rung the bell again but he had called and knew she was expecting him.

"Officer Libka, please come in and close the door behind you."

He did as requested and followed her from the stone foyer into the great room that was wood flooring, most likely parquet. She was svelte and tall, five foot ten Warren estimated, and moved with a fluid grace. The entire time on stone and wood she moved soundlessly. Warren surmised that she was barefoot but he couldn't tell because her pants had bell-bottoms and her blouse sleeves matched. The material was black, red, and yellow in overlapping rectangles on a white background and as she moved it rippled and made it look as though she was on fire.

"What can I help you with that I didn't earlier this morning, Officer?" Ingrid said as she settled herself on a sofa tucking her legs under her (she was barefoot) and leaving him to choose a seat.

"Wahl, Mrs. Swartz …"

"Ingrid, please."

"Pardon me, ma'am but my upbringing just won't let me do that while in uniform if you don't mind."

Ingrid shrugged.

"Anyway, Mrs. Swartz, I remember that you were awakened by Jennifer's call this morning and might not have been thinking clearly. Also it is possible that you have knowledge of something that you wouldn't want Jennifer to know."

Ingrid looked at him quizzically.

"Let me start at the beginning and we'll get to that part. When is the last time you saw or talked to Gladys Wilson?"

"I think I saw her two days ago in Alpena but I can't be certain it was then or a few days before. I did talk to her yesterday briefly. There is an Audubon Society meeting she wanted to take me to but I demurred. I'm not really a bird person."

"But she is?"

"Yes, she loves the birds. I think she has ten bird feeders on her patio. But then one or two of them are just for squirrels. She tries to keep them away from the bird feeders but it doesn't work. Never does."

"So you do know about birds?"

"Just from what people have said and what I have read from time to time."

"So to last night. You didn't see or talk to her?"

Ingrid shook her head. But there was something there he couldn't place.

"Jennifer said when she went to bed about nine or so her mother was in the living room reading."

"She loves to read."

"What does she read?"

"Does that have something to do with her disappearance?"

"I don't know. I'm just trying to get the entire picture."

"She reads mysteries, suspense, and thrillers, I think. I prefer biographies."

"Did she have any special friends she might have gone to see without telling her daughter?"

"You mean, did she have a lover?"

"Yes, ma'am."

"Ridiculous. She and Tom were the perfect pair."

"There's always a chance of a flaw in the most perfect looking diamond."

Ingrid almost glared at him. He thought he caught a flash of fury but it passed quickly.

"Did the explosion wake you up last night?"

"What explosion? I don't think I heard anything."

"On Hibbard Pond, just off Timber Point," and Warren gestured in the general direction. "They're saying it was a meth lab."

"It was a met …," Ingrid stopped but he could have finished it for her "…eor." "A meth lab? Sounds a little ridiculous to me."

"Yes, I agree but that's what they're saying."

"Do you think that Gladys was there?"

"No, ma'am. Just asking questions," *and getting unspoken answers* he finished to himself.

"Well, Gladys didn't do drugs."

"You said that like she's dead."

"Did I. I didn't mean to. I was just saying that if it was a meth lab she wouldn't have anything to do with it."

After leaving the Swartz house, Warren sat in his car pulled over West Path and went over the interview again trying as much as possible to do it word for word. She knew more than she was saying. She knew it was a meteor yet she denied hearing it. And her makeup was sloppy, like she wasn't used to it and was trying to cover something up. Tired eyes maybe. Could be she is the one with the lover. Warren decided that he would have to keep tabs on this lady.

Chapter 21

After talking to Officer Libka, Jennifer walked back to her house, deep in her own thoughts. *Where was her mother? Was she alive? Had she been murdered? Where had she gone?* Her mind tugged at something buried deep inside but couldn't pull it loose. A female cardinal circled around her head chirping excitedly but she didn't notice. Also not recorded by her mind, a rabbit sat in the middle of the driveway and watched her pass within two feet and didn't move.

After locking the door, she dumped the mail on the table and went to the refrigerator. From the freezer she got three pieces of pizza left over from a trip to town with her parents when they had dinner at JJ's. Then retrieving her backpack, she started her homework. Normally it would be done in study hall but that time was taken up with the counselor. She had just finished her algebra and was starting English when the phone rang.

"Hi, daddy," she said excitedly.

There was silence on the other end for a moment.

"Sorry, Jennifer," said a female voice. "This is Earleen McBruce."

'Oh," Jennifer sounded dejected and then perked up. She liked the McBruces. Dugal McBruce and her father had become friends through the Hibbard Pond Sportsman initially and discovered they shared a bond of a common vocation – both were or had been truck drivers. Earleen was one of the most beautiful women she had ever met, even for an "old" lady.

"Hi, Mrs. McBruce. Mom's not home."

Again a moment of silence as Earleen struggled with what to say.

"I know, Jennifer, and I sorry. You father called Dugal a few minutes ago and asked if we would check up on you."

"I'm fine. I'm doing my homework. Just talked to Officer Libka, he's with the sheriff. I think he's in charge of the case. He said he had talked to a lot of people today, but right now mom's disappearance is an enigma. He didn't say that. He said 'puzzle'."

"I guess you mean that they don't know anything."

"That's what he said. He talked to the neighbors, and Mrs. Swartz, and Gert at the store, but didn't learn …" She paused as a thought hit her. "He didn't learn anything that he can tell me. You know how the police are. Until they know for certain, they won't say a word. 'The facts, ma'am, just the facts.' That's what that Detective Friday on that old police show said."

"Dragnet. You watch that?"

"No, but they spoof it all the time on late night talk shows and Saturday Night Live."

Earleen laughed. "Yes, you're right. Do you have supper?"

"Yes. I'm thawing some leftover pizza."

"Okay, you can come over here if you want."

"Thanks, but I'm fine. I have things to do and I want to find my mom's eBook reader. Maybe what she was reading will have a clue."

Earleen laughed again. "We know you can take care of yourself. You're your mother's daughter. But if you need anything, we can be there in five minutes."

"Okay, but I think I'll be fine."

"Well, just a suggestion. This is something I always did when Dugal was away. Keep your cell phone by your bed in case you need to call."

"Good idea. Thanks."

No sooner had she broken the connection then the phone rang again.

"Hello," Jennifer said more cautious this time.

"Hi, sweetie," her father said. "What's happening?"

"Oh, I just talked to Mrs. McBruce. She's nice. She said I could come over for dinner, but I'm thawing pizza."

"Any news?"

"No." They both were quiet for a moment.

"I talked to Officer Libka, he's in charge of the case, I think. He said he talked to a lot of people today but didn't learn anything. At least nothing he would tell me. Maybe he would tell you though."

"What, you think because you're a kid he wouldn't tell you if he found out anything important?"

"Yes."

"I don't think so. I just talked to the sheriff and he said they had no solid leads."

"So they have leads?" Jennifer was suddenly hopeful.

"No, he didn't say that. He just used police talk."

They chatted for several minutes and she told him about her day. She was about to break off when … "Oh, I almost forgot." And she told him about the doe and the birds, especially the pileated. "Then when I walked to get the mail. A squirrel nattered at me just two feet away. I could have touched it."

Her father said nothing.

"Daddy, what's wrong?"

"Oh, nothing. It's just …"

"Just what?"

"Your mother has that animal magic. I've watched her feeding the birds sometimes when she didn't know I was looking. You know how people get parrots to sit on their arms."

"Yes," said Jennifer trepidatiously.

"Well, one day, there was a pileated on the suet feeder where you saw that one today. She held out her arm and the bird looked at her for a minute, cocked its head and then flew and sat on her arm."

"Wow!" exclaimed Jennifer.

"I think she talked to it asking it to do that and it understood her."

"Mom can talk to the birds? Like Dr. Doolittle!"

"Well, this one time at least she seemed to."

"I wonder if I can do that."

"Possibly, sweetheart, but it might take time."

After they hung up, Tom Wilson sat in his truck cab and thought about what his daughter had told him. Jennifer had always liked animals but had never had the ability that Gladys had. Now Gladys had disappeared and Jennifer had the ability. Tom didn't know what to make of that.

Chapter 22

After her homework was completed and her dinner eaten, Jennifer went looking for her mother's eBook reader. She looked near her mother's favorite chair but it wasn't there. She checked the cushions and under it but there was nothing. She thought her mother always kept it by her chair. *Maybe she had taken it to the bedroom to read.* So she went and looked. It wasn't there. She checked the computer because that is how the eBook reader was charged. The charging cord was there, plugged into one of the computer's USB ports but no eBook reader. It was starting to be a real mystery. *Maybe she had taken it with her when she went out.* So she went to the garage. She searched the car from top to bottom, under the seats, in the glove compartment, in the map compartments on the doors. Nothing. *Maybe the forensic team had found it and taken it for evidence.* That seemed reasonable. *Who were those guys? Oh, yes, Rich Walker and Bob Roberts.* She would have to check tomorrow. As she started to leave the garage, something caught her eye. At the back of the garage, near the front of her mother's car, were plastic bins, like medium-sized rectangular plastic garbage cans where her mother kept the birdseed. She kept small amounts in that metal trash can near the feeders with the top chained down, but these containers contained about fifty pounds of birdseed: mixed for the regular feeders, corn kernels, corn on the cob for the squirrel feeders and sunflower seeds. Those were for the birds but the squirrels loved them and were difficult to keep out. She went to the first container labeled "Mixed" and took off the top. It was supposed to flap open because it was intended to be used as a kitchen trash can but her mother always took the top off so she did also. Looking inside she saw mixed birdseed consisting of red and white millet, corn bits, sunflower seeds and other fillers. She was about to put the top back on when something strange caught her eye. In the middle of the seed, was a narrow ridge about half an inch wide and eight inches long – just like the narrow side of her mother's eBook reader. She stuck her hand in, grabbed something hard and pulled it out. The eBook reader in its blue, white and black plastic protective cover. Now very excited, she was closing the access door when she remembered she hadn't put the cover back on. Her mother wouldn't be pleased, so she returned and put the lid on.

In the house, she settled herself in her mother's reading chair and turned on the eBook reader. When it turned on, it was in library mode where the books on the reader were listed. The second one down caught her eye: *The History of Witches.* What a strange book for her mother to be reading. She selected it and found that her mother was at location 911 (no page number given):

> Of her actual appearance, divested of
> her infernal attributes, no better description
> could be desired than that given by Reginald

Scot in "The Discoverie of Witchcraft": –
"Witches be commonly old, lame, bleare-
eied, pale, fowle, and full of wrinkles;
poore, sullen, superstitious, and papists" –
(it is perhaps unnecessary to point out that
Scot was of the Reformed Faith) – "or such
as know no religion; in whose drousie minds
the devil hath goten a fine seat; so as, what
mischief, mischance, calamitie or slaughter
is brought to passé, they are easily persuad-
ed the same is done by themselves, imprint-
ing in their minds an earanest and constant
imagination hereof. They are leane and de-
formed, showing melancholie in their faces
to the horror of all that see them. They are
doting, scolds, mad, devilish."

Of course she laughed at this. Her mother most certainly did not fit this description. She was a beautiful woman.
But most witches she knew about (like the Wicked Witch
of the West in *The Wizard of Oz)* certainly did fit that mold.

She went back to the beginning of the book and read
the Foreword:

Lest any reader should open this volume expecting to read an exhaustive treatise
on witches and witchcraft, treated scientifi-
cally, historically, and so forth, let me dis-
arm him before hand by telling him that he
will be disappointed. The witch occupies so
large a place in the story of mankind that to
include all the detail of her natural history

within the limits of one volume would need the powers of a magician no less potent than was he who confined the Eastern Djinn in a bottle.

She laughed at that remembering the story of Aladdin and the genie (Djinn) in the bottle. *The History of Witches* was an old book written in 1908 according to the Foreword. It must be popular if someone had gone to all the trouble to put it in eBook format because it had to be scanned page by page, formatted, and checked for accuracy. Nowadays the programs used to convert the printed word into something like a Microsoft Word document were very sophisticated and often got everything perfect. Jennifer knew this because she often used their scanner and the computer to get needed excerpts for her school papers rather than having to type them in. But when they had first come out, they weren't nearly as accurate.

She read a couple of pages and found the material about witches fascinating. But the question still lingered: Why was her mother reading about witches? She couldn't tell if it was a library book or something her mother had bought. Curious she checked the last pages of the book and found a list of references. One or two of them had been underlined. She moved the cursor of the reader to the underlined book and saw a command: click to read highlight. So she did: "This looks like an interesting book." And the highlight for the next book took her breath away: "I have to get this one." The title of the book was: *The Witch's Crafte and Her Spells*. Why would her mother want to know about spells? Was she trying to be a witch? Or was she a witch?

That was a chilling thought that seemed not to be so surprising but Jennifer didn't know why.

She noticed that the date on the highlight was two weeks ago. Plenty of time to get the book from the library or from someplace on the web like Amazon.com, her mother's favorite source for things. The book was not listed in the eBook reader's library shelf. It was an old book, published in the early 1800s when there was still a real interest in this country about witchcraft. However recently, the hot thing, at least among teenagers, was vampires. She had always thought vampires were stupid. Somehow witches seemed a lot more interesting.

If her mother didn't have it as an eBook, she would have tried to get a hard copy. She went to the computer and pulled up Amazon.com in the browser. She searched for *The Witch's Crafte and Her Spells* and got a hit. Someone was selling the book for $10,000. Her mother didn't have that kind of money. Or did she? She noticed that the greeting at the top of the browser page was: "Hello, Gladys. If this isn't Gladys click here." She didn't. Instead she clicked "My account" and then "Order History." The page switched to where a person would enter a username and password and the part "I am a certified user" was filled in although she couldn't see the password. So she clicked on it and her mother's order history came up. The last thing ordered, just about one week ago, was *The Witch's Crafte and Her Spells.* She was stunned. She didn't bother with checking the price but ran out of the house to the garage.

Chapter 23

Throwing off the lid to the mixed birdseed, she plunged her hand in, searching as she pushed her arm deeper into the seeds as far as she could reach. Nothing. She was taller than her mother by two inches so her mother should have shorter arms – certainly no longer than hers. The next bin was kernel corn and into it her arm went. Again as far as she could reach. Nothing. Then it was the sunflower seeds turn, the bin was only half full. The search revealed nothing. She was disappointed. In some ways her mother was a creature of habit so not finding anything meant she had a different place but that didn't ring true. In a funk she replaced the lid on the sunflower seeds, then the corn but she didn't see the cover for the mixed bird feed. Then she spotted it lying on the far side of a bag of sunflower seeds. Of course, she would have purchased more since she was beginning to run low. Just as Jennifer had deduced, the bag of sunflower seeds had been opened. Plunging her hand in, she searched down and when her arm was in up to the elbow she felt something. Not a book but something slippery, like plastic. Grabbing it tightly she started pulling up. Whatever it was, it wouldn't come easily. It was fighting back or so it seemed. It got easier as it moved toward the top of the bag and suddenly it burst out, bringing sunflower seeds with it. The release was so sudden that Jennifer stumbled and almost fell and indeed dropped whatever it was, which landed on the floor loudly. Picking it up from among the sunflowers seeds that had come out with it, Jennifer turned and ran out of the garage, only shutting but not locking the door behind her. It is easy to forgive her; her mother certainly would, in the excitement of her discovery.

In the house, the door locked and bolted behind her more for the secrecy of the discovery rather than the security provided, Jennifer put the parcel on the kitchen table and stood looking at it. Whatever it was, a two-gallon zipper freezer bag protected it. Inside the bag, Jennifer could see a silver rectangle inside another freezer bag, this one folded around the object so that it would easily fit into the outside bag. Her hands shaking, Jennifer opened the outer bag and removed the object. Looking at it through its plastic bag container, she could see that the silver was aluminum foil. Turning it over she saw two dark green strips on either end of the rectangle and another near the middle forming a huge capital I. It must be important because her mother had taken great precautions to protect it. Trepidatiously she unzipped the second bag and removed the foil wrapped object. This was the first time she had noticed how heavy it was. About the size of a regular piece of paper, it was about an inch and a half thick. Looking carefully at the green strips she realized they were duct tape, with the end cuts even – obviously made with scissors. Jennifer backed away from the table, turned and walked to a counter, her eyes never leaving the object for fear that it would vanish in a puff of smoke. Fumbling with her hands she opened a drawer and found the roll of dark green duct tape she knew would be there. Then she returned to the table and held the roll of duct tape against the tape on the object. It was a perfect match in color, at least to her eyes. She looked at the roll of tape and found the end, her eyes leaving the object for the first time since she had removed it from the freezer bag. The end was easily found because her mother always used one of the plastic tabs found securing bags of potatoes and other things to make the end easy to find. As Jennifer knew it would be, the end was an even cut and would match one of the ends of the three pieces of tape on the package. The question now was "Should she open the package?" No, that wasn't the question because she was going to open the package. The question was "Could she put it back together so that her mother wouldn't know she had opened it?" She quickly decided she really didn't care. If her mother were mad Jennifer would explain why she had opened it – not because she was curious (a little – no, a big – white lie) but because she was trying to find out what had happened to her mother.

Her decision made she sat down at the table and stared at the object – might as well acknowledge it for the book she knew it was: *The Witch's Crafte and Her Spells.* Carefully lest she damage the book, she pulled on one of the duct tape pieces making the bar at one end of the I. Jennifer could then see the end of the foil where her mother had folded it. On each side there was a little triangle where the foil had been folded under. She looked at it carefully so that she could reproduce it. The other piece of tape also came away cleanly revealing the same two folds. Taking a deep breath, Jennifer removed the long piece of tape revealing the fold that her mother had made with the ends of the foil wrapping around the book. Everything was pristine, no wrinkles at all. Her mother had been very careful and Jennifer would be also. Even though she knew that the foil could not be used again, she was extremely careful in folding back the flaps and the triangle folds. Then she unfolded the long flap and grasped the two ends and pulled them apart. It was indeed a book, dark black cover with gold writing on it. She turned the book so that she could read the writing: *The Witch's Crafte and Her Spells.* She smoothed the foil back and opened the book. There was a piece of white paper lying on the piece of black paper that was the flyleaf of the book. Handwritten on it was the following:

Enjoy this book and use it well.

It is my gift to you.

Chapter 24

There was no signature. Jennifer exhaled and realized that she had been holding her breath. Clutching the cover in her left hand, she turned the white sheet like a page and then the black sheet revealing the title page:

The Witch's Crafte
And
Her Spells

There was nothing about a publisher or any other information. Looking at it carefully, Jennifer realized the reason: It was handwritten not printed. It was done in calligraphy like Bibles were done by monks before the invention of the printing press by – who was it? Gutenberg? No, that was moveable type but everyone thought it was the printing press. Before Gutenberg had invented a way to make the letters individually and be held in place, pages were hand-carved on a block of wood.

Jennifer turned the page, expecting to see a table of contents or other information ordinarily found at the beginning of a book. Instead she found a page with hand-drawn pictures in circle around a word she did not recognize. The pictures were of leaves, leaves with berries, sprigs of weeds or flowers, and a toadstool or mushroom. She turned the page finding nothing on the verso or left hand page. On the recto or right hand page was a drawing of what looked like a piece of ivy with red berries. Below it were two words and under that a paragraph. Jennifer assumed that the two words were the name of the plant and the paragraph was a description. She turned the page and found that (as on all succeeding pages) the verso was blank but everything was on the recto. She giggled to herself realizing that she was using those terms rather than left and right because they had been studying that in English class. As she paged through the book she saw pictures like the first but different shaped leaves in various shades of green and berries of different colors. There were pictures of sprigs of weeds or flowers, nuts, and mushrooms, toadstones as well as other strange looking fungi. All had what she thought to be their names below the picture and a paragraph describing the flora. One page in particular drew her attention but she did not know why. It was a mushroom (or toadstool, she didn't know which) with a thick dark purple stem and a white bell shaped top with purple sworls. *Sworl?* Jennifer thought. *Why would I think "sworl"? It's a swirl.* Around the edge of the top there were small v-shaped indentations. Hanging from one of these was a drop of dark purple liquid. Jennifer realized that there was an indentation below each sworl. *Huh?* Jennifer thought. *I did it again!*

Forcing herself away from the page and not understanding why it had captivated her so much, she continued on and finally came to another page announcing a different chapter, she assumed. On it were many glass vials containing different color liquids arranged in a circle and in the circle was a word.

Turning the page, she saw a picture of a glass vial (Jennifer knew it was crystal) containing a pink solution. Below that was writing, like a title but Jennifer had no idea what it said – the language was strange. Under the title was what Jennifer took to be a list of ingredients because she knew this was a potion of some kind and this was followed by what she assumed to be directions on mixing the potion. *Like a cookbook,* Jennifer thought.

The next page was another potion, only green, then a red one with a heart on the vial. *A love potion.* There was a dark purple one and a black one with a skull and cross-bones. *Poison.* Actually there were several of those. She continued through the potions chapter until once again she was attracted to a page. This one had three drawings at the top. The center picture was a vial containing a purple liquid and on either side of the drawings were disks. The picture in both was that of a cobblestoned city street. However, in the one on the left only parts near the edge of the disk were distinct, the interior was blurry and the center was indistin-guishable. The picture in the right hand disk was sharp and focused. She glanced at the potion's title and froze. She recognized the first word. Putting a pencil to mark the page she flipped back until she found the purple mushroom. Its name was the first word of the potion. She couldn't read the directions (if that was indeed what they were), but there were only two ingredients, the mushroom and something else but she didn't recognize the word.

Finally she flipped on and realized she was nearing the end of the book when she found another chapter title page.

This time the pictures around the title were of human (or she supposed human) figures all with their left hand in the air and something in front of them – a red ball, an orange sun, and a sword. When she turned the page, the picture at the top caused her to stop. It was of a person, sex indeterminable, with the left arm in the air. In front of the person was a ball of what appeared to be fire. Under this picture was another showing a person in profile, left arm raised, and in front of the person were several versions of the fireball increasing in size, larger as the distance from the person increased. Then a picture of the ball throwing pieces out – *It exploded,* thought Jennifer. A fireball spell. The writing under the pictures was just four words. Under those four words written, in what she thought was pencil, were the same words but broken into what Jennifer assumed were syllables because letters of the words were separated by "•". One of the words had three syllables and one of the words, the last, only one. One of the syllables was written in capital letters and she understood that to be the stressed syllable. She sounded out the syllables as best she could, because the letters were like her own alphabet, but nothing happened and she breathed a sigh of relief. On the next page, the picture was again a figure with the left arm in the air and a shield, or what Jennifer took to be a shield. Beneath that picture again was a profile view of the figure and in front of it a huge shield that would hide the figure completely if viewed from the front, and under that two words. Again in pencil underneath someone had broken the first word into three syllables but the second word was one. Jennifer looked at the writing closely and thought it was her mother's. Again she tried to pronounce the words but nothing happened.

At this point Jennifer happened to look at the clock and noted that it was almost 11:30 and she had to be up at 6:00. She closed the book, hastily rewrapped it in the foil using new duct tape to cover the seams. Then the package was put back into a bag that she zipped closed, folded over and put into the second two-gallon bag, and it was closed. She hurried out of the house to the garage not even noticing that the access door was unlocked. Trying to stuff the package into the seeds was impossible. So she took a small bucket her mother used to carry seeds and laboriously filled the bucket many times with seed from the bag that she then dumped into the plastic bin containing sunflower seeds . When she thought she was deep enough, she took one last bucket full, set the book upright in the bag and poured the bucket of seeds over it to hide it. Then she took buckets of seeds from the plastic bin and filled the bag to the proper level. It was only then as she checked to be certain that all was right, that she noticed all the seeds on the floor. She found the dustpan and brush her mother used to clean up dropped seeds and swept the seeds up. She also picked up a lot of dust so she carried the dustpan outside and to the patio where she strewed the contents. Once the dustpan and brush were back, she closed the door and locked it.

Back in the house, she locked herself in and hurried to her bedroom, turning off lights as she went. She was too tired to put on her pajamas so after removing her blouse, jeans and socks, she simply collapsed into bed trusting her alarm to wake her.

Chapter 25

Small lights shone over the doors to the post office, the funeral home and the library. At 2:00 in the morning there were no lights on in either the Hibbard Corners General Store or Helen's Hair Quarters. A dark blue SUV with no lights on rolled silently to a stop just past the Hair Quarters. The driver sat quietly in the vehicle and watched and listened with windows rolled down. There were no sounds. After a few minutes the driver's door opened but there was no interior light. The driver got out wearing a long robe with bell sleeves and a hood. Retrieving a bag from the car, the figure walked quickly to the door of Helen's Hair Quarters. Taking a spray paint can from the bag, in one motion the figure quickly painted a circle and then an inverted five-point star making pentacle. Putting the can back into the bag, the figure removed a second can and used it to draw a red V with outward horn like protrusions from the top of each leg and then two dots for eyes.

Stepping back, Ingrid looked at her artwork of a Judas Goat. *Not perfect but it will do. The North Witch will get the message*. She hurried back to her SUV, got in and drove south on East Hibbard Pond Path. It was the long way but she didn't want anyone to see a vehicle leaving and returning.

* * *

Jennifer sat up abruptly in her bed. In front of her, as though on a television screen, she could see what Ingrid was doing. When Ingrid had gone, Jennifer whispered some words she didn't know, wouldn't have understood nor remembered. Then she used her right arm and first traced the pentacle as Ingrid had done it and then the symbol of the goat, symbolic of Satan. As she did so, the paint on the door disappeared in just the way it had appeared. There was no trace of Ingrid's warning.

Her job completed, Jennifer lay back down and closed her eyes. She had never been awake and would remember nothing in the morning.

* * *

Ingrid drove all the way around the lake, passing the East Witch's driveway, turning on to South Path and then North Path, passing the South Witch's house, and finally turned into her own driveway. The entire time she had not seen another vehicle but that was not unusual for that time of night. Her only fear had been that she would see a sheriff's cruiser.

At the end of her driveway, she pushed the garage door opener and by the time she got to the house, the door was up. She drove into the garage and closed the door. The two cans of paint were put back into the paint cabinet and the robe was folded, put into a plastic bag and hidden in an out-of-the-way place. Entering the house she smiled to herself wishing she could be there in the morning when Mrs. T-G saw her front door.

When the garage door had come down and settled, any watcher (and there were none) would have seen that Ingrid's version of the Judas Goat (also known as Sigil of Baphomet) appeared on the door in just the manner she had drawn it on Mrs. T-G's door but it was larger – the circle went from the top of the door to the bottom.

The next morning dawned crisp and clear, the start of a warming trend that indicated the end of the winter and melting of the ice on Hibbard Pond. Ingrid decided to walk to the end of her driveway and get the paper. On cold or snowy mornings she afforded herself the luxury of driving that short distance. On the way back she was deeply engrossed in one of the stories on the front page and did not notice the door until she was about to turn on the walk to her front door. Then she saw it in her peripheral vision, turned to look at it, and screamed. Fortunately the neighbors didn't live close. She couldn't believe what she saw. It was her sign. She knew it was. How did it get here? She had no answer to that. But she did have a solution.

Hurrying inside she got a white candle and put it in a silver candlestick and then placed it in the middle of the kitchen table. Lighting it, she sat down and looked into the flame and tried to pull its protective powers around her. Soon she felt that she was within the candle's flame and said:

Craft the spell
In the fire
Craft it well
Weave it higher
Weave it now
Of simmering flame
None shall come
To hurt or maim
None shall pass
This fiery wall
None shall pass
No, none at all

Finishing the spell she felt herself within its sphere of protection. Leaving the candle burning she donned old clothes and went to the garage. She found a can of white trim paint in the paint cabinet; her husband had been a keeper of extras. Armed with the can, a paintbrush, and a stepladder she attacked the door vigorously. It took an hour to cover the symbol and the paints didn't quite match but you had to look close. Fortunately Karl always bought the best paint. She would wait until good weather and then paint the entire door again. Maybe a pale green instead of the proverbial white. She had just finished cleaning up and putting things away when the phone rang.

Hurrying inside she picked up the phone just as the answering machine clicked on.

"Hello," she said breathlessly.

"Ingrid, it's Helen. You'll never guess what's happened?"

Ingrid smiled to herself. She knew what had happened.

"Gretchen McCaulay just left."

What? Not the door?

"Who's she?"

"Oh, she's the wife of John McCaulay, the local DNR officer."

What? No outpouring about her door?

"Oh, yes, I remember." But she didn't.

"She told me that when the ice clears, U.S.G.S. divers are going to recover the meteor."

Ingrid said nothing. She couldn't believe what she was hearing. Nothing about the door.

"That means they'll find Gladys' body," Helen continued.

"Maybe not. We don't know what happened to her."

"Yes, but her body is down there somewhere."

"It could have floated anywhere. Maybe the meteor actually hit her and burned her to a crisp." *One could always hope.*

"You think?"

"I don't know. I think that we just do as we planned and don't get involved."

"You're right. Always the level headed one. The news about Gladys disappearing isn't out yet."

"The sheriff probably has it under wraps trying to figure out what happened." *Good luck with that. But what about your door?*

"Probably. Gert hasn't heard a thing. You know how she blabs."

Yes, indeed.

"Anything else on the news front?" Ingrid said trying to get Helen to tell her about the door.

"Nothing that I can think of."

Your door?

"Okay, keep in touch."

The idea about diving to retrieve the meteor didn't sit well with Ingrid despite her attempt at levity. That and the symbol on her door made her decide that today happy hour started at, she checked the clock, 11:15. *Hell, it's five o'clock somewhere!*

That night at the same time when the Sigil of Baphomet or Judas Goat had first appeared on Ingrid's garage door, it came back. It didn't bleed through the concealing white paint. It was painted afresh. And the red was blood.

Chapter 26

The alarm clock jolted Jennifer out of a deep sleep. She knew she had some weird dreams that night but couldn't remember them. She took a quick shower, keeping her hair dry because it looked all right up in a ponytail. She dressed and quickly ate a bowl of cereal before hurrying to catch the bus. She cut through the woods to save time and found herself looking for the doe but didn't see it. Passing by the evergreen copse, she looked in and saw the doe lying there looking at her. The doe got up and stood there un-afraid.

"Good morning." *What's her name?* Jennifer thought and then said, "Feebee." The doe walked toward her until Jennifer could reach out and touch its head, which she did. "I've got to go," Jennifer said as though the deer could un-derstand her and hurried through the woods to East Path. The school bus was already sitting at the stop with stop signs out and flashers on and Jennifer saw Jimmy Lukas getting on. She waved at Lucy, the driver, and ran to the stop and got on the bus.

"Oversleep, Jennifer?" Lucy asked with a smile.

"Yes," Jennifer said, "I had a bad night."

She quickly chided herself for lying and then realized that it was a bad night. Her dreams had been nightmares, full of monsters and witches throwing fireballs and wielding huge swords.

She went through her morning classes in a daze and welcomed the lunch break, buying lunch for the first time in several weeks because she hadn't the time to make it. Usually she showered the night before, but she had been so entranced with the spell book she hadn't done that. At the end of the day, she put the books she needed into her backpack and headed for the waiting school bus, lost in thought and walking slowing. Suddenly she realized that she wasn't in the correct hallway but was in the science wing outside the chemistry lab. Looking in, she saw a box on the teacher's lab desk and went into see what was in it. She found herself look at a box of test tubes with plastic stoppers. She reached out and took two of them, immediately secreting them in her backpack. Then she turned and raced from the room and toward the bus.

Once again sitting by herself by choice, she thought about what she had done. *How had she gotten to the chemistry lab? Why had she gone in and why had she stolen the test tubes?* She had never stolen anything in her life if you didn't count taking a few cookies without her mother's permission. She found herself shaking her head in disbelief.

"Bad day?" somebody asked.

That brought her out of her reverie and she looked up to see Muddy Waters across the way looking at her.

"Yes," she said. "Actually a bad couple of days."

Muddy nodded at the empty seat next to her and moved onto it.

"I understand," he said. "There are all sorts of rumors but they all seemed to hinge around your mother."

Jennifer stared at him.

"Is that the problem?" asked Muddy.

Jennifer nodded.

"I won't pry," he said, "but I understand. If I had a problem with my mother, I'd be upset too."

They sat there quietly, Jennifer feeling better having someone sit by her even if they didn't talk. When her stop came, Muddy moved back to his seat and Jennifer got up.

"Thank you," she said and Muddy smiled.

Jennifer crossed the road and walked toward her house. She started to cut through the woods and then remembered the mail. She hurried to the mailbox but there was nothing there and she cut into the woods hoping to see Feebee. It was almost as though the doe was waiting for her. She was standing near the copse watching Jennifer make her way through the woods.

"Hello, Feebee," Jennifer said and the doe turned and walked toward a rotten stump about twelve feet away. Halfway there Feebee stopped and looked back at her and then shook her head as though to say *Come on.* Jennifer followed Feebee to the stump where Feebee used her hoof to clear some leaves from the bottom of the stump. What was revealed made Jennifer stare in disbelief. It was a purple mushroom like the one she had seen in the book last night. Getting down on her knees for a closer look, Jennifer saw that there was a purple drop of moisture running from one purple sworl. Instinctively Jennifer opened her backpack and removed one of the test tubes. Uncapping it, she stuck it under the indentation in the cap just as the drop reached and, after only a momentary hesitation, dropped into the tube. Jennifer quickly capped it and put the tube into the backpack.

She felt Feebee nudging her and moved out of the way and watched as the doe ate the mushroom and then moved off as though saying *You've done your part and I've done mine.* Jennifer got up and continued through the woods. As she neared her home she saw two men standing in front of the garage. One she immediately recognized as her father and she broke into a run screaming, "Daddy." She flung herself into his arms and they stood there for a moment clutching each other. When they broke the hold, Jennifer noticed that the other man was Officer Libka. Jennifer looked at him hopefully but he shook his head sadly.

"I was just telling you father that we have nothing firm to go on," Officer Libka explained. "I have talked to many people today from all around the lake and nobody has any idea of what your mother has done or where she may have gone."

"So there is absolutely nothing," her father said.

Officer Libka looked at him and then shrugged.

"There are one or two possibilities, very slim but I really can't say anything about them."

"You mean they're the kind of things you could catch somebody up on?"

"Yes," Officer Libka said. "Just some details that may help us eventually."

Chapter 27

As Jennifer and her father entered the house, the tele-phone rang and they stopped in their tracks. It rang a se-cond time and they looked at each other. On the third ring, Jennifer ran to it and picked it up.

"Hello," she said anxiously wanting to add "Mother."

It was a woman's voice but not her mother's.

"Jennifer, this is Mrs. Gilmore, from across the street."

"Yes, ma'am," Jennifer said deflatedly.

"I hate to bother you, but my husband had to go to Lincoln and I would really like a cup of tea. I can't … well, I shouldn't use the stove because of my eyesight. Would you mind coming over and making me some?"

Jennifer knew that her mother always helped out Mrs. Gilmore. She was a nice lady even though her husband was a grouch.

"No, I don't mind," Jennifer said, trying to sound cheerful. "I'll be right over."

Jennifer told her dad what she was going to do and he left the room saying he had to unpack.

"Put your dirty clothes on top of the washing machine and I'll do them when I get back," Jennifer called after him.

Then she opened her backpack and took out the two test tubes. The one with the drop of purple mushroom dew, as she thought of it, she put into her pocket. She got out the bottle of white vinegar and poured about a tablespoon of it into the other test tube that she then capped and put into her pocket. After she put the vinegar away, she got her jacket, put it on and left the house.

The door to the Gilmore house was ajar but Jennifer knocked and then entered the house when Mrs. Gilmore answered.

"Hello, Jennifer, and thank you," Mrs. Gilmore said from her chair in the living room. "I should have had Don do this before he left but I forgot."

"No problem," Jennifer said. "I've got my homework done and daddy and I are going out for dinner tonight at the Old Mill."

"The tea's in the …"

"I remember," Jennifer said. And she did because she had been over with her mother several times to help Mrs. Gilmore out. *Macular degeneration must be a terrible thing,* Jennifer thought as she walked into the kitchen.

She put the teakettle on to heat, got out a mug and a tea bag, and was about to open the refrigerator door to get the squeeze bottle of lemon that she knew Mrs. Gilmore wanted in her tea when she stopped. From the depths of her mind came the thought that lemon juice and what she was going to put into the tea didn't react well together. She got out a tablespoon and a teaspoon from the silver drawer. Then she took the two test tubes out of her pocket and looked at them. The purple dewdrop had not broken apart and had not smeared the sides of the tube whereas the vinegar had left legs on the sides where it had sloshed as she hurried across the street. The teakettle started to whistle and

Jennifer turned off the heat. She opened the teabag and put it into the cup and poured hot water in to within a half inch of the top.

Holding the tablespoon level in her left hand, she picked up the test tube of vinegar and pulled the cap off with her teeth. Then she carefully measured out and poured exactly two teaspoons of vinegar into the tablespoon. Re-capping the vinegar tube, she put it down and picked up the tube with the purple dewdrop. Uncapping it with her teeth, she carefully tilted the tube to pour the dewdrop into the vinegar. She found herself holding her breath as the purple dewdrop slid down the side of the test tube and, pausing only slightly, dropped into the vinegar. It seemed to settle to the bottom of the liquid and then started expanding as little tentacles reached out. Then suddenly the liquid in the tablespoon was all purple. There was a little hiss, a bit of mist rose from the liquid and the tablespoon warmed in Jennifer's hand. Then the liquid turned opaquely white. Jennifer poured the liquid into the tea and stirred it with the tablespoon, which she then rinsed, dried and put away. Putting the teaspoon into the mug, she carried it into the living room.

"Did you remember the lemon?" Mrs. Gilmore asked as she accepted the mug.

"Try it," Jennifer said smiling.

Mrs. Gilmore stirred the tea with the spoon, as she always did although there was never any need, and put the teaspoon on the table between her chair and her husband's. Holding the mug with both hands she lifted it to her lips and took a sip. A broad smile crossed her lips and she took a larger drink.

"This is marvelous," she said smiling at Jennifer. "What in the world did you do to it?"

"Nothing special," Jennifer answered, *just added a little magic potion.*

That thought stopped her because she suddenly realized that she had not thought about what she was doing with the purple dewdrop. It had all seemed so perfectly natural.

"Be certain that you drink it all while it's warm," Jennifer admonished Mrs. Gilmore. "It's more healthful that way."

On her way back home, Jennifer looked at the woods next to the garage and saw Feebee standing just at the edge. She waved to her and the deer turned and went back into the woods. Jennifer continued between the house and the garage to the patio where the birds were chirping excitedly. She replenished all the bird feeders that needed it, enjoying the way the birds flitted around her chirping excitedly. One chickadee even landed on her shoulder and did a little preening before flitting off to get a sunflower seed that it took away to stick into a crack in some tree and then open with its beak. Feeling much better than she had in two days, Jennifer walked back to the house looking forward to dinner out with her father, never thinking that she was subconsciously accepting the fact that their family was now permanently two.

Chapter 28

The next morning when Ingrid went to get the paper she was shocked to see the Judas Goat on the garage door again. However this time it was different, the red had run. When she looked closely, it appeared to be still wet and she whirled around to see if someone was watching her reaction. They couldn't be far away. But she didn't see anyone.

"I'LL FIND OUT WHO YOU ARE AND MAKE YOU PAY FOR THIS," she screamed. To herself she thought, *Oh, Karl, what am I going to do?* Then she turned back to the sign and the still damp red paint. She touched her finger to it and it was in fact still wet. She smelled it and immediately wretched. She had smelled that smell often enough – it was blood (goat's blood in fact although Ingrid could not tell that.) She raced into the house and got a bucket of water and poured ammonia in it. Carrying the bucket and a rag, she returned to the door and managed to clean the blood away leaving only the inverted pentacle. She was out of paint and would have to get some more.

She backed her car out of the garage and then pressed the button to lower the door. She watched anxiously as it came back down, expecting the goat's head to be there again but it wasn't. She breathed a sigh of relief and headed for the hardware in Ossineke going through Hibbard Corners on the way. She parked next to the general store and went in ostensibly to buy some cornbread since it was Friday, but in reality she wanted to see the front door of Helen's Hair quarters. It was pristine white. She almost turned around and left without buying anything but that would have looked bad.

"Morning, Ingrid," Gert greeted her cheerfully as she entered the store. "Did youse hear that the U.S. Navy is going to dive and get that meteor?"

"No, I didn't," Ingrid said. "What I heard was that the U.S. Geographical Survey was going to dive and get the meteor or whatever it was."

"Really?"

"Yes, I heard it from Gretchen McCaulay."

"Oh, wells I try to remember."

"Can I get four pieces of cornbread, please?"

"Just four? Hardly seems like enough."

"It's just me," Ingrid said.

"Oh, right. Sorry," Gert said apologetically and put five pieces in the bag in the way of a peace offering. "Oh, I gots some with jalepeño in it if you want?"

"No, I'm spicy enough. Thanks." And Ingrid handed her a five.

Gert laughed, gave her the change. "Have a nice day."

"I'll try," Ingrid said and meant it.

In the Ossineke hardware, Ingrid explained that she needed to cover paint that bled through but she didn't know what kind it was. Karl had done something before he died and it hadn't been done right.

"Karl not do something correctly?" the clerk said. "That's a first."

And he'll be rolling over in his grave being accused of such a thing, Ingrid thought.

She was given a primer guaranteed to prevent bleeding from just about anything and a gallon of the best covering exterior enamel they had. *Probably the problem,* Ingrid thought. *I used just house paint, not enamel.*

"Is this latex base just as good as oil?" she asked.

"Yes, ma'am," said the clerk.

Back home, the goat still had not reappeared, for which Ingrid was truly thankful. Changing her clothes, brewing a pot of coffee she put into a thermos, she assembled primer, enamel, brushes, a tarp in case she got messy, stepladder and a lawn chair because it was going to be a while. She starting at the top and was planning on working her way down. Her plan was to do the entire door and that goat was not going to come back!

"Nice day for painting."

Ingrid was so startled she almost fell off the stepladder. Turning and looking she saw it was Joe, the UPS man holding a package.

"Hi, Joe. Didn't hear you."

"It's so nice, I decided to walk in." Joe was in shorts. *Pushing the season,* Ingrid thought.

"I wasn't expecting anything."

"Well, Amazon doesn't usually make mistakes. Why are you repainting the door?"

Ingrid looked at him and then at the door with the inverted pentacle only partially covered.

"You don't think I should cover that up?" Ingrid said.

"Cover what up, Mrs. Swartz?" Joe asked.

"You don't see anything?"

"White garage door being painted white again."

"Seriously?"

"Seriously, Mrs. Swartz. Have to go. Extra heavy load today. Enjoy yourself, Tom."

Tom? Oh, Tom Sawyer.

Ingrid climbed down from the ladder and looked at the door. The inverted pentacle was there plain as day. Was Joe blind? Or was she the only one who could see it? To answer that question she would have to ask someone else, but that would involve a lot of questions.

She heard the sound of a car on the driveway and turned to look. A purple van was coming down the driveway. *South Witch!*

Ingrid walked to where the van was parked. Jane Eyre Polli (aka South Witch) was in the van.

"Morning, Ingrid. What are you doing?"

"Painting my garage door," *you ninny.*

"Doesn't look like it needs it."

"Really? What do you see?"

"A white garage door being painted white."

"Okay, yes, you're right. I am painting it green because I like green."

"Ah, the color of love. New man in your life?"

"No, I just like green."

"Reason I stopped was to tell you that the U.S. Coast Guard is going dive for the meteor."

"It's the U.S. Geographical Survey."

"Oh, Martha said …"

"Well, Martha's wrong. I got it from the DNR's mouth."

"Okay, don't take my head off. Got to run. We ran out of vodka last night and Rolli's a little under the weather so I have to run to Alpena. The Cracker Barrel is the only store around here to carry what Rolli likes."

With that, Jane Eyre backed the van adroitly out and onto West Path and headed north. Ingrid turned and looked at the door, still seeing the black inverted pentacle. *What the hell, I must be going nuts.*

Ingrid plugged on with the job finishing in the late afternoon. After cleaning up, she poured herself a generous libation, heated a frozen dinner, and tumbled into bed. In the middle of the night, at precisely the same time as previously, the Judas Goat reappeared complete with goat's blood.

Chapter 29

Ingrid was now convinced that someone was out to get her and that someone had more power than she did and that her protection spell was not strong enough. She needed help. With Gladys dead, she didn't know anyone else that had any power. Except for the Ice Bear.

That night, just about midnight, she had her family room set for her calling. The candles were lit and she was standing at the top of the pentacle, facing her stairway. Fortunately she had not removed the Chippewa chant from her smart-phone. She was dressed in her white gown and had her black robe over it because that had been the way they looked on the lake. Carefully she recited the chant and waited. Nothing happened. She recited the chant again. Nothing happened. Something was wrong and she couldn't figure out what it was. Frustrated, she decided to try to reach Karl.

She closed her eyes as she had always done and tried to relax. Breathing deeply and slowly concentrating. She had no idea how long she did this, every time had been different. Sometimes it was easy and sometimes it was difficult. Suddenly the room turned extremely cold. As cold as the grave, she thought. This had never happened before. It was never this cold. She continued her meditation, not daring to look until she heard a hissing sound she could not neglect. She opened her eyes to take a peek and what she saw made her gasp. A mist was covering the floor of the family room to the height of about a foot. It seemed to swirl around the room and then began to coalesce at the other end of the pentacle. She watched in amazement as it gathered in between the two vertices of the inverted pentagram. Then a form seemed to rise from the mist. It was the Ice Bear and in his mouth he held a fish made of ice just like him.

When the Ice Bear had fully materialized, he tossed the fish into the air, caught it and ate it in two bites. Then it looked at her.

"You summoned me again?"

The manner in which the Ice Bear said this made it sound like "this better be good."

"Yes, I need help."

The Ice Bear looked at her and then shook itself before answering. Flecks of ice showered the room, many hitting her. They stung, just like real ice.

"Are you in need?"

"Yes. I need help."

"What kind of help?"

"Someone is threatening me and I need to know who."

"And what will happen when you find out?"

"I will make them pay."

Again the Ice Bear shook itself and again ice showered the room. Ingrid noticed that when it landed, it melted and left little puddles.

"This land is a land of peace. My mantra is that I help people in need but I can bring them no harm. What you are asking of me, I cannot do. For telling you who is, as you say, threatening you would then bring them harm."

"But they put this awful sign on my garage door."

"What awful sign?"

"The Judas Goat."

"That sign is not a dangerous threat."

"But the goat is drawn in blood."

"Goat's blood to draw a goat. What could be wrong with that?"

"But it is a threat."

"Was it a threat when you put in on the North Witch's door?"

Ingrid stared at the Ice Bear in shocked disbelief.

"I ..."

"It was a threat that was wrongly made and so it was returned to you."

"How do I get rid of it?"

"Get rid of the evil in your heart. That is as much help as I can give you. Until you have ridded yourself of evil, do not summon me again. Even if you do, I will not come for I will know."

With that, the Ice Bear shook itself once more spewing pieces of ice in all directions and then dived into the mist and disappeared. The mist followed it as though it was water being sucked down the drain of a sink. Ingrid stood there for a moment trying to understand what the Ice Bear had said. One thing she knew for certain was that the Ice Bear could not help her against the force that was assailing her. Therefore, she decided, it must be black magic and she cast a spell to protect her from black magic,

Power of objection,
magic of deflection.
Assist me in this task be done,
banish this darkness with the power of the sun.

Satisfied that she was now protected, she turned to other things. Ever the fastidious housekeeper, Ingrid immediately wiped up the water from the melted ice shaken off by the Ice Bear. But whatever shape the puddle was in, a grey outline of that remained on the floor, sofa or wherever it had landed. She tried every product she had, as well as many old wives' remedies, but nothing worked. After an hour of scrubbing, she sat back on her heels and thought about it. *What if it is another thing only I can see?* Of course, the only way to find out was to have someone over and see if they noticed anything. But then how would she explain?

She pondered again about what the Ice Bear had said: *Get rid of the evil in your heart.* Did he mean that when I got rid of the evil I would no longer see the Judas Goat? Well, time would tell about that. When she got rid of the North Witch, the evil in her heart would be gone! Then the sign would be gone. But until then she was going to need help. And for that she turned to literature.

When she got up the next morning, she went out to see if the painting had reappeared. Indeed it had but there was something new. At the bottom of the door, lay a small white cat, more a kitten than a cat. When it heard her curse at the Judas Goat on the door, it had gotten up, stretched and scampered over to her and rubbed against her ankles. She looked down and saw the kitten.

"Scat, you little beast," Ingrid said brushing it away with the soft kick of a foot. But the kitten came back. Ingrid pushed it away again and hurried to her front door, the kitten close behind her but not close enough to get in the door before it closed. Or so Ingrid thought for when she entered her kitchen to make a pot of coffee, she heard a plaintive mew and looking down saw the kitten. She didn't like cats, but this one seemed to be different. This one actually liked her, rubbing itself against her ankles.

"Okay. You can stay, but only for a day or so." She got a saucer out of the cupboard, poured in some milk, added an egg that she mixed with the milk and put it on the floor. The kitten fell to it with relish.

Ingrid had no idea how to take care of a kitten and didn't know why she had even adopted it, but here it was. It seemed to be attached to her by a string, trailing along, often at a run, wherever she went. It was on a trip to the lower level to get a book that he got his name. She had gone down the stairs without a thought and was on the landing when she heard a plaintiff mew and looked up to see the kitten standing at the top of the stairs looking down.

"Come on," she said. "You can do it. Just one step at a time."

The kitten cocked his head to one side and then backed up until she could just see the top of his head. Then he seemed to race forward and just at the top of the stairs turned into a white ball that rolled off the top step, hit the next one, rolled forward, fell and rolled until it reached the landing where she stood laughing.

The kitten unrolled from the ball, got up, looked at her and mewed.

"Well," Ingrid said, "you're just a little snowball with four legs."

The name stuck.

Not everything was so obvious though. When she went back upstairs Snowball was still on the landing where he had remained while watching her get the book she was after. She started up the stairs and heard Snowball mew.

Looking back she said, "Let's see you roll up the stairs."

When she reached the top and looked back Snowball was still at the bottom. She turned and was walking toward the kitchen when she heard his plaintiff mew and looked down to see him sitting beside her. She shook her head and went on, him trailing.

Later she was in the kitchen and felt something tug at her trousers. Looking down, she saw Snowball looking up and when he noticed that he had been seen, he turned and started for the doorway. Getting there he looked back and saw Ingrid still standing there watching him. He returned to where she was, sat and looked up at her.

"What?" she asked.

Snowball headed back to the door and looked back at her halfway but she hadn't moved so he returned. Looking up at her, he mewed and then raced back toward the door. Sensing that he wanted her to follow him, she did and he went to the front door and sat. Curious now, she opened the door and Snowball rolled out and then ran to the edge of the porch and disappeared. She waited and in a few minutes he reappeared running from the far end of the porch and into the house. She hadn't seen how he had gotten up. This procedure happened two or three times a day, once after she had arisen, then midday, and in the evening. She knew that he was using the flowerbeds as his toilet.

For food, initially she gave him tuna that he seemed to enjoy and on her first trip into town she got a bag of kitten chow. He seemed happy to drink water and even turned up his nose at milk though he had liked it earlier.

Chapter 30

The ice had been off Hibbard Pond for two days when the Hibbard Marine barge (a pontoon boat stripped of all but the steering console moved to the center rear of the deck) drifted to a stop almost exactly where Zeb Pyke had marked the location of the meteor strike. Two U.S.G.S. (United States Geographical Survey) divers dropped anchors on long ropes to the bottom of the lake to hold the barge in position.

"Beautiful day for a swim," Ryan Jirik said.

"If you're a fish or polar bear," replied John McCaulay.

Ryan laughed and then started pulling on his dry suit. Despite the warm spring day, he and the other two divers were wearing heavy polar fleece long underwear to help keep them warm in the depths. Each put on a Viking dry suit by first applying talcum powder to their wrists to help maneuver through the watertight seals. Once the waterproof zipper was closed, only hands and part of the face were left exposed. Each diver checked his Buoyancy Compensation Device (BCD) or vest, which contained forty pounds of weight and their air tanks. Finally each put on pre-heated insulated gloves and closed the locking ring effectively sealing water out. Ryan would not make the dive to retrieve the meteor but was to serve as the emergency diver. Tim Nelson and Tom Niger had logged many hours of dives, most of them in the Great Lakes, and were used to the depths. They had the newest gear, with communications systems between them and the surface. Their facemasks covered all the bare area of the face not covered by the suit so there would be no problem with the cold.

"We have half an hour on the bottom," Tim said, "and if this location is anywhere close to accurate, we'll find the meteor unless it is something other than metal. According to witnesses the path would be from here to the east so that's how we'll do it."

"We'll get it up with balloons," Tom explained to McCaulay. "We'll put it in a net, attach a weather balloon that we'll fill with enough air to get it moving, and then let it go. The air will expand as it rises and it will be up quickly. We, on the other hand, will have to take a couple of decompression stops if we are down longer than about twenty minutes."

"How are you going to locate it?" John asked.

"Well, as Tim said, it should have some metal in it and so our metal detector should find it easily."

"How quickly?" Tim asked, knowing that as usual they would make a bet.

"I'd say 12 minutes, fifteen seconds," Tom said.

"Closer to 15 minutes, twenty five," Tim said.

"You're on. Usual stakes?"

"Yep, T-bones."

The two had a good laugh and finished putting on their gear. As there was no railing on the pontoon other than at the stern, the two stepped off the sides of the pontoon and into the water. Once in, and certain that all was working well, Tim led the way down holding onto the forward anchor rope. They had activated their lights before starting down knowing that at 100 feet they would be needed. On the bottom, both looked at their GPS units and started swimming eastward, each holding a metal detector. It was at 10 minutes, 22 seconds that Tim said, "Got a strike." And less than thirty seconds later, "Bingo."

He was quickly joined by Tom and the two of them looked at a wide furrow in the sand. At the west end it was about three feet wide and continued on for some twelve feet as it narrowed down to about six inches and was maybe three feet deep.

"I can taste it now," Tom said gleefully as he started for the narrow end of the furrow where the meteor's remains would be.

"Hold on a minute," Tim said pointing off to the side just a bit.

"What?" Tom asked, flippering over to join him.

Tim was looking at something black protruding from a mound of sand, which the meteor's impact had thrown out of the furrow. He swam over and tugged at it and then recoiled as though bitten by something.

"Houston, we have a problem," Tim said.

"What's that?" Ryan responded.

"I think we are going to need law enforcement," Tim said. "We have a body down here."

Following the call, the two divers sent up the weather balloon with just a little air and they kept the line attached to a two pound weight to hold it in place. On board the pontoon, the anchors were weighed and the pontoon moved to a spot ten feet away from the weather balloon and the anchors were lowered again. Once that was done, the two divers started their assent leaving the weather balloon tethered to one of their diving weights.

At that time, with the safety of the divers taken care of and the spot marked, John McCaulay called the sheriff's office.

"Good morning, Alcona County Sheriff's office, how may we be of assistance?"

"Good morning, Barbara Ann. John McCaulay here."

"How's the water?"

"Cold and deadly I'm afraid."

"Deadly!" Barbara Ann's voice turned serious. "What do you mean?"

"The U.S.G.S. divers say there is a body down at the site of the meteor."

"A body? Let me transfer you to the sheriff."

There was a brief pause, then "Nathanial here, John. You say a body?"

"Yes. Apparently buried in the sand thrown up by the meteor hitting the bottom."

"Any idea about sex?"

"No, once they knew it was a body, they quit. They say there is a hand, small. Teenager or small person. Cannot say more than that," and he filled Nathanial in on the discovery.

"Okay. Hang tight. I'll get a team there with a deputy as soon as I can."

Nathanial's first call was to Chet Willis, head of the Alcona County dive team.

"Morning, Chet."

"Not again."

"Afraid that's the report. The U.S.G.S. divers report finding a body buried in the sand thrown up by the meteor."

"That's deep isn't it?"

"A hundred feet give or take."

"They didn't disturb anything did they?"

"They hadn't started recovery yet. They were just at the site and one of them noticed something black waving from under the sand. When he pulled at it a hand was revealed and they stopped. They're on their way up. The site is marked and the Hibbard Marine barge is anchored there."

"Okay, I've got four guys I can call. How'll we get out to the barge?"

"I'll have one of our men run our whaler over to the East Bay Launch. Also, I'll get Warren Libka to accompany you."

"Warren? He works at night, doesn't he?"

"Yes, but he is working on a missing person case and this just might be a discovery in the case."

"But not the kind you hoped for."

"Nope."

Chapter 31

"Morning, Delores. Is Warren about?"

"Morning, Sheriff. He's sleeping," Delores said in a whisper.

"Well, I'm afraid he has to get up."

"Important, is it?"

"Yes, I believe it concerns Gladys Wilson."

"Oh! Just a minute."

"Wait."

"Yes."

"Have him call me when he is fully awake."

"Certainly, Sheriff. Bye."

Delores hurried down the hallway to their bedroom in the back of the house. She cracked the door quietly so as not to awaken him suddenly and tiptoed to the side of the bed.

"What's up?" Warren said before she even touched him.

She wasn't surprised because he was a light sleeper and used an eyeshade despite the dark blinds and curtains.

"Nathanial needs you. He says he believes it's about the Wilson woman."

Warren rolled over and sat upright in bed, jerking off his eyeshade.

"Gimme the phone."

"He said to call him when you were awake."

"Well, I'm awake."

Delores handed him the portable phone and Warren pushed a speed dial number, swinging his legs over the side of the bed.

"Barbara Ann, it's Warren."

"Just a minute."

"Morning, Warren," Nathanial said.

"Where do you need me?"

"East Bay launch on Hibbard Pond. The U.S.G.S. divers went down to retrieve the meteor this morning and found a body covered by sand that was thrown up. They saw a hand, small. Teenager or young adult."

"Okay, forty minutes."

"That should be good. Rich Walker is taking the whaler over and Chet Willis is getting divers. The barge from Hibbard Marine is anchored at the spot."

It was thirty-five minutes later that Warren's cruiser pulled into the large parking area at the launch. The whaler was in the water tied up at one of the two DNR docks. There were four people standing on shore. Warren recognized Rich Walker but didn't know the others. Putting on his black baseball cap with the Alcona County Sheriff's Department logo emblazoned on the front, Warren walked toward the four as a pickup truck with another man appeared in the lot.

"Morning, Rich," Warren drawled as he approached the foursome. "I'm Warren Libka," he said extending his hand to the man who appeared to be the oldest of the group. "You must be Chet Willis."

"Yes," Chet answered. "And this is Skip Andrews. The young lady is Susan Schwartz and the fellow that just pulled in is Fred Fithe. Soon as he gets his gear on board we can shove off."

"You dive?" Susan Schwartz asked.

"No, I can stay afloat, but I'm not really a water person. Well, I don't mind being on the water but not in it."

"Tally ho," Fred Fithe said as he set his scuba tanks down.

"Well, the gang's all here, let's get going," Chet said. "I'll tell you what's going on as we go out."

The six of them boarded the whaler making it tight with all the gear.

"We'll come back in by shifts," Chet explained to his team as Rich Walker backed the whaler out. "We've got a possible body covered with sand in one hundred feet of water. That's priority number one. There are two U.S.G.S. divers who were down to recover the meteor that hit ten days ago and uncovered the body. They'll serve as emergency backup for you three. After we have the body aboard, you'll recover the meteor. There should be time unless it's too deep in the sand. If it is, then we'll have to let the U.S.G.S. do it."

"How far from entry to the site?" Skip Andrews asked.

"Ten feet more or less. After they found the body, they marked the site and moved the barge."

"Shouldn't be any problem unless uncovering the body is difficult."

"Shouldn't be," Chet said. "It's only covered with sand that the meteor threw up. The divers said you could pretty much define the body's outline. Also being only ten days and the water so cold, there shouldn't be much decomposition."

Warren had been listening and watching the whaler's progress. He had spotted the barge when they had pulled out and headed for it.

"The body's marked by the weather balloon," Rich Walker said. "I'll tie up on the west side of the barge."

"Did you lose or win?" Warren asked.

"Lost," Walker said, "At least according to Bob. I like the cold."

Rich Walker and Bob Roberts always flipped an imaginary coin when there was an onerous task or a cherished one. They had started this when neither of them had a coin, so Walker came up with the idea. The flipper thinks of heads or tails and then flips the imaginary coin and the other person calls his choice. People would think that the flipper could cheat, picking the way he wanted it to turn out but the two were good friends and wouldn't cheat on the other. Each had admitted that at times it was tempting.

The U.S.G.S. divers grabbed the bow and stern lines that were tossed and the whaler was made fast to the barge. They had moved their gear to the back and out of the way but were still wearing their wet suits since they were back-up divers. One of them would be more fully dressed when the dive started in case of an emergency.

"I dived here last summer," Fred Fithe said. "It was cold then, too."

"Colder now but probably not much difference," Chet said.

When the dive team was dressed, they entered the water and followed the line tethering the weather balloon down. Nearing the bottom, Susan started taking pictures to document everything for the forensics team. Once the area had been photographed, Skip and Fred started removing the sand using garden trowels. They moved the sand away from the hole where the meteor was. Each trowel of sand was filtered through a screen as they looked for anything that didn't belong on the bottom of the lake, but they found nothing. Because the sand was not packed down, it was an easy job and went quickly.

At one point the light that Susan was holding jerked and the two men looked up from their task. She had turned away from them and was shining the light around. Then she turned back. Both men resolved to ask her about it on the surface. In ten minutes they had the body uncovered and realized that it was a woman. (It was Gladys' body but they didn't know it.) They couldn't tell the people on the barge because they didn't have the communication equipment that the U.S.G.S. divers had. Fred swam back to one of the barge anchors where there was the basket and body bag, with a rope attached for retrieval. He brought both back to the body and the two men put the body into the bag and strapped it in the basket. Skip tugged on the rope twice and the two U.S.G.S. divers started pulling the basket up. Skip and Fred guided it back under the barge and then the basket was headed for the surface.

Moving back to the hole the meteor had made, they commenced digging the sand out and within minutes found the meteor. They put it into the bag provided by the U.S.G.S., attached a second weather balloon, and filled it with air until it was buoyant enough to rise to the surface. All the time they had been doing this, Susan had been faithfully recording their work. With the meteor on the way to the surface, the three divers returned to the anchor ropes and started their assent, Fred and Susan on one and Skip on the other. Skip looked at his dive watch and saw that they were on the bottom nineteen and a half minutes out of their allotted twenty. He smiled with smug satisfaction.

On the barge, the U.S.G.S. divers had pulled up the basket with the body bag and gotten it out of the water and onto the pontoon. Warren had unzipped the bag and looked at the body. Since his investigation had started, he had carried a picture of Gladys Wilson with him and it was easy to make the identification.

It was with a heavy heart that he called to file his report. "Sheriff, the body has been recovered. I've made a tentative identification that it is Gladys Wilson."

There was a moment of silence from the sheriff.

"What in the hell was she doing out on the ice when that meteor hit?" the sheriff mused.

"That's the big question," Warren said. "When we get the body to the funeral home, we may have some answers but probably a lot more questions."

With the help of the U.S.G.S. divers, the body was moved to the whaler. Warren Libka had called Wallace Hibbs at the Hibbard Corners Funeral home and he was on his way with a hearse.

"Hey," Tim shouted. "The meteor's up." Warren and Rich saw that he was pointing to a weather balloon about ten feet from the other one. Warren and Rich Walker took the whaler around, retrieved the meteor and took it back to the barge where it passed into the custody of the U.S.G.S. divers. Then the whaler headed for the East Bay launch site. Wallace Hibbs was waiting and they carried the body bag to the end of the dock where Wallace had a gurney waiting. After fastening the body to the gurney, Wallace got it into the hearse and headed for Hibbard Corners with Warren in his cruiser right behind. Rich Walker headed back to the barge with the whaler to bring back the Alcona dive team.

When the dive team reached the surface, they were greeted with a look at the meteor. It was about eight inches long, and looked like what one thinks of as a comet: round at one end and then tapering back. It was brown, black and yellow, shiny all over, and weighed between five and ten pounds.

"Wasn't very deep in the sand," Fred said. "I thought it would really be buried deep."

Ryan Jirik explained, "First, it was slowed down when it hit the ice which was probably two feet thick, then it had to go through 100 feet of water and the force would build up as it went deeper, just like a skydiver who meets more resistance as it falls. In the skydiver's case it is air pressure but in this case it was water pressure."

"Makes sense," Fred agreed.

The three got out of their gear, bagged and loaded it on the whaler, and the four members of the dive team headed back to the launch.

"Thanks for the help," the two dive teams expressed to each other on parting.

"Hey, Susan," Fred said as they were underway. "What happened down there?"

"When?" Susan said and then realized what they were talking about. "It was crazy. Suddenly I felt really, really cold and then swear I felt something bump me. When I turned I thought I saw a big shadow in the water but it was nothing."

"Certainly had us going," Skip said.

The anchors were pulled and John McCauley headed back for the East Bay Launch where Chuck Shulmann, owner of Hibbard Marine, was waiting with his pontoon trailer. Up in the parking lot, Rich Walker was putting the finishing touches on securing the whaler to its trailer. The Alcona dive team was nowhere to be seen.

"Sorry we couldn't get any fishing in," John McCaulay said to Ryan Jirik.

"You'd lie about the sizes anyway," Ryan said as the two parted.

Chapter 32

Wallace Hibbs backed the hearse into position against the loading dock and was getting out just as Warren pulled in. Together they got the gurney out and wheeled it through the door, down a short hallway and down the ramp to the preparatory room. Parking it next to the prep table, Wallace set the brakes. Both men donned protective clothing including surgical masks and latex gloves. Unzipping the body bag, they lifted Gladys' body out and onto the prep table. While Warren was moving the gurney back up the ramp and near the loading dock doors, Wallace got out a digital camera and took pictures from all sides.

When Warren returned to the room, Wallace was standing there looking at the body.

"Do you know her?" Warren asked.

"Never had the pleasure. You?"

"Unofficially, she's Gladys Wilson."

"Ah, the missing woman. You recovered her from the meteor site?"

"Yes."

"Wonder what she was doing there?"

"That's the $64,000 dollar question. Along with that is how she died."

"Well, we might have an answer, or at least a partial answer, when we get her clothes off. This black outer garment looks like a cloak of some sort."

"Like a monk's robe with those bell sleeves," Warren said as they started to remove the cloak.

"Or a witch's," Wallace said and they looked at each other.

"Stranger things have happened," Warren said. "And witchcraft might be an explanation of why she was out on the ice."

The robe removed, Wallace hung it up on a hanger where it started dripping on the floor.

"I'd like to throw all these clothes in a dryer," Wallace said, "but the forensic boys wouldn't like that."

"Nope, they'd run you through an old fashioned dryer," Warren said, a sly grin on his face.

"What do you mean by that?" Wallace said.

"The wringer," Warren said and chuckled.

After Wallace had snapped the obligatory photos, they took off the heavy red sweater Gladys was wearing. That was almost as easy as the robe because it unzipped. Next was a red and black plaid woolen shirt that was obviously too big for her, again removed after photos were taken.

"She certainly was dressed for the cold," Wallace said. "But I doubt this is hers."

"Probably Tom's," Warren said.

Under the woolen shirt was a blue silk turtleneck and under that a winter underwear top. As Wallace started pulling it up revealing Gladys's naked abdomen, Warren asked, "Do you ever feel as though you're invading their privacy?"

"You mean the bodies?"

"Yes."

"I did at first, and do when I know the person, but most of the time it's just an inanimate object. I have to treat it that way or I couldn't do the job."

Photos were taken before the removal of each piece of clothing and of her naked lying on her back. They turned her over and shot photos from the rear.

"No real signs of bruising. No gunshot wounds, no sign of strangulation, bondage or anything." Warren said as Wallace pulled up a sheet to just above Gladys's breasts.

"Not surprising," Wallace said. "If she was there when the meteor hit, it didn't hit her. The explosion when it hit the ice would most likely have thrown her into the air and probably some distance away. The ice she hit would most likely have knocked her out, if she wasn't killed, and then she would have drowned on her way to the bottom. The cold down there would have prevented any bruising. She would be close to frozen pretty quickly."

There was a buzz and Wallace moved to a box on the wall and pressed a button.

"Who is that knocking at my door?" Wallace said.

"It ain't the big bad wolf," Rich Walker said in reply.

Wallace pressed a button that opened the door to the loading dock letting him in.

"I'd like to get a TV camera there, and at the front door, but just don't have the money. Have to stick with old technology."

"Nice looking woman," Rich Walker said when he arrived. "Any idea on cause of death?"

"None, other than a guess at drowning. I think we need to send her to Blodgett in Grand Rapids," Wallace replied.

"I agree," Rich said.

"When will you take her?" Warren asked.

"Day after tomorrow, if the family can ID her tomorrow. I'll give them a call and set it up."

"Well, let me know," Warren added. "I want to be here."

The three men bagged the clothes that hadn't been hung up and then bagged those that were hanging, each piece in an individual bag, each labeled. Then Warren and Rich Walker carried them out the loading dock door and put them in Rich Walker's SUV parked along the road with the whaler in tow behind it.

"Let me know what you find," Warren said.

"Where you headed now?" Rich Walker asked.

"Home to get some needed sleep," Warren said.

* * *

The next morning after his night shift, Warren Libka stopped in the sheriff's office to update him on the investigation.

"Doesn't appear to be any indication of foul play. Wallace says that any bruising would have been negated by the cold water. He'll send the body to Blodgett tomorrow after it is identified. I'll go along unless you have someone else."

"No, you need your sleep. Long way there and back."

"Walker and Roberts have the clothes. Nothing strange there except for the witch's cloak."

"Witch's cloak?" the sheriff said.

"That's right," Rich Walker said as he rapped on the door and stepped inside. "Her other clothes are ordinary.

Wool shirt that probably is her husband's. But the outer garment was a black cloak with a yellow flannel lining, probably for warmth. The cloak had a hood and bell sleeves. Typical thing you think of a witch or monk wearing although a monk's would be brown."

"And made out of rough cloth like burlap," Warren injected.

"That's right," Rich Walker agreed. "The cloak appears to be homemade. I'm saying that because there are a couple of imperfections in the stitching. Nothing major but caught under close examination." He continued giving himself a pat on the back.

"Also there is an embroidered pentacle on the right breast."

"Pentacle?" This from both Warren and the sheriff.

"Yes. It's a circle with a five-point star with one point at the top. Standard kind of thing that you see in movies when the witches gather to cast spells."

"How would you get something like that done?" the sheriff asked.

"One of those fancy sewing machines," Roberts said. "You can scan a picture in and then choose the colors to use. You set the material where you want the pattern to start and watch it go."

"Does Gladys Wilson have a machine like that?" The sheriff asked Warren.

"Don't remember seeing a sewing machine in the house," Warren said and Rich Walker agreed. "I can ask when I get the clothes identified. Jennifer and her father are coming to the funeral home this morning to officially ID the body.

Chapter 33

Jennifer and her father climbed the steps to the front of the Hibbard Corners Funeral Home holding hands. They had parked in back, walked to the front and stood there for a couple of minutes looking at the doors, not saying a thing. They had gotten a call from Wallace Hibbs an hour before. He had explained that a team of divers from the U.S.G.S. had discovered a body on the bottom of Hibbard Pond when they had gone down to retrieve the meteor that had smashed into the lake two weeks before. Members of the Alcona County dive team, under the supervision of Deputy Sheriff Warren Libka, had recovered the body of a woman who seemed to match the description of Gladys. He had asked Tom to come to make identification, but Jennifer had insisted that she be there also. Tom hadn't wanted to have his daughter face this egregious task but had finally agreed.

Jennifer looked at her father and smiled; then the two of them went up the stairs. Tom opened the door and followed Jennifer inside where Wallace Hibbs and Warren Libka awaited them.

"I am sorry to have to ask you to perform this identification," Officer Libka had said.

"It is never easy to have to see the body of a loved one for the first time," Wallace Hibbs said. "Is your daughter going to be with you?" he asked Tom.

"Yes, I am," Jennifer said, firm in her resolve.

"Let me take your coats," Wallace said. He hung them up and then led them into the chapel, which was the former nave of the church. Wallace Hibbs was a big man, easily weighing three hundred pounds with most of it below his waist. In high school he was referred to as "The Whale" and it was not a kind reference. As they went down the side of the chapel toward a door that opened onto a ramp leading to the preparatory room in the basement, Wallace said, "It is quite cold at the bottom of Hibbard Pond at this time of year, still close to freezing, so the body has not suffered any decomposition. Of course, I haven't done anything yet and won't until she is properly identified."

Jennifer grasped her father's hand tightly with both of hers as they walked down the ramp behind Wallace followed by Officer Libka. Reaching the bottom Wallace opened the door into the preparation room and preceded them inside. They saw a gurney covered with a sheet and could discern the outline of a body underneath. Wallace walked around to the other side of the gurney, reached over and took hold of the top of the sheet on their side.

"Are you ready?" he asked.

Jennifer looked at her father, smiled weakly and looked at Wallace Hibbs.

"Yes," she said although she really wasn't.

Wallace drew back the sheet with a facility that belied his size. The last thing Jennifer remembered before she fainted was the unnatural appearance of her mother's face.

The cause of her fainting was not her mother's face but the sudden influx of hidden memories into her consciousness.

She saw her mother standing at the foot of her bed in a swirling mist of white and felt the bone chilling cold. Bits of the conversation with her mother replayed itself in her head.

"Calm yourself, my daughter," her mother's spirit said. "I don't have much time. The Ice Bear has granted me this final wish, but I only have a moment."

"The Ice Bear?"

Who was this Ice Bear?

"Yes, the others were lucky."

"They should be dead, too," Jennifer said that in a way that one could sense she wanted them dead.

"No, Jennifer, there is no reason for them to die. But you need to watch for one of them for I don't trust her."

"Who?"

"The West Witch."

"Who's she?"

"Ingrid Swartz."

"She's a witch?"

"As much as I am."

Her mother was a witch!

"Yes, I am and so are you."

"I'm a witch? I have no powers."

"Until tonight your powers have been latent, but with my passing they have been unlocked sooner than expected."

"What powers?"

"You will learn all in good time. For now you must heed my warning. Beware of the West Witch for she will try to kill you."

"Kill me? But she's your friend."

"Yes, but she has evil inside her. I have sensed it recently."

"But the other two?"

"They are harmless. They have no powers."

"But you and she do?"

"Yes. Mine are for good, hers I am afraid are for evil unless she is careful. That is why you need to watch. I need you to protect North Witch and South Witch."

"I am fifteen years old. How am I supposed to protect anyone?"

"You will be granted some limited powers to use until my friends are safe from the West Witch. When you need them you will know what they are and how to use them."

"But who are the other witches?"

That nagging question went unanswered as the mist disappeared into the floor.

She remembered that the little purple mushroom is known as the Purple Terror. It grows in rotten logs and stumps in the late winter months. During its growth it is extremely poisonous to anything that eats it. In maturity, it collects its poison and releases it in one gelatinous drop. Once free of the poison, the mushroom is extremely healthful to pregnant mothers but the plant dies within half an hour. Mixed with two teaspoons of pure alcohol, the liquid turns crystal clear and is virtually tasteless. One-quarter teaspoon can kill in excruciating agony within five minutes and there is no known antidote. However, mixed with two teaspoons of white vinegar, the liquid turns opaque white and mixed with a hot liquid it is said to cure "middle blindness" and is most beneficial if consumed while the liquid is still hot. However, if so much as a drop of lemon juice is in the liquid, the benefits are nullified.

Chapter 34

Jennifer opened her eyes and found herself looking into her father's anxious face. She smiled and tried to sit up but he restrained her with a hand on a shoulder.

"Take it easy," he said, concern in his voice. "I was afraid this would happen."

"I'm fine. It wasn't seeing mother. I was prepared for that," Jennifer tried to explain.

"Then what?"

"Memories," Jennifer offered and hoped that would be sufficient and it was. She knew that she could never tell her father of her mother's appearance, her revelation of being a witch, nor of the Poison Terror. She sat up and found herself on another gurney and shuddered at the thought that a dead person had lain on it sometime. She swung her legs over the side and stood up, an anxious father at her side. She saw Wallace Hibbs and Officer Libka standing off to the side talking. They saw that she was up and Wallace came over.

"How are you feeling, my dear?"

"Fine, thank you. Can I see my mother?"

"Do you think that's wise?" Wallace asked her father.

"It's what she wants," her father said.

Again Wallace Hibbs drew back the sheet. Jennifer looked intently at her mother's face. There was a dark bruise at her hairline. She pointed to it.

"What's that?" she asked looking at Wallace Hibbs.

"One of several bruises on her body," he answered uncertain of how much he should say to the young girl.

"Is that how she died?"

"I am not certain," he replied cautiously. "As I explained I haven't had a chance to do an examination. She might have drowned or possibly had a heart attack. There are a variety of possibilities."

"We don't think there was foul play," Officer Libka injected. "There are no visible wounds that we could identify as being deadly."

"Like a gunshot?"

"Yes, or strangulation. But other than that we have no clue."

"How will you find out?" Jennifer's father asked.

"Well, in a case like this, I believe that a more qualified person than I should do an autopsy," Wallace Hibbs explained.

"Meaning what?" Jennifer asked.

"She needs to be sent to Blodgett Medical Center in Grand Rapids."

"Then what?"

"She will be returned here for you to bury."

"She is to be cremated," Jennifer's father said. "And her ashes scattered on our property."

"That's fine. The cremation can be done in Grand Rapids and the cremains returned here for a service if you wish."

"Cremains?" asked Jennifer.

"Yes, the term referring to the ashes resulting of the loved one."

"That's too impersonal! We want my mother's ashes and we will have a memorial service here," Jennifer said, not surprised that she was taking command. "When can we do that?"

"It is too late today to get your mother's body to Blodgett. I will arrange for that in the morning," Wallace Hibbs looked at Officer Libka for affirmation and he nodded. "They will take a day or two for an autopsy, then another for the cremation. Not that it takes a day to actually cremate a body, but you have to allow sufficient time." Jennifer and her father nodded in understanding. "Then one day to return here. Let's throw in another day just in case. So what about Tuesday or Wednesday next week?"

"Tuesday," Jennifer's father said. "I am off again on Wednesday."

"And tomorrow," Jennifer said and her father nodded.

"What about her clothes?" Jennifer asked.

"I wanted to ask you about that," Officer Libka said as the conversation moved into his jurisdiction. "She was wearing long underwear (top and bottoms), dark slacks, a blue silk turtleneck, and this wool shirt." And he held up the bag containing the shirt.

"That's mine," Jennifer's father said.

"She had on this sweater," Warren held up another bag.

"That's hers."

"Over them she was wearing this," and Officer Libka held up a long black cape in a plastic zippered bag.

"Don't recognize it," Jennifer's father stated.

"May I look at it?" Jennifer asked suddenly knowing what she would find.

"Certainly, but as it is evidence in a possible crime ..."

"Crime?" Jennifer said incredulously.

"Well," Officer Libka explained, "It is a mysterious death, meaning an unexplained death occurring in a strange manner and, in this case, in a strange place. Until we know the cause of death, it must be treated as a crime."

"Okay, we understand," Jennifer proffered, looking at her father for agreement.

"In that case, if you want to examine the cloak you need to wear latex gloves," as he was explaining this, Wallace Hibbs offered Jennifer and her father a pair but her father refused. Jennifer put the gloves on and unzipped the bag and removed the cloak. The material was dark, some synthetic blend, the interior lining was yellow wool with no design. *That was meant for warmth*, Jennifer thought. There was a hood and the sleeves were belled. *A witch's cloak*. Jennifer was not surprised. She noticed something on the left side of the cloak and ran her fingers over it. She didn't want to make a scene although she knew that the sheriff's forensic team would discover it. She wasn't certain, but she thought that the pattern was a pentacle. That recognition surprised her because before that moment, she hadn't known what a "pentacle" was.

"Have you ever seen this before?" Officer Libka asked the two.

Jennifer and her father shook their heads.

"Did your wife have a sewing machine?" Warren asked Jennifer's father.

Her father laughed, looked at Jennifer and they both smiled.

"She had a difficult time sewing on a button," her father said.

"Do you have any idea what she was doing out on the ice in the middle of the night?" Officer Libka asked.

"You mean the night the meteor hit?" Jennifer asked knowing that was the time he meant.

"Yes."

"How do you know that she was there?" Jennifer knew she had been because her mother had told her but how would the police know?

"Her body was on the bottom of the lake, next to the hole caused by the meteor and it was mostly covered by sand from the hole."

"But wouldn't that mean she was there before the meteor?" Jennifer's father asked.

"We don't think so. We believe that the sand was thrown up into the water and settled back down covering the body which had to get there pretty much just after the meteor hit," Officer Libka explained.

Jennifer and her father looked at each other and then at Officer Libka.

"We have no idea," they said simultaneously.

That ended the questioning. As they prepared to leave, Jennifer went over to the gurney on which her mother's body lay and pulled down the sheet. Leaning over she kissed her mother's head and whispered. "I will do as you asked."

Chapter 35

Now it was grunt work for Warren. Not that it hadn't been before. Talking to people, friends of Gladys, people around the lake who didn't know Gladys. All of that had gained him nothing except for a suspicion that the Swartz woman was hiding something. She was Gladys's best friend. If anyone would know why Gladys had been out on the ice, it would have been her, but she said nothing. Of course, she could have been out on the ice also. Why not admit it? It wasn't a crime! Stupid yes, but not a crime. Now with the sewing machine thing he could go back and see her. But he wanted to know first.

So he started with all the stores around that sold sewing machines, the fancy models, the ones you could program for embroidery. He checked with shops that fixed sewing machines. Two women who lived at the lake had such machines. One said she hadn't sewn in a couple of years. Eyes were bad and she had given the machine to her daughter-in-law. "She lives in Austin. That's Texas." Cross her off the list. The other lady wintered in Florida, left in early December, came back in May after the mud was gone. "Wait till the flowers are up," her friends quoted her. After three days he expanded his search, but there weren't that many places unless you went down to the Tri-City Area (Bay City, Saginaw, Midland) or across the state (Petoskey, Traverse City). Warren thought that was a long way to go to get a sewing machine when you could get it in Alpena. The name "Ingrid Swartz" never turned up.

At the same time that Warren was looking for sewing machines, he was hitting fabric shops looking for the material used to make the cloak. His first stop had been Jo-Ann Fabrics & Crafts in Alpena and he had taken the cloak. The sales lady had identified the types of material so he didn't have to carry it further, but they hadn't sold enough at one time to make anything that big. They carried the black but not the yellow flannel. It was the same everywhere. Nobody carried the flannel, nobody had special ordered it or the black, if they didn't carry that specifically, and nobody had sold enough to make a cloak.

Three days after Gladys's body went to Blodgett, the report came back. Death was not by drowning but by heart failure. Evidence pointed to her being rendered unconscious when she hit the ice and that her heart had stopped with the shock of the cold water. Accidental death by natural causes even if the root of the causes was a little unnatural.

Warren was at a loss – nowhere to turn.

"Somebody knows something," he said to the sheriff. "She wasn't out there alone. Somebody made that cloak. Unless it was a special order somewhere, she didn't get it off the Internet. I got credit card reports with the permission of Tom Wilson. Nothing."

Nathanial Jefferson was quiet for a few minutes. Warren sat there spinning his coffee cup around in his hands.

"Your only lead is this Swartz woman?"

"And that's just a gut feeling. I have nothing to go on."

"Going to confront her about the sewing machine?"

"Nothing else to do until the funeral."

"Agreed. Then we can see who attends and check them out."

So that brought Warren back to the Swartz house. He wanted a search warrant but couldn't get one.

He noticed the pale green garage door. It had been white, hadn't it? He rang the doorbell.

Ingrid opened the door and Warren saw something move at her feet. A ball of white – a kitten.

"I didn't know you had a cat?" were the first words out of his mouth.

"I didn't. He just showed up one day."

"Got a name?"

"Snowball. What do you want, Deputy?"

"Do you have a sewing machine, Mrs. Swartz?" Warren squatted down and tried to scratch the kitten as he said this. "Hi, Snowball." Snowball peered at him from behind Ingrid's legs.

"A sewing machine?"

"Yes, ma'am," Warren said straightening up.

"Yes, I do."

"So you sew?"

"Yes, remember that outfit I had on when you were here before?"

"You mean the one that looked like flames when you walked?"

"Flames? It does? I never …. Yes, that's the one. I made it."

"Does your machine do embroidery?"

"What do you mean?"

"You know, sew pictures of things."

"Oh, yes, it's very modern. My husband Karl bought it for me but I don't do things like that. Button holes but nothing fancy."

"Where did he buy it?"

"Is that important?"

It wasn't. Warren just looked at her. Without a search warrant, Warren couldn't check. But it wouldn't have mattered. Ingrid had hidden the pentacle pattern, and gotten rid of the thread and extra material, all incinerated in the fireplace. If he had wanted to find where the material had been purchased, he would have go to a suburb of Chicago where Ingrid's daughter lived with her family.

"Why do you ask?"

"Well, it is concerned with the death of Gladys Wilson."

"How?"

"I'm sorry. I am not at liberty to say."

It's the pentacle, Ingrid thought. *That's what I get for being so artsy*. Thank goodness it had been the one time she had tried that embroidery gadget except for buttonholes.

"I wish I could help you, Deputy."

At this point, Warren felt something brush his pants and looked down to see Snowball climbing over the threshold. The kitten looked up to see if Warren was watching him and then ran away out of sight. He was headed for the room where Ingrid kept her sewing machine but, of course, Warren couldn't follow and didn't even understand that is what the kitten wanted.

"Frisky little kitten," Warren commented.

"Yes. Is there anything else I can do for you?" Ingrid asked.

"No, ma'am."

"Good day then."

In his cruiser Warren sat thinking, trying to piece things together. With all her sewing abilities, she could have made the cloaks with no problem. She had the machine that could do embroidery. Why didn't she? In this case, two and two didn't make four. Didn't even come close.

Chapter 36

The day of Gladys's memorial service was a beautiful crisp April day. Jennifer was happy because it was the kind of day that a celebration of someone's life would be held. It was not a day for good-byes because Jennifer knew that she could never say good-bye to her mother. She and her father were there early sitting in the front row looking at an urn that only temporarily contained her mother's ashes. Since they were going to be spread elsewhere, there was no need to buy an urn but rather they were in a zip lock bag inside the urn. They had decided to be the first there and wait until after the service before greeting attendees. They had asked the minister of the Presbyterian Church to conduct a short service in the middle of which Jennifer would give a memorial address. If it were so construed, that was to be her way of saying good-bye. Her father had acceded to her wishes because someone had to do it and he couldn't bring himself to do it. Not that he was grief stricken (that had passed with the identification of his wife's body, as it had with Jennifer), but because he was a man of few words.

Neither of them looked behind them to see how many people were there because they were afraid that some of them had come because of the morbidity and notoriety of Gladys's having died when the meteor hit. The one thing that the rumor mill had missed, and for this both were exceeding thankful, was that she was wearing a witch's cloak. The Alcona diving team probably knew what she was wearing although underwater it was likely they just knew it was a black cloak. Her corpse had been put into a body bag to be brought to the surface and it remained in that bag until Wallace Hibbs had removed it in the funeral home in the presence of Warren. The two of them would have said nothing and most likely the only other people to see it were the sheriff's forensic team of Bob Roberts and Rich Walker. Jennifer had been certain that her father knew what it was (but not about the pentacle), but he had said nothing. If he had asked her about it, Jennifer could have truthfully said that she had never seen it before. So the curious could ask, and someone with no sense of decency probably would, "What was Gladys's doing out on the dangerous ice in the middle of the night?" Jennifer wished that she had some kind of hex that she could put on them but there was nothing in that book that looked like a silence hex. And, truth be told, as hard as she had tried, she had been unable to make any of the potions (except for that with the Purple Terror) or cast any of the spells.

The service started and reached the point for Jennifer's talk. She squeezed her father's hand, stood and walked to the front where there was a lectern, which served as a pulpit when needed. Turning around she saw the crowd for the first time and it was as she feared. Except for the front row in which she and her father sat alone, because it was always reserved for the family and the two of them were all the family that Gladys's had (both of Gladys's parents being only children and her parents dead), every seat in the small chapel was filled and there were several people standing in the side aisles and at the back.

Jennifer wished now that she had written something down but had thought it best to speak from the heart. Now words seemed to have fled but she had to say something. She smiled at her father and then looked at the crowd seeking friendly faces. There were the Gilmores, she looking radiant and he smiling – he never smiled. Ah, the McBruces both looking at her confidently; he winked at her and the tension eased a bit. Behind them someone familiar, not an adult – Muddy Waters, sitting with a man and a woman (his father and mother) and a young girl (his sister). She fastened her gaze on him and began talking – to him:

"Thank you for coming. It is difficult to lose a family member. Especially for a child to lose a parent. My mother Gladys was a wonderful woman who loved life, especially her birds. She fed them every day during the winter and she taught me to love them also. She taught me many other things – how to cook, wash clothes, all the things that a mother should teach a daughter. She was wife, a wonderful wife, to my father."

Her gaze moved from Muddy to her father. She smiled at him and he at her.

"He won't say it but I know, because I am his daughter, that he now has a terrible hole in his life, a vacancy in his heart. I do, too. But I know that when I graduate from high school, she will be there. When I graduate from college, she will be there. When I get married, she will be there. When I have my first child, she will be there, holding my hand, coaching me through labor." *And she will be*

there when I make my first potion – I know she was there –
and when I cast my first spell.

Her gaze then moved over the audience until it found the face she wanted – Ingrid Swartz.

"When I have a problem and need help, she will be there. When I need courage, she will be there. When I need knowledge, she will be there."

That was intended as what it was: a threat. She didn't know if the West Witch would know it, but the new East Witch was giving her fair warning: *Watch out. I know who you are.*

"My mother's life was too short. Cut off because of a terrible accident. But she will not be forgotten."

Unbidden and unwanted, tears welled up in Jennifer's eyes and she left the lectern and went to sit by her father who put his arm around her and they stayed close for the rest of the service.

Chapter 37

Earleen McBruce and several others of Gladys's friends had arranged for a potluck luncheon to be held at the township hall just a half-mile east of Hibbard Corners on Huron Road. The Presbyterian minister had announced this during the service. Jennifer and her father had gone out the door to the loading dock where one of Wallace Hibbs' part-time employees was waiting with the funeral home sedan. They had just turned east on to Huron Road from Grouse when Jennifer's father said, "We forgot to get your mother's ashes."

The ashes had been in a zip lock bag and Wallace Hibbs had put them in an ornate cremation urn that was placed on what had been the church's altar since there was no casket.

"I have them," Jennifer said, patting the duffel style purse that she was carrying. She hadn't had any purses of her own and this one had been her mother's. Her father looked at her in amazement, but Jennifer just smiled and didn't offer any explanation. If her father had asked how she had gotten them, she would have been truthful and said, "I just wished them into the bag," and that is exactly what she had done. During the service she had wished that her mother was with her, just shortly before her eulogy, and shortly thereafter she had felt a slight movement in the bag and the ashes were there. She had then carried the purse with her when she went to the lectern. Her father had grown used to the things that his wife had done seemingly by magic and had long ago accepted them, so he didn't ask about the ashes. It didn't bother him. He just accepted that women had a way of doing things.

Inside the township hall, they were greeted by several of the women who had worked during the service organizing things. They offered condolences and suggested a spot where they could stand to receive their guests. Her father had excused himself to use the men's room, but Jennifer knew that in reality he was going to take a swig or two from the flask he had brought with him. She didn't mind because he wasn't a big drinker and she knew that this would help calm him. She wished that she had something herself, then patted the bag with her mother's ashes and realized that was all she needed. She smiled at her father as he returned seeming much more relaxed than before.

The first people to enter were the Gilmores who spotted them and hurried over. Jennifer was surprised to see Mrs. Gilmore walking firmly and not using a cane or walker.

"It's a miracle," she said to them. "And we have your mother to thank."

"What do you mean?" Jennifer's father asked.

"A few days after Gladys's went missing, I noticed that my eyesight seemed to be improving. I got an appointment with my ophthalmologist and he told me that my eyesight had improved by twenty-five percent. The macular degeneration was being reversed somehow and he had no medical explanation for it. A week later it was fifty per cent and yesterday ninety. Your mother had always told me to have faith and she was right."

"Of course, we thank the Almighty," Don Gilmore said, "but we also have to thank your mother and you," this he directed to Jennifer.

"Me?" Jennifer said, trying to appear disbelieving, although inside she was turning cartwheels.

"Yes, you have always been nice to us, just like your mother. And you came over and fixed that special tea for my wife …"

"There was no special tea," Jennifer said. "If there was, it was there all the time because I used your own tea."

"Well, it certainly tasted special," Mrs. Gilmore said.

Jennifer started to say something to direct their thoughts elsewhere but she didn't need to.

"Regardless of what happened," Don Gilmore said, "My wife's eyesight is better and that has lifted a big burden from me. For years I have been so worried about her eyesight and had become a grouch. I know that and I'm sorry. Feel free to bring in my mail anytime."

With that the Gilmores hurried off to find a place to sit. *Hope they don't make a big deal out of me making her tea,* Jennifer thought.

The next couple to come in was one of the ones who had been standing in the back and had been classified by Jennifer as troublemakers. She expected one of them, the husband she had thought, to start questioning them about what her mother had been doing out on the ice. As they neared them, Jennifer looked the man straight in the eyes and thought, *Keep your mouth shut.*

"We so sorry about your wife," the woman said to Jennifer's father. "And your mother, of course," she added when her husband didn't say anything. She looked at him expectantly, but he was staring at Jennifer with a dumbfounded look on his face. His wife grabbed his hand and led him away.

"I thought you were going to ask her what her mother was up to out on the ice at that time of night," the woman said.

"I couldn't," the man replied, thankful that he could speak.

"What do you mean, you couldn't," the woman said.

"I couldn't open my mouth," he replied in truthfulness.

"Oh, you ass. All talk beforehand but when the time comes, you're just a wimp."

The man said nothing because he knew that he was in the doghouse and it was going to take something special to get out of it, but he had no idea what he could do.

Jennifer was a bit concerned by what had happened. She certainly hoped that they wouldn't make a big deal out of it to friends because as she remembered from reading *The Book of Witches*, it didn't take much to get in trouble.

Who was that? she thought. *Oh, yes, Joan Peterson, the witch of Wapping, who was hanged at Tyburn in 1652, convicted as a witch just on someone's opinion. It seemed that a black cat had wandered into a neighbor's house and scared the woman. She had sought counsel of the village baker of all people. A baker! What could a baker know about witches? The baker had expressed his opinion that the cat was Joan Peterson whom he had seen pass by his door only moments before the cat had appeared. At the trial (that was convened based on that opinion), the baker had also expressed that he himself had never been frightened by a cat, but that this particular one had terrified him. That had done it. He'd been terrified by a black cat, ergo Joan Peterson had to be a witch. There couldn't have been a jury found at that time who would have found her innocent.*

Jennifer resolved to keep her thoughts to herself for the rest of the day.

Chapter 38

Several more couples came through expressing condolences, but none of them appeared to have any thoughts of animosity. The next person was a tall woman with long straight glossy black hair, a thin olive colored face with high cheekbones, and flashing black eyes. She was dressed in a black pantsuit with a white blouse open at the neck. Jennifer could see a pendant hanging from a chain around her neck and thought it was turquoise.

"I'm Rachel Whitehawk," she said extending her hand to Jennifer's father. None of the other couples had bothered to introduce themselves. "I'm Owen Whitehawk's wife – he is the postmaster. I knew your wife through several different organizations. She was a wonderful woman and I will miss her."

Then she offered her hand to Jennifer, looking her straight in the eyes. "You also are special, Jennifer. If I can ever do anything to help you, do not hesitate to call me."

The woman's touch sent a warm sensation through Jennifer and she knew at once that Rachel Whitehawk was a witch and knew that she was one also. Jennifer also knew that Rachel Whitehawk was not The Witch of the North or South.

"Thank you," she said. "I won't forget."

The next couple was another that Jennifer didn't know and she sensed that her father didn't either. They reminded her of Tweedle Dum and Tweedle Dee from *Alice in Wonderland.*

"I'm Jane Eyre Polli," the woman said to her father, "and this is my husband Rolli. I didn't know your wife well. In fact, I hadn't met her until just a few weeks before …" and she waved her hand not knowing what to say nor wanting to say the wrong thing. "I liked her a lot."

Then to Jennifer, "She thought you were special. Talked about you all the time," and she touched her cheek. It was an ordinary touch. For whatever reason, Jennifer knew that this woman had no powers and wouldn't get any; but (how she knew this she didn't know) Jane Eyre Polli was The Witch of the South.

"Thank you," Jennifer said.

The McBruces were next.

"Thank you for arranging all this," Jennifer said to Earleen.

"You're welcome. I wish we had known your mother longer. She was special."

Jennifer nodded in agreement knowing that Earleen had no powers and was not The Witch of the North.

Then came several more couples, a few they knew, some they didn't. Jennifer knew at least two of them were there only to get the food and had never known her mother, but she didn't say anything. There was no reason to do so and cause a scene. It was harmless anyway because at these gatherings there was always plenty of food.

Then came Muddy Waters with his parents and sister.

"This is my mom Jessica and my father Stefan and my sister Katie" Muddy said politely introducing them to Jennifer, who responded, "Pleased to meet you." Then she turned to her father. "This is Muddy Waters. I told you about him and how he stood up to that nasty girl who said I was running away because my father beat me. And these are his parents. This is my father, Tom Wilson."

"Pleased to meet you," Tom said shaking hands with Muddy's parents. "You certainly take after your mother, don't you, young lady." This last directed to Katie. Then to Muddy's father, "You have the farm on Creek Waters Road ...say," he said looking at Muddy. "You're the boy who saved that Amish lad's life, aren't you?"

Muddy blushed not liking the limelight, at least not at this time.

"Yes, sir," he said, "But he saved my life, too."

"And helped Muddy win the fishing tournament with Big Burt," Katie blurted out and quickly shut up when admonished by her mother.

"Gladys's used to go to the farmer's market over at the ARA (Alcona Regional Area) grounds," Tom Wilson said to Muddy's mother. "She liked your bread. Well, we all liked your bread. That French Rustic whatever."

Muddy's mother smiled graciously and the Waters moved on.

Next was another tall woman with beautifully coiffed hair. She had on a patchwork blazer with a white tee-shirt underneath and clean stonewashed blue jeans.

"I'm Helen Trumball-Grant. People call me Mrs. T-G. I run Helen's Hair Quarters," she said offering her hand first to Jennifer's father and then to her. The hand was firm and squeezed hers in a reassuring and consoling manner. "I cut your mother's hair. I know she cut your hair. If you ever need a cut, I'll be glad to do it, no charge." With that she was gone.

Jennifer looked after the powerless Witch of the North as she walked away. *I just might do that,* Jennifer thought. *You're the person who could tell me what my mother was doing out on the ice.* In addition to knowing that Mrs. T-G was The Witch of the North, she also knew that she had driven her mother's car home that night. She took all these insights for granted and was not the least bit troubled by how she knew them.

The last person in line was the one that Jennifer didn't want to see but knew she would.

"I'm so sorry, Tom," Ingrid Swartz, said to Tom extending her hand. "She was my dear friend and I am going to miss her terribly." *What a liar,* Jennifer thought.

"Thank you, Ingrid," her father replied, personally happy that this condolence line was over. "She liked you a lot. That one outfit you made for her was special. You really have a way with cloth."

"It was nothing. Just a little something I whipped up."

Yeah, like the witches' cloaks with the embroidered pentacle. I'll bet Officer Libka would like a look at the software for your sewing machine, Jennifer thought.

Then The Witch of the West turned to her. Jennifer thought that her green eyes were flashing a warning: *Look out for me, you little witch. I'll destroy you with one wave of my broom.* At that thought, Jennifer almost laughed it was so silly. But she wasn't scared and, for whatever reason, didn't think she should be.

"Your mother was a dear," Ingrid Swartz said to her. "She thought you hung the moon. She kept telling me how **special** you are."

As she was saying this, she had taken Jennifer's hand. Ingrid's was cold – ice water or grave cold – and it made Jennifer shiver inside. *Mother was right*, Jennifer thought. *This woman is evil.* She sensed a power in Ingrid. A different power than that she had felt in Rachel Whitehawk, not necessarily stronger but different. There was definitely something evil about this woman. Something that she had to be careful about. She needed to put up wards. *Wards? What are those?*

"Yes, I know," Jennifer replied. However what she meant was, "I am special and you better watch out." But Ingrid didn't understand. She just smiled and walked away confident that she could handle the little impudent bitch without any problem. Especially once she could summon someone or something to help her. And that was only a matter of time.

Chapter 39

The lake was smooth that afternoon, for which Jennifer and her father were grateful. Dugal McBruce had launched his pontoon this afternoon to take them out to the spot where Gladys had died. There were only the four of them: Jennifer, her father, Earleen and Dugal. It was chilly but the sun was warm. As they motored slowly from the East Bay launch, Jennifer watched the shoreline because she hadn't seen it this early in the year. Most of the docks and boat hoists were still pulled up on shore, but there was the occasional one already in the water. When she commented on that, Dugal had said, "Die hard fisherman."

"Is there a season for anything this time of year?" Tom had asked.

"Not really. Most fish spawn now and the DNR in its infinite wisdom, and I mean that seriously, wants the fish to have the chance to produce offspring. That's what keeps this lake alive."

"So what are those people after?"

"Don't know. Perch are always in season so maybe they're after them. Other than that, I guess you'd have to ask them."

The trip out to the location took about twenty minutes simply because Dugal went slowly so they wouldn't all freeze to death. He had marked the location obtained from the sheriff's department (and his friend Zeb Pyke) on his GPS.

"We're coming up on it," he said slowing the motor and finally cutting if off. The pontoon continued to glide from its forward momentum but when it stopped, Dugal said, "As close as we're going to get."

Jennifer pulled a plastic bag from her duffel purse and she and her father went to the front of the boat.

"This is only half," Jennifer said to her father as she handed him the bag. "I divided them back at the township hall. We'll spread the other half at home."

Tom looked the bag and its nondescript contents.

"Just doesn't seem like this is all there is left," he said as tears welled up in his eyes.

"It's not, Daddy," Jennifer said. "There are memories. As long as we live, she'll be alive. I meant it today when I said she will be with me. She's with you, too. All you have to do is think about her."

Tom looked at her, wiped the tears away and kissed her on the forehead.

"You're right, of course," he whispered softly as he took a deep breath and let it out. "I can feel her," and he did.

He kissed the bag and then opened it, letting its contents fall onto the water.

"Good-bye, my love," he said watching the ashes sink beneath the water. Ordinarily they would float until they became wet but these ashes sank beneath the waves immediately. Jennifer and her father stood hand in hand as each of them mentally said their good-byes giving the ashes time to sink one hundred feet to the bottom. Then they went back to their seats.

Without a word, Dugal started the motor and turned the pontoon around heading back to the East Bay Launch. Jennifer and her father helped him load the pontoon back on its trailer. Then leaving the McBruces to secure it before returning it to its winter home until early May when they would launch it for the summer, Jennifer and her father drove home with Jennifer at the wheel.

"You're doing a good job, Jennifer," her father said. "I haven't been with you for a while, but I'll bet you could pass your driving exam today."

"I wish I could," Jennifer said. "With you gone, I'll have to rely on someone else to get around."

"Well, those someones are the Gilmores. They told me they would be happy to go with you if you needed shopping or anything. The McBruces said the same thing."

"It's so nice to have friends," Jennifer said.

Her father laughed and Jennifer looked at him trying to figure out what was funny.

"I'm laughing at the change in Don Gilmore. I can remember back when you were little, he was a regular guy and then he became a crab. Couldn't put my finger on it until today but it sounds as though it all had to do with deterioration of his wife's sight."

He was silent for a minute.

"Wonder what caused her sight to come back?"

Jennifer said nothing knowing that the question was rhetorical.

After parking the car in the garage, Jennifer and her father walked toward the bird feeders in the back yard. As they approached, the birds and squirrels scattered and her father stopped.

"The birds were your mother's special friends," he said to Jennifer. "Now they're yours. I think you should do this alone."

Jennifer understood and walked forward. Usually the birds would be chirping and flitting about but today they were quiet as though they knew this was a solemn occasion. When she was in the approximate center of the bird feeding area, she stopped and opened the zip lock bag she had been carrying. She looked at it silently for a moment and then lifted it into the air in preparation for the release of its contents. There was a whirr of wings and a pileated woodpecker swooped down and grabbed the bag in its beak. Then it flew around Jennifer as Gladys's ashes fell out.

Both Jennifer and her father watched this in stunned silence. When the bag was empty, the woodpecker dropped it in front of Jennifer and alit on the suet feeder. Immediately the reverent silence of the birds was broken as they all chirped their songs. Then, their memorial service over, their feeding began. Jennifer looked at the pileated woodpecker and found her looking back. Jennifer curtsied, pulling out an imaginary dress. When she stood up, the woodpecker gave forth with one of its trademark calls and then started eating the suet as though nothing had happened. Jennifer walked back to her father and took his hand and the two of them watched the birds for a moment before turning and entering the house.

Chapter 40

Jennifer parked the car in back of the Hibbard Corners General Store where there was a small parking area. Her father had left that morning on another run and when she got home from school she had called Helen's Hair Quarters to see if she could get the promised haircut. Mrs. T-G had told her she had nobody from 3:30 to 4:30 so to come ahead. Jennifer knew she was taking a chance driving the car because she didn't have a driver's license but in her mind there was no choice. She had to find out why her mother had been out on the ice. She was satisfied that she not raised any concerns with that couple at the reception after the memorial service because she had talked to them later and both were very congenial, especially the husband who had not looked frightened or otherwise askance.

Opening the door to Helen's, she saw Mrs. T-G sitting in one of the chairs reading a magazine. She looked up and saw Jennifer and smiled.

"Jennifer, how nice to see you," she said getting up and indicating that Jennifer should sit down, which Jennifer did after hanging up the light jacket she was wearing.

"That was such a nice service," Mrs. T-G said as she put the protective cloth around Jennifer's neck, pulling her long hair out. "You gave a marvelous memorial talk. I was very impressed."

"Thank you, Mrs. T-G. I was very nervous."

"I'll bet you were. I don't like talking in front of people. I mean I talk all the time in here, but that's expected, but talking to a crowd. No way! Now, you just want a trim? The ends evened up?"

"Yes, please."

Mrs. T-G brushed Jennifer's long tresses to get any snags and snarls out.

"You have beautiful hair, Jennifer."

"Thank you. Mrs. T-G, what were you and mother doing out on the ice that night?"

Mrs. T-G stopped her brushing momentarily and then began again but more slowly.

"I don't know what you mean."

"I think you do, Mrs. T-G. Someone saw you bring mother's car home. She didn't recognize you but I know it was you."

"I ..."

'You see, one thing is you left the entry door to the garage unlocked. We never do that."

The brushing stopped.

"Are you going to tell the sheriff?"

"Was there a crime committed?"

"Only a crime of omission. We could have told someone that your mother had been out there under the ice. I'm so sorry."

"That's over and done. I want to know why she risked her life going out on the ice in the first place. The fact that she died the way she did was a freak accident. She knows that."

"What? She knows …"

"She believed in life after death and so, if she is right, she knows what happened. Knowing mother, she would hold no malice." Jennifer hoped that her explanation helped her out of that awkward moment.

"Yes, I understand."

Mrs. T-G moved around in front of Jennifer.

"You really don't want a haircut, do you?"

"No."

Mrs. T-G moved to the front door, turned the sign to "Closed" and pulled down the shade. Then she removed the protective towel around Jennifer's neck, turned her other chair to face Jennifer's and sat down looking at Jennifer. She took a deep breath and let it out.

"It all started with a visit to the post office."

Mrs. T-G told her about hearing the legend of the Ice Bear from Owen Whitehawk.

"After those two boys left, I asked Owen whether the legend was true. He shrugged and said, 'All legends have some basis in fact.' So I asked him where I could find out more about it and he gave me the name of the old man who had told it to him. The first day I could, I drove to Mt. Pleasant and found the old man."

She laughed as she remembered her meeting, "Are you familiar with the saying 'older than dirt'?"

Jennifer smiled as she replied, "Mother used to say 'older than God'."

"That works, too. That was my first thought when I met Soaring Eagle. He was in an office at the Soaring Eagle Casino."

"Was it named after him?"

"Don't know," Mrs. T-G replied. "Could have been, his grandson runs it and lets him use one of the offices. When I announced myself to the doorman, he directed me to the office.

"Soaring Eagle was sitting behind the desk. He had a blanket with an Indian design over his shoulders. Under it was a buckskin shirt. His hair was black, tinged with white, and pulled back in a ponytail. I don't think there was a smooth place on his face what with all the wrinkles. His skin was coppery red. I judged that he spent a lot of time in the sun. However, it was late fall so it was cold which was probably why he was inside. I think that I surprised him in the middle of a nap since he had a sleepy look on his face. I had to knock twice before he answered. I introduced myself and told him why I was there.

"'You want to know about the Ice Bear?' he asked. I told him that I heard the story from Owen Whitehawk. 'It is not a legend many people know because it took place on a deep lake and most lakes are not deep enough to qualify and therefore the story is not really of interest'. I asked, 'Is there a ceremony that is performed to call the Ice Bear?'" 'There is a chant – that is all,' he replied. I asked him how it went and he said, 'In English it would be, *From all over the Ojibwe land we are from, asking your help. Ice Bear, you of greatness, come visit us, give us your wisdom*'. I asked him to write the Ojibwe words down, phonetically as best he could. He did so and gave me the sheet of paper. He had broken the words into syllables and gave me a pronunciation guide for the vowels. When I got home, I made a sheet on the computer and gave it to the others so they could learn and practice.

"I asked him what it meant to say 'From all over the Ojibwe land'. In particular if that could be representation with standard compass points. He replied, 'No, They come from one of the legends of how the Ojibwa learned the secrets of medicine'. He paused for a minute, closing his eyes and tilting his head back in thought. Then he said, 'When Mi′nabō′zho, the servant of Dzhe Man′idō, looked down upon the earth he beheld human beings, the Ani′shinâ′bēg, the ancestors of the Ojibwa. They occupied the four quarters of the earth—the northeast, the southeast, the southwest, and the northwest'. He paused, opened his eyes and sat back up. 'It is a long story', he said. 'Of no interest to you'. 'Is there any truth to the legend'? I asked.

"Soaring Eagle replied, 'There is truth to every legend. They are stories with a purpose. In the case of the Ice Bear, I believe it is showing that even though one is old, there is still wisdom to share'. He was silent for a moment. 'There is one thing more however', Soaring Eagle said. 'The calling must be made when the ice is starting to go off the lake'.

"'That's dangerous', I said. 'Those in need of help find no fear,' the old Indian said. 'And,' he added, 'it must be halfway between midnight and dawn because that is when the Ice Bear died'. 'But the legend Owen told me was in the middle of the night', I told him. 'Then Owen heard wrong,' the old Indian explained. 'It is as I said … but I could have said otherwise to Owen. I am old – sometimes I forget things'. I asked him how old he was and he said 'I have seen one hundred one winters but only ninety-nine summers'. At this point his head was starting to droop and I knew that my time was over. I thanked him and left."

Chapter 41

Mrs. T-G continued, "Now that I had the information required about the ritual, I needed help. I wanted people who would enjoy a challenge. At that point I didn't know what kind of ritual we would have; witches had never entered my mind. I asked Ingrid Swartz and your mother and they jumped at it. Three might have been enough but your mother explained that the ritual was about people coming from all around the four quarters of the earth, so we needed four people. We were in the shop when that happened and, right in the middle of it, Jane Eyre Polli walked in and heard 'ritual' and 'four quarters of the earth,' or whatever it was we said, and jumped right in. 'What's that about?' she asked. 'Got room for one more?' Your mother and I looked at her a little askance because of her weight. 'It'll be thin ice,' I explained. 'But it's the challenge,' she responded. 'I need some excitement in my life.' So we accepted her. Ingrid wasn't too pleased but there was no backing out. We met at Ingrid's to make preliminary plans. She was the one who brought up witches. Said that it was a secret ritual involving spirits and so witches were a natural. Jane Eyre said, 'But witches are evil. The Great Spirit of the Indians is for good.' Ingrid said, 'There are good witches and bad witches. Remember Glinda the Good Witch from the Wizard of Oz?' She had us there and so witches it became. She said she'd make the cloaks, we just had to pay for the material. I designed the four-pointed star to go with the four corners of the Ojibwa nation – she wanted to make it a pentagram 'because that is what witches use.' We didn't agree, the other three of us. Too much about witches is satanic and we wanted to stay away from that. So when we had decided what we needed, we were glad that we had Jane Eyre because she could carry the ice auger with the least trouble. She had Rolli buy her a treadmill to get in shape and the auger (I think they got both mail order, most likely from Amazon.)

"So everything was set but the date. We felt it best to wait until the time of the legend when the ice was starting to break up because that is when the bear awoke. We knew that it would be dangerous but the argument was made that the DNR banned people on the ice because they took snowmobiles, four wheelers, and trucks out there. It was still safe for walking as long as we were careful. Your mother said we needed something to test the ice and something to sweep the ice clean in case of snow. Being witches, brooms were the obvious answer and your mother made those. Don't know where she got the material or what she used for certain, but she did. I got the rest."

"What about the names?" Jennifer asked.

"What names?" Mrs. T-G seemed bewildered.

"The Witch of the North, etc."

"Oh, again that was Ingrid. To go with the ritual. She suggested we take names of where we lived on the lake (I think she wanted to be The Witch of the West, again because of the Wizard of Oz.) The only one it really didn't fit was Jane Eyre but she went along with being Witch of the South because you couldn't have Witch of the Southwest."

"So what happened?"

"What do you mean?"

"You're on the ice, you're ready for the ritual…"

"Oh," Mrs. T-G said, and explained about sighting the meteor. "I didn't know it was a meteor. I only knew that it was a ball of fire and I knew it was trouble. Later, after Ingrid picked me up from taking your mother's car home, she asked me if we had done it. When I said something about 'maybe if we were real witches,' I think she took exception to it. She didn't say anything but I could sense something – a coldness or chill in the air despite the heater running full blast. We didn't say another word all the way back to my car. Not even good-bye."

"And you've never talked about it?"

"No. I think that we all understood that something awful had happened. It was better to keep silent. I thought that after your mother was found and the funeral, something might change but I don't think so. Yesterday at the luncheon, none of us said a word to the others. At least I didn't and I don't think Ingrid and Jane Eyre talked. Ingrid thought she was something of a twit anyway."

Jennifer thought about the pentacle – no, that was a Judas Goat – which Ingrid had painted on the door.

"So Ingrid was upset with your statement about not being real witches. She hasn't mentioned anything about that? She hasn't hexed you or anything?"

"Hexed me?" Mrs. T-G laughed. "In your dreams. She'd have to be a real witch to do that, wouldn't she?"

Mrs. T-G looked at Jennifer for affirmation and they both laughed. Jennifer knew then that Mrs. T-G didn't have a clue and was as harmless as Jane Eyre. The only danger to any of them was Ingrid. Inside she felt that Ingrid would seek further revenge against Mrs. T-G, but Jennifer was her number one target.

Chapter 42

He had been searching for days. Getting up in the middle of the night, riding his bike round the lake clockwise one night, counterclockwise the next. Going slowly, taking four hours, stopping frequently where there were large clusters of houses but never picking up a signal. He couldn't understand it. The signal (or was it signals?) had been so strong the night the meteor hit and for so long. Hours, it seemed, and then it was gone. He was certain that he had felt something a couple of other nights but never for very long. That's what he didn't understand. Anyone with the power had a constant signal, basically a broadcasting aura. You couldn't prevent it. When you were actually using your powers it was stronger. Like, let's say, your aura at idle time was a pale … what? … let's say, green. When you were actually using your power, you showed an emerald aura. Not that there actually was an aura but it was more a signal, like a radio or television broadcast signal or Wi-Fi. Not strong but present until it was being used and then – bang – broadcastville.

But nothing. Maybe it was the meteor. Maybe it wasn't a meteor at all but some UFO bearing real aliens with powers. He'd heard that the sheriff's department had been out on the ice after the crash. Maybe they found living aliens and took them somewhere. But where? Out of the region obviously. Area 51? Or was Alcona County becoming its own Area 51? He could go over to Harrisville and see if they were there – in jail? Or to Alpena – the hospital? But he didn't believe it. There were people – or at least one – with powers here on the lake. New powers. Strong powers.

Wait! He stopped his bike. Both feet on the ground. Helmet off. There was something. Faint but there. He knew it. East side of the lake. Lots of woods here. Didn't think trees could block a signal, but if it was weak? Wi-Fi signals get blocked, don't they? Strong in one room, weak in the next. He laid his bike off the road where it wouldn't be seen and started walking back the way he had come. Slowly, one step at a time. *Still here. Still here. Gone. Back the other way. Got it again. Still here. Still here.* Ten steps and the signal was there then gone. Back five steps, middle of the signal. *Very weak. Deep sleep probably. Which side of the road?* He had been riding counter clockwise tonight and was headed north on the East Path. No cars. He crossed the road and stopped. *No signal. Back across the road. Signal.* He started into the woods, moving carefully. It was darker than the road. Would be darker in a few weeks as the trees came out, leaves blocking the moon and the stars, what little light they gave.

He moved slowly stopping every few steps, checking the signal. Little by little it increased. He kept looking around peering intently. *A form over there? Animal? No. Stump.* Even moving slowly, he stubbed his toe on fallen logs virtually invisible in the night's gloom. *Should have brought a flashlight. No, too visible. Night vision goggles, like the military. Didn't have them. Didn't need them usual-*

ly. But then he didn't wander the woods at night. Suddenly, unexpectedly he hit something and crashed earthward. Dirt, leaves, twigs. Face down in the leaves. What had happened? He hadn't tripped. Moving too slowly for that. He lay still listening. *Signal still there. Hadn't changed.* Carefully, he pushed himself up, hands and knees, then sat back, but on his heels, and looked around. There, to his right. *Two bright spots. Not really bright but there. Eyes. Animal eyes. Predator? What? Bear? That's all that were here around the lake, wasn't it? Wait? Last fall. That guy's zoo. Animal's released. Didn't they get them all? No. Two missing,* he thought. *Wolf? Yes, wolf. Lobo. Dangerous. What else? Cougar. Yes, a cougar. Rumors it was still around. Farmers missing stock.* He looked at the eyes. *Too high for a cougar? Yes*, reassuring himself. *Too high. Deer! That's it deer. Must have startled it when I fell.*

Satisfied all was well, he got to his feet. Watching the eyes. Brushed himself off. The eyes were gone. *Wait. White spot, bouncing. Ahh, the deer's white tail moving away. Running. Scared. Good.* He started to move forward.

Hoo!

What? Looking around. Searching. For someone.

Hoo!

Oh, an owl. Silly. Scared of an owl.

Hoo!

* * *

Jennifer sat up in bed.

"Who's there?"

Hoo!

An owl. *But why would it wake me? It's not loud.*

Hoo! Who's there?

What? Someone speaking?

Hoo! Who's there?

Jennifer got out of bed and grabbed her cellphone. She had promised her dad that she wouldn't ever be far away from it. He had left while she was at school. Off on another run. Just a couple of days.

Hoo! Who's there?

She hurried to the living room, no lights. Moving carefully she went to the sliders leading out to the patio. The area behind the garage was where the birdfeeders were. Also where her father had his grill. For that reason there were lights for the patio. A floodlight on either side of the door.

Hoo! Who's there?

To the left, back in the woods, tiny dots of light. Eyes. Human? Jennifer flicked on the lights.

* * *

Lights! He stepped back from the edge of the woods where he had been standing. He had just gotten there and could see the outline of the garage and the house beyond. No lights showing. Signal suddenly stronger. Whoever it was had awoken. *Why?*

The lights, there were two, were bright, blocking his vision of the window, door, and the land in between. His vision blinded, he took a step back, turning away, stumbled over something, that was soft and moving. He hit the ground again, half on his left side, half on his front, arm pinned beneath him. *Ouch!* Not the fall. Something sharp at his ankles. *Ouch!* He kicked out, flailing. *Ouch!* Sharp biting. Scrambling to his feet, he kicked out. *Ouch!* Hitting something solid with his toes. Numb. *Ouch!* The sharp biting. Looking down. Dark form darting away, stopping looking. Green glowing eyes. Low. Four legs. Fox! Run. Darting, hands in front for trees, left, right, jump a log. Bam! Hit from the right. Down on all fours. Ready this time. Up, looking left. White tail bouncing away. *Hit by a deer? Everyone running scared. Bad scene. Power flare. Strong. Dangerous. Nipping at heels. Run.*

Finally reaching East Path. *Where's my bike?* Left. Walking fast. Aching. Out of breath. Not used to all this exertion. Reaching his bike, he picked it up, turning around as he did so. Yip! Yip! Yip! *That damned fox.* Not looking behind, he mounted his bike and began pedaling madly north, away from the power. Staying on the same side of the road, not going out into the open but running away. *Overestimated. Stronger than I thought. Be more careful. Have to come back and check out who it was?*

* * *

When the lights had gone on, Jennifer had been momentarily blinded. Then when she could see she thought she saw movement in the woods.

Intruder! She heard. *Intruder! Who's there?* she thought anxiously. Anxiety peaked. *Protect! Protect! Protect who from what?* she thought. *Intruder!*

The voices she heard were tiny, soft but anxious. Then they faded. She saw nothing.

Chapter 43

Jennifer was sound asleep when her alarm went off and she rolled over and shut it off. Then she lay on her back for a moment.

"What a strange dream," she said half aloud. "As though animals can talk."

Then she was up and moving quickly. In the kitchen, she prepared a dish of instant oatmeal and put it into the microwave to cook. Then she hurried through her ablutions, dried her hair, dressed and went to the kitchen. The oatmeal was ready. She added a tablespoon of brown sugar and a little milk and then ate it quickly. Finishing, she rinsed the bowl and spoon and put them in the dishwasher. Seeing that it was full, she added soap and closed and locked it. She would start it when she got home. Grabbing her light jacket, she picked up her knapsack/book bag and put it on one shoulder. Then she exited the house through the kitchen door and stopped dead in her tracks.

It seemed that hundreds of little voices were saying, "hello." She looked around and saw no one. Nothing except the birds around the bird feeders. But instead of bird songs she heard many little voices, "hello," "hungry," "food," "happy." More intrigued than curious, she walked toward the feeders and stopped when she felt something hit the top of her shoulder. She turned her head suddenly to see what it was and a blue bird flitted away, hovered momentarily and then came back to sit on her shoulder.

"Good morning," Jennifer said.

"Hello," the bird tweeted in reply.

Jennifer's mouth dropped open.

"You talked," she said to the blue bird.

"You heard," said the blue bird and then flitted away.

Jennifer pinched herself and it hurt, so she knew she was awake. She turned away from the feeders and hurried into the woods so that she wouldn't miss the bus. Ahead of her she saw Feebee and gave her the usual, "Good morning, Feebee," and heard "hello" in return but this was different. This was in her head. She started toward her and then heard, "Intruder Dark" in a different voice. Turning she saw nothing and then she heard it again, "Intruder Dark" and she looked down to see a red fox looking up at her.

"There was an intruder," Jennifer said, a statement not a question. "I wasn't dreaming."

"Intruder Bite" the fox said.

"You bit the intruder?" Jennifer questioned.

"Hit Down" this from Feebee.

Jennifer turned to face her. "You knocked the intruder down?"

"Intruder Hit Down" Feebee said and the fox added "Intruder Dark Bite."

Jennifer laughed with pure pleasure at being able to talk to the animals. "I am Dr. Doolittle" and she sang the first verse of the song "If I Could Talk to the Animals":

If I could talk to the animals, just imagine it,
Chattin' with a chimp in chimpanzee,

Imagine talking to a tiger, chatting with a cheetah,
What a neat achievement it would be!

"Babies," she heard the fox said and she looked at the fox that was now eight feet away and looking back over her shoulder. "Babies Follow" the fox said and started trotting away. More curious than intrigued Jennifer followed with Feebee right behind her. The fox led them to an old stump and disappeared in a hole between two roots.

Dropping to her knees Jennifer tried to see into the hole but it was dark. She could hear tiny sounds, yips but not words. Then the mother fox appeared with a kit in her mouth. She dropped it and darted back into the hole and returned with another. Jennifer picked the first one up. Its eyes were open and she knew it could walk but it still wasn't very old. There were four in all and the mother stood proudly by as Jennifer picked each one up for a look.

"I'll have to name them," she thought just as she heard the squeal of brakes and knew that it was the school bus.

She put the kit down and stood up, brushing dirt and leaves from her legs. "Thank you, Mrs. Fox, but I have to go. I'm late." And she took off at a run hearing "Bye" from Feebee in her head.

Chapter 44

Ingrid's search for information on calling forth a powerful being to help her resulted only in a reference to an old lady living in a small rural town in northwest Ohio. There was no method of contact but she did have an address. Now the question was "What to do with Snowball?" Food wasn't a problem but toileting was since Snowball preferred going outdoors. In the end she got a litter box and filled it with unscented litter and in the early morning she headed south.

Five hours later she pulled into the small town where the lady was said to live and, after asking for directions at the local post office, she found the address she was looking for. If anyone in a small town could tell you how to find an address, it was the postmaster. The postmaster had looked at her a little weirdly, but gave her directions. Unlike what she had expected, the house was nicely cared for although there were no flowers or shrubs, but she supposed that was mainly because the house was in the woods at the end of a winding dirt road.

Parking her SUV she sat for a minute trying to get her courage up, wondering what in the world she was doing there. She was startled out of her thoughts by a rap on the window. Outside was an old lady wearing granny glasses, her silver hair pulled back in a bun. She was wearing a ratty dirty looking short-sleeved denim shirt and was peering intently at Ingrid, who pressed the button and lowered the window.

"Well, Ingrid, are you coming in or not?" the old lady said, turned and started walking toward the front door. Ingrid saw that she was wearing a long blue denim skirt, clean and new in comparison to the blouse. Ingrid raised the window and got out to follow her.

"How did you …?" she started as she neared the lady who was standing in her house with the door open.

"You wanted to see me, didn't ya," the old lady snapped. "Who else could you be?"

Ingrid was truly mystified because she had not used her name at the post office and had remained anonymous during her web searches – at least she had tried to remain anonymous, but apparently she hadn't.

"Yes, but …"

"Well, knowing who's coming is something I do. Can't be too careful."

Ingrid entered the house and found that the room she was in was basic. There was a rocking chair in one corner next to a book case filled with books and papers placed in stacks mostly, although a few were standing as books were meant to stand. There were no pictures on the walls and the only other pieces of furniture in the room were a wooden table that had seen better years and four wooden chairs, none of which matched the others or the table. In the corner opposite the rocking chair was a wooden bucket and next to it was a broom with twigs instead of straw.

That's like the ones that Gladys made, Ingrid thought.

"Yes, it is," the old lady said. "Have a seat I'll get us some hot tea. You need something after your long drive from Hibbard Corners. Five hours and seventeen minutes wasn't it? That's not counting your stop at the post office for directions."

The old lady disappeared through a doorway with Ingrid staring after her, mouth agape.

"Sit down and close your mouth or flies will get in," came from the other room. Ingrid did as she was told.

The old lady returned in a few minutes carrying a chipped pottery plate with some nondescript cookies in one hand and in the other two mugs, one pottery bearing the logo of the Toledo Mud Hens (an International League baseball team made famous by the comic strip *Crankshaft* written by Tom Batiuk and drawn by Chuck Ayers) and the other an enameled metal cup, blue on the outside, white on the inside. The old lady set the plate and mugs down in the middle of the table, picked up the Mud Hens cup and motioned Ingrid to take the other.

"Don't ha' no milk or sugar and the lemon gone bad. Cookies are stale but I don't get food stamps till Monday."

Ingrid took the enamel cup noting that it was chipped in several places, the handle was dented and the interior white, which she could see was cracked.

"They call them cracks 'crazing,' " the old lady commented. "Supposed to be good if you got a collectors item which this ain't." She picked up a cookie off the plate and balanced it on the rim of her mug and the handle. "Always been partial to Crankshaft," she said indicating the mug. "You read Crankshaft?"

"No, I ..."

Douglas Ewan Cameron

"No mind. Now what exactly do you want?"

Ingrid's mind struggled to find the words.

"I … I've been hexed?" she finally stammered.

"You mean that Judas Goat on your garage door?"

Ingrid nodded, words not close to coming.

"You put it there. What's the hex?"

"I put it there?"

"Well, who'd you think?"

"But I put it …"

"Where it wasn't proper, didn't belong. You think that Mrs. T-G deserved something as drastic as that?"

"Well, she …"

"Said she wasn't a real witch."

"She said we weren't real witches."

"Words. 'We' meaning her and you. She ain't and you're questionable."

Ingrid stared at her and for the briefest moment considered leaving. She didn't know why she had come.

"Don't go running off just yet," the old lady said. "There still things we need to chat about."

"I don't …"

"There are powers at work up there where you live. Old powers that have nothing to do with witches."

"Old powers?"

"Injun powers."

"Indian?"

"You think only white folk got powers? All races, colors got powers. Some good, some evil. Injun powers mostly good."

Ingrid just stared at her.

"Wells, you talked to that Ice Bear, didn't cha? He told you he was good and couldn't help ya."

"How do you know all that?" Ingrid was dumbfounded.

"Cause I am a real witch, you ninny."

"And I …"

"Yes, you got powers. Surprises me, it does, but so it seems. There is something I can sense. Not strong."

"I can speak to my husband." *At least I try.*

"Ah, communicating with spirits – at least trying. That don't necessary mean you have witch-type powers. Lots of folks can do that and they ain't witches."

"But …"

"See, you don't understand. People know I got powers. They call me 'Broomhilda' round here."

"Comics?"

"Yes, it's all many of them know."

"Is Hilda your name?"

"No, 'tis Haggis."

"Haggis?" Ingrid stifled a snicker.

"Oh, you may laugh. Everyone does. My father had a sense of humor. Wanted a boy. I was sixth of six girls and he had had it. Said I looked like haggis and that was my name."

Ingrid did laugh.

"Did he keep trying?"

"Nae, he gave it up, I guess. Mum never said."

"Was he Scottish?"

"Naturally, I was born there."

"In Scotland?"

"Where else? A small village. Me mum was a healer. Least that's what they called her. Never a witch because there in the highlands witches are evil. They get killed without a second look."

"Still?"

"Well, I can't say, it was some time ago."

"When?" Ingrid was suddenly curious."

Haggis looked at her as though trying to decide. Then she shrugged.

"Seventy-nine."

"Years ago?" *It couldn't be 1979.*

"Nae. T'was longer than that."

1879? 1779? Don't ask.

"Your accent is ..."

"A mixture. It drops in and out. I've lived a lot of places. Stay till it gets unfriendly and then I fly away."

Instinctively Ingrid looked at the broom in the corner.

"Nae," Haggis laughed. "I doesn't fly on a broomstick. That's for folks who wants to think that's what witches do. True, some do, but now adays I prefers my hog."

Ingrid looked at her incredulously. "A pig?"

Haggis laughed.

"No, my dear. It's me Harley."

Ingrid laughed picturing Haggis, wearing a witch's hat and a cloak, riding down the freeway on a Harley Davidson having to hold the hat on with one hand.

"T'would be a funny sight, that one you're thinking," Haggis said. "Pardon me, but mind eavesdropping is a habit hard to quit."

Ingrid sat up and tried to keep a blank mind.

"I'll try not to peek," Haggis said, "but 'tis difficult. More tea?"

Ingrid hadn't even touched hers but suddenly felt thirsty and took a sip.

"This is very good," Ingrid said, taking another swallow.

"Well, finish it up, and I get a hot cuppa," Haggis crooned.

Ingrid did as she was bidden and handed the cup to Haggis who hurried into the other room and soon returned with a steaming cup that she set down in front of herself as she retook her place. Ingrid looked at her quizzically.

"Oh, it's for you, my dear," Haggis said. "You'll need it to clear your head fore you start back to Hibbard Corners."

And indeed, Ingrid did feel strange.

"What was in that tea?" she asked beginning to feel a little warm and numb.

"Just a little herb or two. Nothing dangerous, believe me. But helpful to me to see if you deserve – more qualify then deserve – what you want to ask me for. You see, dearie, witches, for the most part at least, deal more with herbs and stuff. Oh, true, there are spells to cause palsy, ruin crops, and things that people report. But not all is to cause trouble. As I said, me mum, God rest her soul, was a healer."

God rest her soul? Ingrid thought.

"Oh, yes, me mum's dead these fifty odd years. She was living in France at the time. Me dad's been dead much longer. He didn't have any power, and if you don't, you live a normal life."

"So you die naturally?"

"Or by accident like your friend Gladys or by malicious intent. They really did drown 'witches' and burn them at the stake. Most of the 'witches' they drowned or burned t'weren't really witches. They was just normal ladies trying to help folks or accused of being witches because people ken they were."

"But Gladys ..."

"Ahh, she was a real wonder. One of the best I've ever met."

"You knew her?"

"We all did."

"All?"

"Yes, there is a coven – yes, that's the term we use that's been usurped by the pretenders. A coven of us in lower Michigan and this corner of Ohio. She was from here, did you ken that? No, guess you didn't. Can't speak now, can you?"

Ingrid found that she couldn't.

Chapter 45

"You're a strong one. Hadn't suspected that. Usually it works faster than it did with you. Guess you have more power in ye than I thought. Yes, she was from a place not far from here. Probably older than you thought too, but that's no matter."

Haggis got up and started toward her and Ingrid suddenly found that she couldn't move. Haggis leaned in front of her and raised each of her eyelids one at a time peering into each eye as a doctor might, but a doctor would have used a light that Haggis didn't need.

"You be ready. Do you feel all right? You can answer me but only truthfully."

"Yes," Ingrid found herself saying. "Warm."

"Good. Now I'm going to put you through some tests to see if you are worthy of what you want to know."

Worthy?

"Might not be the proper term but what you want, and what by our bond I am bound to give you, if you can handle it properly."

And if I can't?

"Then this visit will never have happened. You will think you had tea with a nice old lady who wasn't a witch at all and you'll have no idea why you even bothered to drive down here. Or maybe you'll just discover that you were missing a day completely. That will make you wonder why you bothered to get a litter box for Snowball, which he doesn't need by the way. That's a special cat you have. Don't know where he came from any more than you do, but I do know he has powers I don't understand. You wonder things about him, right?"

Yes.

"Like how does he get up stairs. You've never seen him climb them, have you?"

No.

"That's cause he don't."

What?

"That's right. He just sort of disappears at the bottom and reappears at the top."

He teleports?

"You a Trekkie?"

No. Ingrid felt a little pinch in her mind – well, maybe not so little. *Yes, sort of.*

"I guess it could be that, but there is no machine involved. He just does it. When you get home, provided you pass my tests, you'll find that he hasn't used the litter at all. He just goes outside. He could do that all the time but I guess he doesn't want to frighten you. I guess I'll have to make you forget that. He wouldn't appreciate it if you knew.

"Now let's have some fun."

Fun?

"Well, you might not think it is. See this stuff I gave you sort of unlocks your abilities, those that you have but don't use cause you don't know how. When I find out what they are, I'll know if you can handle what I will tell you. If you can, then I put what you need in your mind but I'll lock everything back until you need it. Understand?"

No. Yes. I guess.

"I feel that way too, sometimes. Now, let's start easy. That cuppa tea over where I was sitting. It's your tea so it should be in front of you. Why don't you get it."

It wasn't a question, it was more of a command.

Ingrid tried to stand but couldn't. She tried to reach but couldn't. Frustrated she looked at Haggis, her eyes being all that she could move.

Get it?

"Yes, bring it to you."

Ingrid looked at the tea and tried to get it to move to her.

"Nae, that's telekinesis. That's not a witch's power. Picture it in front of you. A hot steaming cuppa sitting right there."

Ingrid closed her eyes and thought, picturing the cup sitting on the table between her hands. *Plink* she heard. Opening her eyes she saw the cup of tea sitting between her hands.

"Very good. That was fast. Now let's try something you can't see. Bring the broom to stand on the table."

I can't ...

"Then we're done."

Wait.

Haggis was silent. Ingrid closed her eyes and tried to picture the broom standing on the table. She saw it but didn't hear anything. Opening her eyes she saw a clean table except for the cup of tea.

It didn't work.

"Try it with your eyes open."

I can't picture it with my eyes open.

"Try."

Scritch. Swish. And the broom flew by her and stood on the table in front of her.

"Put it back."

Ingrid found herself thinking, *Go back,* and the broom was gone.

Haggis reached down and picked up the cup and said, "Drink it all at once," as she put it against Ingrid's mouth and started tipping it. The liquid was warm and pleasant and she easily managed to drink it all. The cooling warmth spread throughout her body and then was gone and she found she could move again.

"You surprised me," Haggis said. "I didn't think you could do it."

"So can you help me?" Ingrid said.

"First, let me ask you a question," Haggis said as she took both cups and went out of the room to return in a minute with two steaming cups of liquid. She set the enameled cup in front of Ingrid and took the Mud Hens cup with her and sat at the other end of the table.

"It's just tea," Haggis said. "Cross my heart."

Ingrid smiled and picked up the cup. It was beautiful tea.

"Thank you. What's the question?"

"What did the Ice Bear tell you?"

"About what?"

"About getting rid of the Judas Goat. That's what you want help with, isn't it?"

"Yes." *The truth but not the whole truth.*

"Well, what did the Ice Bear tell you?"

"That he couldn't help me."

Haggis looked at her as though waiting for her to complete her answer.

Ingrid swallowed hard.

"That he couldn't help me unless I got rid of the evil in my heart."

"And you cannot do that?"

Ingrid thought about it and when she did, the loathing she felt for Mrs. T-G swelled up and took over, strengthened by her grief for the loss of her friend Gladys.

"No, I can't."

"Hate is a terrible thing," Haggis said. "It can destroy a person if they are not careful. Hate can be overcome by love if one wants."

"There is no love there."

"Very well. In my position as a teacher, I must give you what you want. But I also must warn you. With this summoning you will make, there is a price. The price may be too great."

"What is the price?"

"I cannot tell you because I do not know. When you have performed the incantation, if it is successful, you will learn the price. At that time it is too late to turn back."

"I understand."

"I hope you do. Drink your tea."

Ingrid lifted the cup to her lips and drank deeply.

The small house in front of her had been beautiful, but it was now a rundown shack. The windows were smashed, the shutters gone from one window, and the other had one shutter intact and the other hanging by just one fastener.

The door hung on one hinge and the shingles were half off the roof and there was a huge hole in it caused by the limb of an oak tree that was still attached to the tree and lying on the roof.

"What happened?" she said aloud, suddenly realizing that she was in her car, with the door open. She got out and with great caution approached the front door of the house. She peered inside and what she saw inside was a shambles: The floor had holes; there was no furniture; and spider webs were everywhere. In the middle of the floor sat a gray mouse, looking at her expectantly.

"Boo," she said and the mouse scurried away, disappearing through one of the holes in the floor.

"Haggis," she called out tentatively but there was no answer.

She walked back to her car, got in, and backed out the twisty road because there was no place where she felt she could safely turn around. When she back out onto the road, she saw that the mailbox, which had been upright and painted a dark green, was lying on the ground, its pole half broken, and was rusty as though it had been that way for several years. Poked into the ground in front of the mailbox post was a For Sale sign but other than the words "For Sale" she could make out nothing. She sat there in a quandary and replayed the visit with Haggis in her head. When she got to the end, when she was drinking the last of her tea, she remembered the setting for the ritual she was to perform and the incantation. She also remembered Haggis's last words: *When you have performed the incantation and it is successful, you will learn the price. At that time it is too late to turn back.*

Chapter 46

Jennifer had basically just walked through the kitchen door when the roar of a motorcycle shattered the afternoon's quiet. By the sound, she sensed that it had turned into her driveway and then she heard it being shut off. Curious she looked out the window in the kitchen door as she had when Officer Libka had first arrived. Sitting in the driveway was a huge black Harley Davidson, a "hog" as they are popularly called. It was adorned with flames on the front and back fenders. The rider was small person wearing a black helmet with flames leaping out of the visor. The rider, either a woman or a cross dresser, was wearing an old sleeveless denim shirt and a new looking long denim skirt underneath which Jennifer could see black motorcycle boots. As she watched the rider removed her helmet and Jennifer was shocked to see the face of an old woman wearing granny glasses, her white hair pulled back in a bun.

Who on earth is that? Jennifer wondered as the old woman dismounted and placed her helmet on the seat. She then opened the saddlebag compartment behind the seat and removed a denim duffle handbag. As she started for the house she waved and Jennifer waved back, more out of shock than anything else. As the woman approached Jennifer opened the door.

"May I help you?" she asked.

"You certainly can, Jennifer, and I can help you."

"Excuse me if I seem rude, but who are you?"

The woman laughed. "My name is Haggis and I am an old friend of your mother's. May I come in?"

Jennifer stood aside and Haggis entered the kitchen.

"I am a little parched from driving, may I fix a cup of tea?"

And without an answer and without asking further, she went and pulled the teapot out of the cupboard, filled it with water, and set it on a burner she had turned on although Jennifer didn't remember her turning the knob.

"You knew my mother?"

"Yes, sorry to hear of her passing. It happens to all of us."

"Where did you know my mother?"

"In Ohio where she grew up."

"She never talked about you," which was true because Gladys hadn't talked about her childhood very much.

"No, don't 'spect that she would," Haggis said as the teapot started to whistle – *that was quick*, Jennifer thought. Seeming from nowhere she produced two mugs, one a ceramic one with the logo of the Toledo Mud Hens and the other a battered metal cup with blue on the outside and white inside.

"You will join me, wouldn't cha?" Haggis said as she set the enamel cup by the chair where Jennifer's father usually sat and went to the other end of the table and took the seat where her mother had sat, that now was Jennifer's place as the woman of the household.

Jennifer just stood there mouth agape, not believing the audacity of the woman and the speed with which the water had come to a boil.

"Don't just stand there, have a seat and close your mouth before you let the flies in," Haggis intoned. "Sorry I didn't bring any cookies, but I left home in a kindda hurry. You got any?"

Jennifer went to the cupboard and took out a plastic container with some ginger snaps and Lemon Crisps from the Hibbard Corner's General Store.

"Ah," Haggis said when Jennifer set the opened container in front of her. "I love Gert's cookies."

Still in mild shock, Jennifer took the indicated seat.

"Cookie?" Haggis said, sliding the plastic box toward her. It stopped just in front of her. "Drinks your tea before it gets cold."

In a daze, Jennifer picked up the enameled cup and raised it to her lips but just before she drank, she put the cup down. Haggis looked at her in surprise.

"What's in this tea?" Jennifer demanded.

"Just Earl Grey," Haggis said.

"No, there is something else. Not a tea. An herb perhaps but definitely not part of the tea."

"I'm impressed," Haggis said.

"By what?"

"Well, I served this same brew to Ingrid Swartz earlier today and she didn't sense anything wrong."

"Ingrid! She's evil," Jennifer almost screamed.

"Yes, she is," agreed Haggis. "And she might get more evil unless you can stop her."

"Me? How can I stop her?"

"Jennifer, I believe you have powers that eventually will rival or best mine. You'll have to confront her when the time comes, but you won't be alone."

"Are you going to help me?"

"No, this is a problem that has to be taken care of by local people."

"Who? The sheriff?"

Haggis laughed. "The sheriff? Bless me, child, but he be libel to get blown away before he could open his mouth. This woman has powers she doesn't know yet and she needs to be stopped before she can summon aid and before she can gain more power."

"Summon aid? From whom?"

"Beelzebub or one of his underlings."

"The devil? How did she learn to do that?"

"Well, 'mongst witches there is a rule that when someone wants to learn a spell of which she is capable, she has to be taught. I was the teacher."

"How did you learn she was capable?"

"When she was under the control of the potion, her mind opened and I asked her to do some simple things but enough to convince me that she could perform the ritual that summons Beelzebub or one of his demons."

"What test?"

"Well, put that metal cup in front of me."

Jennifer started to stand up with the cup in her hand.

"Nae, not that way. You have to use your magic."

"What magic?"

"That exactly what Ingrid wanted to know. So I asked her to do what I am asking you to do."

"Move the cup? Telekenisis?"

"Nae, make it be there and then be here. Use your mind."

As Haggis was saying this, the enamel cup disappeared from in front of Jennifer and reappeared on the table in front of Haggis. Jennifer looked at it her mouth agape. "Did I do that? "

"T'weren't me," Haggis admitted.

"But I didn't do anything – I mean – say anything. I thought but that was all."

"And that's all there is to do. You have powers you have just begun to discover."

"But how will I learn about them."

"You get someone to help you."

"Who?"

"One of the other witches of Hibbard Corners."

Chapter 47

"How long have you know Haggis?" Jennifer asked.

When she had gotten home from school, the phone had rung, and it was Rachel Whitehorse. "A mutual friend has suggested that we talk," Rachel had explained. "Who?" "Someone who has a hog," Rachel replied.

They were walking in the woods across East Path from Jennifer's house. The hunting acreage belonged to a friend of her father's who had given Jennifer and her mother permission to walk there. It had been their favorite spot and they would walk and talk about mother and daughter things.

Before Rachel could answer the question, Jennifer heard a small voice saying "Intruders."

She looked and saw a chickadee sitting on a nearby bush. "Intruders," it said again.

"Friend," Jennifer replied.

"What?" Rachel said in amazement. "You tweeted."

Jennifer looked at her perplexed. "No, that would be rude and I don't even have my phone with me."

Rachel laughed. "No, I mean you sounded just like a bird."

"I did? I thought I just said 'friends.' "

"No, you sounded just like that chickadee," at this point the chickadee landed on Jennifer's shoulder and cocked its head, looking at Rachel almost apprehensively, Jennifer thought.

"Friend," Jennifer said again.

"Friend," repeated the chickadee and flew away.

"You can talk to the birds?" Rachel asked incredulously.

"Yes, but I thought I was talking in words," Jennifer replied smiling.

"No, you definitely tweeted, chirped or whatever."

"It happened just the other night. Well, it started longer ago than that. The day of my mother's funeral the birds started being unafraid of me. They wouldn't scatter when I went to feed them and would sit on my hand or shoulder. There's a deer, too, apparently making its home in our woods, waiting to give birth. She doesn't run away from me. Oh, and a fox with four kits. They're adorable."

Rachel was looking at her, mouth agape.

"Unbelievable."

"My mother could do it, I think. She never said so but the birds never flew away when she would feed them. I never thought about it, but now I remember."

They had stopped walking when Jennifer had tweeted but now they resumed continuing their slow pace.

"Back to what you asked," Rachel said. "Haggis came to see me shortly after I met your mother."

"Oh, that was my next question," Jennifer said.

"I had had a bad night. One of my children was ill, running a high temperature. The doctor said to give her baby aspirin, with a dropper, and watch her temperature. She was crying so I picked her up and sat in the rocking chair in her room. She wouldn't stop and suddenly I heard myself singing to her. Usually I can't sing worth a hoot. I didn't know what I was singing. The words were strange, but she calmed down and went to sleep. I sat there with her singing and rocking, and half an hour later her fever was gone."

"Was it a spell?"

"I have no idea, but it must have been. It just came into my head. The next morning I stopped in to see Owen on my way to do some shopping and I had her with me in a basket – my mother was watching her brother. On the way out the door, your mother came in and started to hold the door. She looked at the baby, as most mothers do, and then looked at me. 'Oh,' she said. 'Did you know that you could do that?' indicating my daughter. I was surprised and said, 'No.' She introduced herself and asked if she could send a friend to see me and explain to me what I had done. I was hesitant but she was so concerned – not about my daughter but about me – that I agreed. Two days later Haggis showed up."

"Did she test you?"

"Yes, gave me something in the tea she brewed. Made me 'teleport' – I can't think of another word for it – a cup and a broom. I tried it later and couldn't do it."

"The tea relaxed you and opened your mind. I think you could do it with some practice."

"And you?"

"Same thing." It was basically the truth, there had been something in the tea but she hadn't drunk it. She had tried to move the broom later and had been able to. But she wasn't about to admit it to Rachel.

"Is there a Chippewa name for witches?" she asked trying to change the subject.

"Yes, if I were a member of Midewiwin I would be a *medewiwin*."

"What is Midewiwin?"

"It is the Grand Medicine Society, a secretive religion. Its practices are called 'mide' and a male practitioner is a *midewinini*."

"I know a little about Indians and they have a great store of lore. Do you know the history of Midewiwin?"

"Yes, let me tell you a story. It starts with the creation of man but not Adam and Eve. In the beginning, Gichi Manidoo (that's the Chippewa name for the Great Spirit) made the mide manidoog (that's spirits). He created two men, and two women and made them rational beings. He paired them, and from this sprung the Anishinaabe (the Odawa, Ojibwe, and Algonquin peoples). He placed them upon the earth, but they were frail and subject to sickness, misery, and death, and he knew that if he did not provide them with the Sacred Medicine they would soon perish.

"Between Gichi Manidoo and the earth were four lesser manidoog and Gichi Manidoo talked to them and told to them the mysteries by which the *Anishinaabeg* could be helped. This was like a chain letter because he spoke to one giving him all the details; that one communicated the same information to the next, and he in turn to another, who told the fourth. They all met in council summoned in the four wind manidoog. After discussing what would be best for the Anishinaabeg, these manidoog agreed to ask Gichi Manidoo to give the Mystery of the Sacred Medicine to the people.

"Gichi Manidoo went to the Sun Spirit and asked him to go to the earth and instruct the people as had been decided upon by the council. Taking the form of a little boy, the Sun Spirit went to the earth and lived with a woman who had a little boy of her own.

"After the fall they went away from the village to hunt, during the winter this woman's son died. The parents decided to return to the village and bury the body there. As they traveled along, they would each evening erect several poles upon which the body was placed to prevent the wild beasts from devouring it. The adopted child—who was the Sun Spirit—would play about the camp and amuse himself. Finally he told his adopted father and mother that he was sorry for their sorrow and told them that he could bring their son back to life. Naturally the parents were amazed and wanted to know how he could do this.

"The adopted boy hurried with them to their home village, where he said, 'Get the women to make a wiigiwaam (wigwam) of bark, put the dead boy in a covering of wiigwaas (birch bark) and place it on the ground in the middle of the wiigiwaam.' On the next morning after, the family and friends went into this wiigiwaam and seated themselves around the corpse.

"After some time, a bear came toward the wiigiwaam, entered it, and sat before the dead son and said, 'ho, ho, ho, ho.' Then he passed around it counterclockwise with a trembling motion, and as he did so, the body began to quiver. Four times the bear encircled the body with the quivering increasing as he did so and at the end of the fourth circuit, the son came to life again and stood up.

"The little bear boy then remained among the Anishinaabeg teaching them Midewiwin mysteries. Then because his duties were complete, he needed to return to his spirit home. Since they now possessed the Midewiwin, the Anishinaabeg would have no need to fear sickness. He also said that his spirit could bring a body to life but once, and he would now return to the sun from which they would feel his influence."

Jennifer listened intently to the story.

"The bear is interesting. The Chippewa must believe that a bear is sacred."

"Yes, but not because it is big because a beaver is also special. Each is a keeper of the doorway to one of the levels of the Midewiwin."

"You mean there are different levels?"

"Yes, as you learn more and become a better healer, you move up on the levels of knowledge. There is a ceremony for the achievement of each level."

"Sort of like scouting or the military."

"Yes," Rachel agreed, "but it is so much more mystic. Midewiwin is more like a religion."

"So the members of Medewiwin are healers and they keep their secrets. In a way, because this seems so mystic, they are like witches."

"Yes, but the Medewiwin are revered, not feared."

"If people understood the good that witches can do," Jennifer said, "maybe witches wouldn't be feared."

"That will take a while, I think," Rachel said. "Because witches have long been associated with the devil and people will have to forget that."

Suddenly they both stopped and stood as an animal might stand sniffing the air, but it was other senses that were being used by the two women. After a moment or two they looked at each other.

"I think the game is afoot," Jennifer said.

"When you need us, all you have to do is send a summons."

"How …"

"You'll know and we'll come."

Chapter 47

When Ingrid had returned home from her meeting with Haggis, still wondering if it had really happened, it was too late to get the ingredient she needed (more wanted than needed) for the summoning rite. She was welcomed by Snowball as she entered the kitchen from the garage.

"Why hello, fluff ball," Ingrid said, as the kitten rubbed against her ankles. "Did you miss me?"

Apparently not, for as she reached down to pet the kitten, Snowball raced over to his almost empty food bowl and mewed plaintively.

"Ah," Ingrid acknowledged, "you just want me for the food."

After complying with the kitten's request, she turned off the light and headed for her bedroom followed closely by Snowball. After performing her bedtime ablutions and changing into her pajamas, Ingrid tumbled into bed and was asleep almost immediately. Down in the kitchen and totally ignored sat the kitty litter box, still pristine from kitten additions just as Haggis had promised.

The next morning, eight o'clock on the dot, she called the local IGA to see if they knew anyone in the vicinity who had goat meat for sale. The phone was answered by a youngish sounding lady who, upon hearing the request, shouted to a coworker, "Hey, Henry, got any goat meat?" There was a muffled answer, and she said into the phone, "We don't, sorry." And the phone went silent.

So it was to the yellow pages where she found the number of a local meat processor.

"Bennington Provision," came over the line from a scratchy voice.

"Do you slaughter goats?" asked Ingrid.

"We don't do any slaughtering," Scratchy Voice said. "Youse got to do the slaughtering yourself. You got a goat you need slaughtered?"

"No, I trying to find some goat blood," Ingrid answered bluntly.

There was silence on the other end of the line.

"Is this a prank call?" Scratchy Voice asked.

"No, I need some goat blood."

"Got some cow blood," Scratchy Voice offered. "Would that do?"

"No, it's for a science project," Ingrid explained, having come up with this as she had contemplated how to explain things. "My grandson wants to compare the blood of different animals for a science project."

"Well, I've got cow blood," Scratchy Voice offered again.

"She's already got cow blood."

"I thought you said it was youse grandson," Scratchy Voice said.

"Oh, bother," Ingrid said. "Thanks for your help," and she started to hang up the phone.

"I know a farmer who raises goats," Scratchy Voice said just in time.

"Who?"

"Jakob Glouchester."

"Where does he live?"

"Royston."

"Royston? Where's that?"

"North of Hillman. Small town just north of Hillman. You just follow F-21."

"Do you have an address?"

"No, but he has a big sign, four by eight, I think. Says 'Glouchester Farm.' "

"Do you have a phone number?"

"No. He doesn't believe in them."

Armed with this precious bit of information, Ingrid headed out. An hour later she passed the first sign announcing her arrival in Royston. It rivaled, actually excelled over, Hibbard Corners only in the number of buildings – eight, all houses. Not a store to be seen. Fifteen minutes later she was several miles north of Royston (city limit signs only about a hundred yards apart) and not a sign of or for Glouchester Farm. Fortunately her cell phone had a signal.

"Bennington Provisions," said a basso profundo voice.

"Do you know where Glouchester Farm is?"

"Hey, Burt," shouted Basso Profundo. "Where's your cousin's farm?"

Ingrid heard a muffled answered.

"Royston," Basso Profundo said.

"Where in Royston?"

"Lady wants to know where in Royston," Basso Profundo shouted and received a muffled answer.

"Burt says it's a mile and three-eights west on 628."

Ingrid hung up without a thank you. Ten minutes later she entered Royston from the north and almost immediately saw two signs: One on a high post saying "County Road 628" and a dingy battered semi-arrow shaped sign pointing to the right with faint lettering proclaiming "G o ch st r F rm." Country Road 628 was paved and just about a mile and three-tenths from F-21 she saw an equally shabby sign pointing right to a dirt road. In the distance were several farm-looking buildings.

When she reached them, she saw an unpainted wood-sided house, gray weathered by age, sitting in front of a barn, apparently made in the same manner. As she got out of the car, a skeleton of a man sauntered out of the house and stood there watching her, his clothes hanging on him like sackcloth. He was wearing bib denim overalls with just one strap fastened over a seemingly moth-eaten denim shirt with the pocket half ripped off. A scraggly scruff of a beard covered his protruding lower jaw above which a wild hair mustache was presided over by a beak nose on either side of which were dark beady eyes shielded by bushy scraggly eyebrows. Wisps of yellowish gray hair protruded from a filthy Detroit Tigers baseball cap worn incongruously at a tilt emulating C.C. Sabathia of the Yankees.

"Youse lost or come to give me a good time?" the man's voice seemed to cackle. His left hand was stuck into his bib and there was movement under it as though he was scratching himself. Ingrid was thankful that the hand was not stuck any lower.

"Do you have a goat?" was her reply not in response to either of his entreaties.

"A goat? What's you want a goat for?" This retort punctuated by a big wad of spittle that he sent off the porch into a scraggly bush struggling to survive but now probably doomed.

"Don't really want a goat, I want some goat blood!" Ingrid hadn't moved away from her SUV feeling that she might need it quickly as a refuge. Something about this near-death visage troubled her.

"How's about some cat blood instead?" the man crooned as his left hand drew a dirty yellow kitten from out of his bib. Ingrid thought that the kitten matched the man's emaciation.

"No, goat blood."

"Well, I got's me three goats but I needs them for milk and more goats," the man said, dropping the kitten to the porch and stepping off it in her direction. Instinctively Ingrid cowered back against the SUV.

"I'll give you a hundred dollars," she offered.

"Let me see it," the man said stopping five feet from her, his beady eyes scanning her head to toes, probably envisioning her naked, she thought and couldn't repress a shudder. Not daring to take her eyes off the man and almost wishing she hadn't come, her right hand reached into the SUV grabbing for her purse. Finding it, she brought it out, grasping it with both hands, then opening it and finding her money clip – it had been Karl's. Removing the bills, she thrust them out at him. He reached for them but she drew it back.

"It's all there," she managed to squeak out, "when I get the blood."

"How much blood?"

"A quart."

"I ain't gots a jar."

"I do," Ingrid said and the man turned and started toward the barn, waving his bony arm indicating that she should follow. Putting her purse back into the car, she retrieved a plastic shopping bag containing an empty mayonnaise jar and followed him, lagging ten feet behind as he disappeared into the barn's gaping entrance. She stopped short at the entrance to the barn because it was like another world – clean and orderly, nothing like the outside. The floor was swept, tools and equipment hung on the walls or placed orderly on the floor. In a straw-strewn clean pen on the right side of the barn were three goats, two adults and one young one. The man opened the gate to the pen and picked up the little one, which kicked and bleated. After closing the gate with a free hand, he reached out and snatched the bag from her, at which point she turned and walked outside the barn, not wanting to witness the bloodletting.

"Where's me money," she heard the man's cackling voice ask about five minutes later. Turning she saw he had the bag thrust out at her in one hand, smears of red on the plastic, his bib and shirt showing splatters of the same color. His other hand, showing no signs of red, was thrust toward her, fingers wiggling in anticipation. Grabbing the bag with her right hand, she threw the money at him and ran to the safety of her SUV. As she backed down the dirt road, she looked back and saw him on hands and knees picking up the money. Maybe she would add him to her list of projects once she had her ally.

The man finished picking up the money and counted it, discovering that she had paid him $135.

"Well, I be," he muttered to himself. "Hope's she's happy as I am."

He walked into the barn stopping about halfway down where a newly slaughtered sucking pig was hanging from a hook over a barrel into which the last of its blood was dripping.

"Shame to waste a good kid when I was getting ready to do a pig anyways," he said as he opened the gate to a nearby stall. The young goat stood looking up at him and bleated.

"Come on, let's get you back to your mother," he said as he picked the goat up and started toward the front of the barn.

Chapter 49

When Ingrid returned home, Snowball greeted her but immediately was apprehensive about the smaller cooler she had taken to put the jar of blood in to preserve it. Intrigued with his manner, she put the cooler down in front of him. He sniffed it and then growled and hissed, arching his back and making his fur stand on end. Wanting to see what he would do, she bent down and opened the lid of the cooler. Creeping forward Snowball smelled the jar, repeated the hissing and arched back and then fled from the room. Laughing, Ingrid put the jar of blood into the refrigerator but left the cooler on the floor to permit further investigation by Snowball. This was more for her enjoyment than playtime for the cat.

More important was the other item that she needed – again that she felt she needed: a proper gown. She had the beautiful silk white one that she had worn when attempting to communicate with Karl but that was simply not a proper color when dealing with the Evil One. Black was what she needed and she had, stored away, enough of the finest silk in the deepest darkest black anyone could imagine. She pulled the pattern out from her collection in a package that said baby gowns, which it also contained, and started to work. It took her two hours to cut the pieces and by then the long day left her exhausted, so she left the pieces sitting with the pattern sheets attached and went to the kitchen to fix dinner. There was a strange smell in the kitchen, she noticed immediately upon entering and she quickly traced it to the cooler. Looking down she saw that Snowball had expressed his dissatisfaction with the cooler leaving both urine and fecal matter. Wrinkling her nose in distaste, she carried the cooler to the kitty litter pan and dumped the contents in, not noticing that they were the first such contributions. She carried the cooler to the laundry room, rinsed it out and the filled it with water and added a cup of bleach to sterilize it.

After dinner, she fell asleep on her bed watching television and didn't stir until the next morning. But her night was filled with dreams. First, there was the ghostly image of Karl at the foot of her bed waving his arms wildly as though trying to get her attention. His mouth opened and closed as though screaming. Finally he just faded away into nothing. Second, there was the image of Jakob Glouchester in his barn with a long knife – a long evil looking knife – held in his teeth like a pirate and he was tying some animal up by its hind legs but she couldn't see what type of animal because Jakob's head blocked the view. Then he took the knife and made a slashing motion and blood squirted out and he tried wildly to capture it in the jar. When he turned around as though to go out of the barn to give the jar to her, his face was covered with blood and he was laughing wildly, waving the jar in one hand and a wad of money in the other. Then he faded into blackness and the image of Karl returned again just as before, but his time his image was spattered with red as though he had been the one to slaughter the animal, not Jakob Glouchester. As Karl faded, blackness around him burst into flames and a ghoulish image in red and black appeared. It resembled a man with horns and pointed ears and behind him a barbed tail waved wildly like that of an excited puppy. She knew that it was the Evil One, but his face constantly morphed between Karl's and Jakob Glouchester's with Karl gesticulating wildly and Jakob laughing and waving money and a jar of what she thought to be blood but appeared to be more like cloven hoofs, four little cloven hooves. Finally the vision vanished and she slept undisturbed. When she awoke sunlight was spilling into the room through half open curtains and Snowball was sitting on the foot of the bed looking at her with his little head cocked as though he was contemplating something.

She lay there looking at him for only a moment because she knew that today was a day that was going to change her life – it was the eve of the first anniversary of Karl's death and it would be the eve of his rebirth and her becoming a powerful force in the world of witchcraft. She hurried through her morning ablutions and breakfast that she might have skipped but knew that she needed the sustenance to accomplish her goals this long day. First item was to finish her gown and the first item on that agenda was to do the embroidery. From under her bed she pulled out a clothing storage box and removed from the bottom her embroidery attachment for her sewing machine and quickly attached it. Then from the bedside table drawer she pulled out the family bible and opened it to the first book of Samuel, Chapter 28, about the visit of Samuel to the Witch of Endor. Lying on the open page was a small flash drive that contained only one file – the embroidery pattern for the pentacle. She inserted this into her sewing machine and downloaded the file. Selecting the appropriate piece of black silk material, she removed the pattern tissue paper held on with pins and put the piece into the hoop that she then fitted into the embroidery attachment. After installing the black silk thread, she watched as the machine stitched what would become an inverted pentacle when the gown was completed.

That done, she removed the embroidery attachment and began to sew together the gown. She was careful and worked slowly but efficiently and by early afternoon had the gown completed. Then began the final preparations in the downstairs. The glass top table was moved and the rug rolled up and laboriously moved to one side so that she had easy access to and from the stairway. Then she went to the kitchen to retrieve the blood. She found the entry to the kitchen blocked by Snowball who arched his back and hissed at her. Stepping over him she almost fell as he seemed to appear underfoot as though by magic. He appeared at her foot with every step and she had to slide him out of the way. Finally reaching the refrigerator, she opened the door and took out the jar of blood. When she turned around, she looked at her feet so that she would not trip over Snowball, but he was nowhere to be seen. She was certain that he would show up on the steps, but he didn't. It was as though he was tired of the game and had gone off to other kittenish pursuits.

In the family room, she used chalk to sketch out the goat's head that would turn the inverted pentacle into a Judas Goat. Then she put a dab of Vapor-Rub under her nose and donned a surgical mask followed by latex gloves. Kneeling on the floor in the center of the pentacle and opening the jar of blood, she began to fill in the outline. It wasn't easy as the blood didn't have the consistency of paint but she quickly became used to its texture and finished her painting with the last bit of blood in less than an hour. It didn't look quite right but it would have to do. Picking up all the materials used in the painting, she put them into a plastic trash bag and carried it upstairs and out to the garage where she placed it into the trash can. Downstairs in the family room, Snowball crawled out from under the couch and sat looking at the result of Ingrid's efforts with his head cocked to one side as a painter might when viewing his work in the stereotypical stance with one thumb up but, of course, Snowball didn't have a thumb. Then he carefully walked around it and moved to the foot of the stairs. He looked up and then seemed to disappear.

When Ingrid walked out of the kitchen heading for her bedroom to take a short nap in preparation for the late night, Snowball was sitting at the top of the stairs and followed her to the bedroom. This time when she drifted off to sleep with thoughts of her coming ritual running helter-skelter through her head, there were no dreams, no warnings. What damage there was to be done had already been done.

Chapter 50

Jennifer sat bolt upright in bed. It was dark ... the middle of the night. She knew that something was terribly, terribly wrong. She sensed someone or something in the room.

"Who's there?"

There was no answer, yet the sense persisted. She peered into the darkness but could make out no forms.

Then, near the foot of the bed, there was a soft light that grew brighter and brighter until a warm glow permeated the room. She watched something materialize at the foot of the bed, becoming more and more distinct as the glow became brighter and brighter until the room was filled with its warm luminescence. What she saw was startling.

It was like a hologram, a little scene she looked at from almost from above but not quite. She could see a wood floor on which there was a pentacle – no, not a pentacle, a Judas Goat, the goat's head in red. Red blood.

Goat's blood, she thought, *at least that is what it should be.* And there were runes, also made with the same blood, at the points of the star. There were candles or something with flames at each of the points of the star.

Off to one side, not in the symbol at all, was something small and white – a kitten. Then a figure moved into the middle of the Judas Goat. Jennifer looked closely and realized that it was Ingrid Swartz. She was dressed in a long black gown – and she was holding a candle and appeared to be chanting. She didn't know what was happening but whatever it was, it was bad. Evil. Terribly Evil. She had to stop it. Getting out of bed she reached for her robe and found instead a cloak that she thought was her mother's, but this one was white. No, not white, silver. It shimmered even in the darkness of the room. Putting it on she wanted to pull it closed to cover her shorty pajamas, but then realized she wasn't wearing them but instead had on a gown of white. Walking to the foot of the bed to get a better look, she watched as the hologram moved to the floor. She looked at it for a minute and then instinctively pulling the cloak's hood up over her hair, she stepped into the hologram.

"What are you doing?" she said to Ingrid as she appeared in Ingrid's family room, apparently having walked through the glass wall that looked out onto the lake.

Ingrid turned and amazement filled her face. "You! Jennifer? What …" In awe she saw Jennifer clearly, standing there in a shimmering silver cloak, the hood up around her face, but a face that wasn't dark but lit up by an emanation from the cloak. As amazing as that was she was more amazed by seeing perhaps seven forms standing behind her, some in white and others in black or … they were so dim she couldn't tell.

"Who are those people?" Ingrid asked pointing.

Jennifer turned and looked. The person in front was Rachel Whitehawk dressed in white and as she looked at the others she realized they were the witches of the Hibbard Corners Coven. She recognized them all: Terri Anderson, Gert Pickard, Liz Hughes, Iris Higgins, Heather Dunn-Finney, Kathy Poff, and Jean Alvey. Beyond them she saw another figure, this one spectral – her mother. She turned back to Ingrid.

"They are the witches of Hibbard Corners," Jennifer said.

"And, I assume, you are their leader?"

"Yes, she is," Rachel Whitehawk said.

Ingrid laughed. "You? A child? Leader of a coven of nothing witches?"

"What are you doing, Ingrid?" Jennifer repeated, this time more insistently and with a sternness not of her age.

"I am calling forth someone to help me get rid of the hex that has been placed upon me."

"You placed the hex upon yourself," Jennifer said, knowing that it was true. "And only you can remove it."

"I placed the hex on myself?" Ingrid's laugh was evil, malicious. "Why would I hex myself, child?"

"You didn't intend to do it but when you tried to place evil on Mrs. T-G, the Good in this place refused to let it be done."

"The Good in this place? What Good? The Good that killed my husband? Gave him the cancer? The Good that killed your mother? If all that is Good, than I want nothing of it."

"Nothing gave your husband cancer. It just happened. It could have been in Chicago, Montreal. Any place. It just happened here."

"IT HAPPENED HERE!" Ingrid's face was livid as she screamed these words.

"You can make everything right by forgiving those you think wronged you."

"THINK THEY WRONGED ME? I KNOW THEY DID." Ingrid had gone over the edge.

"Mrs. T-G meant no harm. It was innocent."

"SHE WAS THE REASON. SHE IS GOING TO RE-GRET IT."

"I can't let you do that," Jennifer didn't know how she could stop her, but she had to give it a try. She stepped toward Ingrid.

"Stay there," Ingrid said raising her left hand.

"I can't let you harm ..." Before she could finish, a ball of fire appeared in Ingrid's hand.

Reflexively as Ingrid threw the ball of fire at her, Jennifer put up her right hand and behind her the other witches of Hibbard Corners did the same, standing firm and resolute in the face of imminent death. The air in front of Jennifer seemed to take on opaqueness and the fireball exploded when it hit it, burning fragments leaping outward in every direction except toward Jennifer and the figures behind her.

The flames seemed to envelop the room not shielded by Jennifer's spell, the candles or torches that had been set at the five points of the Judas Goat burst into full flame, and the polyurethane mixture that Ingrid's husband Karl had so carefully made ignited as though it were gasoline. The furniture in the room was set ablaze, as was the carpeting on the stairs and the braided rug carefully rolled up and out of the way. Ingrid was instantly enveloped in the conflagration, her dying scream frozen on her lips. Jennifer watched this scene in amazement and awe, not horror, at what had happened. She had no idea what she had done to create the shield, but it had acted as the one in the book she had read. She realized then that the words calling the spell had been spoken in her head. Behind her the other witches of Hibbard Corners turned and walked out of the room through the glass wall, leaving only the spectral form of her mother standing there.

Off to the side of the Judas Goat, Snowball sat quietly, unaffected by the flames that began to consume everything in the room. Jennifer was astonished to see Snowball suddenly morph into a huge bear seemingly made of ice but oblivious to the flames. The Ice Bear made his way over to Jennifer.

"You have done well," the Ice Bear said. "Evil has been stopped this night. What she was trying to do would have brought horror to the lake and its environs. Now all is well. The beasts of the woods and the fishes of the waters thank you."

Sitting down, the bear reached his front paws up to his head and seemingly into it. He pulled out his skull and offered it to her.

"Why do I want that?" Jennifer asked.

"People like you have altars that are used to communicate with the dead. You will find a need in the future to call upon your mother for aid." The Ice Bear bowed his head in the direction of her mother's form.

"A skull seems to be a necessity in this ceremony and one with a jaw is needed in order to hear the dead speak. I offer this skull, which I no longer need, for that purpose. It also will be a useful means to communicate with me should you find that necessary."

Jennifer took the skull from the Ice Bear who then stood on all four feet and bowed to her, touching his head to the floor. Then he turned and seemed to dive into the center of the flaming Judas Goat. The room was suddenly dark and Jennifer found herself standing at the foot of her bed wearing her mother's black witch's cloak, the lining of which was now a shimmering silver. She still wore the white gown and on her feet were silver slippers. What had seemed a dream she knew to be all too real.

Out on Hibbard Pond, Officer Libka turned his cell phone off, having called 911 and reported the fire. What he had seen he could not explain, just as he couldn't explain what had drawn him to the lake off Ingrid Swartz's place that night. He had seen Ingrid light the candles, if that is what they were, and stand in the middle of them seemingly talking or singing. Then she had raised her left hand and the room had exploded in flames. Now the entire house was engulfed and he knew that the local fire departments would only be able to contain it and prevent it from spreading to the trees. With the death of Ingrid Swartz, his investigation had come to an end with all his questions unanswered and he knew that they never would be.

Douglas Ewan Cameron

Epilogue

It was a warm mid-May afternoon when Jennifer got off the bus. The past few weeks had been quiet and in the household things had settled into a routine. Jennifer and her father (when he was home) shared the household responsibilities and when he was gone, it was up to her. She waved at Muddy Waters and he waved back through the bus's window and at Jimmy Lukas, who had gotten off behind her and was proceeding north along East Path, while she headed south having crossed in front of the bus. She glanced ahead at the edge of the woods where Feebee, now great with fawn, usually awaited her but she wasn't visible. She could be eating off somewhere or getting a drink from the lake, although lately she hadn't strayed too far from the copse of fir trees.

Entering the woods, she heard a faint call and stopped to listen. "Help," was what she heard and she knew it was Feebee. Quickly she moved in the direction of the call and entered the same copse of firs where she saw Feebee lying on the ground, head raised looking at her, a pleading look in her eyes. "Help," Jennifer heard again. "Baby."

Oh, my god, she's giving birth, Jennifer realized, dropping her book bag and moving to the doe's hindquarters. She could see the fawn's legs sticking out and knew from

Feebee's helplessness that something was wrong. *It must be a breech birth*, Jennifer reasoned and realized that she knew this meant that the fawn's head had somehow gotten turned over its shoulder. Kneeling she placed a hand on Feebee's abdomen and started singing a song she didn't know, whose words she didn't recognize. Almost immediately she sensed Feebee relaxing and after a few minutes knew that she was in a deep sleep. It was as though she had been anesthetized.

Taking a deep breath, Jennifer slid her right hand up one of the fawn's legs, inside the birth canal slowly and carefully until she reached the fawn's head that was backwards, over its left shoulder when it should have been between its legs. Sliding her left hand up the other leg and into the birth canal, she carefully pushed the fawn back until the front legs were in enough that she could grasp the fawn's head between the nose and the eyes and then moved it between its legs as it should have been.

Pulling her hands out, she sat back on her heels and realized that she had been singing the entire time. Standing to be out of the way of the fawn's entrance into the world, she knelt near Feebee's head and started stroking her neck, the song changing as she did so. Feebee open her eyes, raised her head and look at Jennifer and her eyes seemed to be filled with relief. Her contractions started again and it wasn't long before the young buck was out. Jennifer breathed a sigh of relief seeing that he was still alive.

With the fawn out, Feebee immediately began to clean it. The young buck then started to crawl up to Feebee's belly and began to search for her nipples and successfully nursed for a few minutes. The entire time Feebee was cleaning the newborn fawn while Jennifer watched in wonderment. After the fawn was completely cleaned and had nursed again, it tried to stand, seeming to heave itself up on its front knees. Then it raised its hindquarters and unsuccessfully tried to stand. After several more attempts, at least one failing because of Feebee's renewed cleaning efforts, the young buck made it to his feet and Jennifer cheered silently. It sank back to the ground and seemed to rest before trying again, this time easier and with seeming greater determination, he took his first few wobbly steps before sinking to the ground. The exertion seemed to have exhausted him and he closed his eyes and went to sleep while Feebee continued her lavish attention.

Knowing that she was no longer needed, Jennifer picked up her book bag and started backing out of the copse. Feebee stopped her ministrations and looked at Jennifer who stopped. Feebee then looked at the fawn and then at Jennifer, at the fawn and then at Jennifer.

"You want me to name him?" Jennifer asked.

Feebee just looked at her.

"Well," Jennifer said. *Rudolph – too trite; Dancer, Prance – no, not for a wild deer; Bambi – wait, what was his father's name? Oh, yes, The Great Prince of the Forest.* "Prince."

With that Feebee went back to her cleansing and Jennifer turned and left the copse.

Wow, Jennifer thought. *If this is what being a witch is all about, I can handle that.* With a happy heart she headed home.

However, on the morrow's horizon, dark clouds were beginning to gather. Deep in the lake in the hole caused by the meteor, there was a disturbance in the water. The Ice Bear was restless in his slumber. Something had once again disturbed the forces around the lake. But the vortex created was brief and the forces steadied and the Ice Bear was quiet once again, waiting to be summoned.

Also by Douglas Cameron

*****

Payback is a Bitch

Chapter 1

They were leaving. I didn't wave. They didn't wave. They didn't even look back! I guess you don't if you've just killed someone. Especially if that someone is your brother-in-law.

I got all this information as I momentarily crested a wave and chanced a quick look through half-opened eyes. Even opening my eyes just a slit and quickly closing them made my head throb.

I tried to relax and float but my clothes were getting heavy – especially my shoes. I mentally kicked myself for wearing sneakers and not boat shoes or sandals. But how was I to know that Howard was going to kill me – okay, make that "try to kill me?"

I felt the next wave carry me to its crest and snuck another peek. The boat was definitely moving away and I could hear the low rumble of its twin Yamaha 150s that suddenly turned into a roar, as Quentin must have pushed the throttles full bore. I just hoped that they wouldn't come round and try to run me over to be certain that the job was done. I didn't think Howard had it in him but maybe Keith did. I didn't know much about Keith – or Quentin for that matter.

Trying to relax, I thought about what had happened to get me into this predicament.

My wife Elise and I were on a Caribbean cruise and headed for Aruba for a week in the sun – a second honeymoon so to speak. Several weeks before, at the suggestion of my wife, I had used the web (a favorite tool of mine) to find a charter captain on St. Nantes. He had picked up Howard,

Keith and me at the pier after we were dropped off from the first tender ashore from our ship, the Caribbean Isle, the flagship of Caribbean Cruise Line. Howard is my brother-in-law – rephrase that – my no-good brother-in-law. Keith is a guy to whom Howard had introduced me on the ship and I asked if he wanted to join my little excursion. He had immediately jumped on board – looking back on it, much too quickly.

We had headed out deep-sea fishing for mahi mahi and anything else that came along in Quentin's thirty-six foot boat. A fast run of forty-five minutes south through two to three-foot emerald blue swells had brought us into the area that Quentin had selected.

"Zere are a lot of fish here," he had said as he baited both lines and set them out and then got the boat slowly up to trolling speed.

We had been offered water, beer, or coke and all of us had selected beer – Heineken in 250 milliliter bottles bearing no regional brewery notation, which I had found strange. Quentin had expertly used his knife pulled from the sheaf in one of the rod holders to remove the caps. Even at 11:00 in the morning, the first draught was welcome. The three of us had touched bottles and wished each other "Taut Lines" and settled in to wait for the first strike that we had decided would be mine as I had organized the excursion.

The sun was high in an azure blue sky and infrequent seabirds crossed our vision as we questioned Quentin about the island and his life. He was a seventh generation island resident and had been fishing all his life, twenty years taking out charters for either inshore (barracuda and an occasional mahi mahi) or deep sea like today. I had chosen the latter, even knowing that its five-hour length would push the envelope getting us back for the last tender to the ship, but that was a chance we were all willing to take. We knew that the Caribbean Isle would not wait for us if we were late since it was not a ship-sponsored excursion. You pay your money and take your chance.

Suddenly the reel to my immediate left began to whine and the rod rattled heavily in its holder. Before any of the three of us could shout "Fish on!" Quentin had throttled back and was halfway to the rod holder. I stood up from my seat in the stern moving starboard to get out of his way, clutching the fighting belt and frantically searching for the snap buckle. "Don't put et on until we have a fish," he had said in his heavy French accent as he explained the technique, "et's bad luck!" Little did he know! Or, on second thought, maybe he did.

I settled back against the rod rack (no fighting chair on this boat) and Quentin brought the rod and snapped it into the holder. I gripped the rod above the reel with my left hand, moved my thumb against the line and starting winding, pushing the line to the right as I did so. Pulling the rod up and cranking it down to keep the line tight, thumb moving left or right guiding the line. Well, at least that is what I tried to do but the fish (mahi mahi, hopefully) had other ideas. The line went out and there was no way to stop it. Then I started reeling line and worked at it, pumping the rod and keeping the line going from side to side. I remember thinking that it would make more sense if these huge Penn reels had a line guide like my freshwater reels did.

The fish was huge and kept taking the line out, erasing what little progress I seemed to make. However, little by little the battle was won and at last, after what seemed like hours because of the adrenaline pumping through my veins but was actually mere minutes, Quentin told me to stop. That was an easy request to obey. Quentin wrapped the line around his hand and started pulling the fish up.

"Get over by the fish for a good picture," Keith had shouted as he had volunteered to be the cameraman on the first fish and I had given him my camera.

I moved a few feet toward the port side where Quentin was at work.

There was a flash of green ...

Chapter 1

"Daws, someone is coming."

"I know, Tres," I replied, "Thanks."

I released the intercom button on the remote I carried and looked at the picture. The car was proceeding toward The House at the End of the Road at a normal speed. My backside motion detector system had been first to acquire the intruder, but the camera would have captured him a few seconds afterward. I had two motion detector units (one on either side of the road) at the far extremities of my property that communicated with the house wirelessly and were solar powered.

I had been living here about six months and the first thing I had done after moving in was to install a security system. It wasn't mine by any means, but I knew how to run it. The system was super high tech, some of the stuff I don't even know if the military had. The windows and doors were all equipped with sensors that would detect them being opened. The windows all had glass breaks. I don't know why I put the glass breaks on because all the glass was bulletproof. All the locks were armed with pick sensors. My keys had chips in them and if the wrong key or a lock pick was inserted, then the alarm would sound. I had given up my landline four months ago and all my communication was done by satellite. A security station in the states would pick up the signal and call me. And if I did not respond, they would contact the St. Nantes gendarmes at the same time as Beecher McFalls, my security man who lived on St. Martin. He was an hour away by private plane but I could not do much better, at least in what he could do for me. The plane could land on the road and he would be at my door in sixty-five minutes tops. We know because we tried.

I had four motion detector systems at the house to pick up any intruders, one under the front deck that watched the front yard down to the slope which dropped down to the Caribbean, one on each end of the house concealed in vegetation and one on top of the carport on the back of the house. But it was the backside motion detector that had found the current intruder – I don't know what else to call him. I am a semi-recluse – except for Tres. I don't get mail delivery and my housekeeper Lynette Duprey had been here only yesterday. "Why no mail delivery?" you might ask. Because there wasn't anyone to write me. All my bills I get on line so all that could possibly arrive by snail mail is crap.

I had an automatic backup generator run on natural gas backed up by a fifty-gallon underground gas storage tank. A wind turbine in the front yard generated the majority of my electricity. It was over to the right side where it couldn't be seen from the front windows or from the deck unless you leaned over at the right end and craned your neck. Anyone who wanted to knock out my security would have to start in the house. I still had landline power but if that supply was severed, I wouldn't even have known it except for the alarm which would sound on my monitor remote which I always had with me, even when I was not home.

I was in the basement exercise room when the current alarm sounded and had just completed my workout. As usual it had started with the weights and ended with the treadmill. Treadmills are basically boring. Well, let's face it, all exercise is basically boring. I had a flat panel TV on the wall and watched CNN International when working with the weights but the treadmill I had in front of the slider and I looked out across the front yard at the beautiful Caribbean, which is basically all I could see from my house or at least the front of my house. I owned seafront property and, as with most of the people who own such, my front yard was between the house and the Caribbean. My "front" door (where any of my few and far between guests showed up) was in the middle of the back of my house.

My exercise room was under the laundry room that was at the far west side of my house, accessed by a staircase that came out at a semi-concealed door next to the kitchen on the front side of the house. I had missed it the first time I was in the house over a year ago but I was not in any shape to really notice hidden passages. I had just survived a grueling, tortuous, unending, terrifying (you pick the adjective) sixteen hours in the water after being "drowned" and left for dead by my no-good brother-in-law Howard and his equally no-good friend Keith. Fortunately, I wasn't drowned and I managed to survive.

Wondering whom the visitor was – let's call him or her that until we know more – I ran up the stairs and almost knocked down Tres, who was coming to get me.

"It's a man. He's driving a Porsche. I don't recognize him."

"Okay, then I probably don't either because you know all the people on St. Nantes that I know. Get your pistol and get down to the control room. If there is any shooting, get into the safe room. Lock it and don't come out until I tell you to."

She didn't question me, just stood on her tiptoes, threw her arms around my neck, gave me a big kiss, turned and ran toward the great room. I was right behind but not at a run. I had a towel around my neck that I had used to wipe the sweat away from my workout. Entering the great room and turning left, I stepped behind the bar, dropped the towel on it and hit a panel on the wall. The door popped open to reveal a safe door about the size of a safe deposit box. I pressed my index finger of my right hand and then the thumb of my left against the security panel, which turned blue, and the door popped open and the drawer slid out. I took the Beretta and its magazine out of the drawer and slammed the mag into the gun with the heel of my hand. I closed the door to the safe and the panel door. There was nothing else in the safe. I racked the slide back, seating the first shell in the chamber.

Thus armed, I went through the great room into the foyer. On my left was the stairway entrance to what was now my control center, formerly a theater. I crossed the foyer and looked at the flat panel screen to the left of the door. I could see a man out there, pacing. He was wearing sandals, white tennis shorts, a black emblemless tee shirt, a matching black baseball cap and reflective sunglasses. I was about to press the talk button to ask what he wanted when he stopped, looked up at the camera, and removed his sunglasses.

I stared in disbelief. I had been wrong. Tres didn't know everyone on St. Nantes that I knew.

The man was Judge Michel Villar.

*****

The Body in the Perch Pond

Prologue

The cold wind whipped the snow in small torrents, dashing it against the ground, the tire, the lantern, his hands, his face – especially the light. Coming in brief gasps the wind caused eddies in the falling snow and whipped the already fallen back into the air obscuring his work. If it wasn't the snow obscuring the wheel lugs, it was the snow whirling in front of the lantern's lens and dimming the light. He cursed his luck. He cursed his lack of electronics. He cursed his hands crippled both by arthritis, the cold and old injuries. If he had a radio – a simple radio – in the truck, he would have (could have) heard about the storm. That is, if he had been able to get a signal but this area was so remote that most signals were difficult to get even in the best of times. But it probably wouldn't have mattered. He still had to get her help.

His half-frozen fingers of his left hand could not control the lug wrench adequately and the half-frozen fingers of his right hand couldn't hang on to the lug nut, which dropped into the snow under the tire.

It wasn't the storm really, he knew, as he groped under the tire for the nut. It was really the tire – bald, over used – it had given out as he hit the last pothole. He knew it was there because he drove the road once a week and he had watched it develop through the long winter.

His groping fingers felt the nut – or a pebble – and closed on it. "Thank goodness," he thought. He had already lost two and losing a third would leave him only two on the wheel. In such treacherous weather, two lug nuts holding on the wheel that helped to power the truck would not have been good.

He put what he hoped was the lug nut into his mouth and sucked at it to clean the snow and ice. It was bitterly cold but there was no alternative. As the snow melted his tongue felt the hole in the object and could discern the sharp corners. His luck was beginning to turn. Spitting the nut into his palm, he turned his head, spat the water and remaining debris into the snow. With his other hand, still holding the lug wrench, he wiped the snow off the lantern's lens and then tried to start the nut onto one of the lugs.

He breathed a sigh of relief as the nut caught and he gave it several turns. He fitted the lug wrench to the nut – easier than the nut onto the lug – and started turning it.

"Need any help?"

The voice from nowhere startled him and he dropped the wrench into the snow. Turning to his left he could make out a form behind a bright beam of light. Beyond that were flashing red lights.

"What?" he stammered but "Cops!" he thought.

"Didn't mean to startle you," the voice said. "We thought you would have heard us stop. My wife and I are on HPCP" – "Hip-Cip" he pronounced it – "patrol and saw your truck at the side of the road. You should have used a flare and had your flashers on."

His mind raced. Things were cloudy, disconnected. Then something clicked and a semblance of understanding formed.

"No – I'm sorry." His eyes returned to the wheel as his hand retrieved the lug wrench and fitted it once again to the lug. "My flashers don't work and I have no flare – didn't mean to be out in this storm."

"Well, none of us should. Can I give you a hand?"

The Samaritan was now crouching at his side. A red and black jacket, red and black balaclava, making his face indiscernible, topped by a HPCP baseball cap. The man's right hand held a powerful lantern the beam of which he directed at the wheel.

"Just finishing," he responded. "Blew a tire on the chuck hole. Had to get my granddaughter home."

Damn! Shouldn't have said that. Too confused. Too cold. Too many things all at once.

The Samaritan's powerful beam moved from the wheel toward the front of the truck.

"We can take her in our truck if you want."

The Samaritan was up and moving toward the cab.

"No." A final twist and the lug was tight. He stood up and put out a hand to arrest the other's movement. He couldn't take the chance – he couldn't let the Samaritan see her. Even after so long, who knew?

"She's fine. The cab's warm and we'll be on our way in just a minute. Thanks anyway."

"You're certain?" the Samaritan said. It wouldn't be any trouble. We have four wheel drive."

"You're mighty kind," he said. "But with the tire fixed, we'll be fine."

The other retreated and he moved to the back of the truck, inserted the tire iron in the jack and started lowering the car.

"If you certain..." the Samaritan said.

"Yes, thank you," he said wishing the other would leave.

"Alright. Be careful. This storm is supposed to hang around for a while and the roads are icy."

"Right. Thanks. We'll be fine. Her home is very close and I'll stay the night."

"Okay - be careful."

The Samaritan turned and focused his light on his truck parked on the other side of the road and made his way to it and opened the door.

******

John got back into his vehicle, luxuriating in the warmth. Glad to be out of the storm. In his rearview mirror he saw the lights of the truck come on as the exhaust belched a plume of black smoke.

"Is everything alright?" his wife Myrna asked.

"Yeah," John said. "Some old guy blew a tire in a pot hole. Says he's taking his granddaughter home. Must not be from around here. Didn't recognize the truck – an old Ford 150, must be one of the first."

John watched as the other vehicle pulled off the shoulder and disappeared into the blinding snow.

"Should we log it?" Myrna asked as she picked up the microphone to the CB.

"Nah," John said. "We've already clocked out. Herb's probably shut down his base. We need to get home ourselves."

"We should never have gone out," Myrna said. "We knew there was a storm brewing."

"Well, we didn't know it was going to hit here or hit this hard," John responded as he pulled off the shoulder. "Who would have guessed that the storm would hit with this fury when we were completely on the other side of the lake. We should have gotten a room at the Dew Drop anyway instead of coming all the way back."

Some fifteen minutes later and not much more than two miles down the road, his headlights picked up the sign at the end of their driveway and he turned into the protection of the evergreens.

"We're safe now, just a quarter mile to home."

"Thank goodness," Myrna said and they smiled at each other.

******

He was anything but safe as the savage winds of this late winter storm whipped the snow against the windshield and caused the light from the headlights seemingly to flicker in and out of existence. He glanced at the blanket wrapped form on the passenger side. "How close that was," he thought. His eyes moved quickly back to the windshield.

The snow seemed to be coming down harder, his windshield wipers could scarcely keep up with it. He was traveling slowly, not more than ten miles an hour when he hit a second pothole. This one was deep and the front wheel bounced in and out and he wrenched the wheel, trying to keep the rear wheel out but it was to no avail. The turning of the wheel started the truck sliding and the rear wheel plunged in, the torque of the slip whipping it against the outside lip putting such a strain on the three poorly tightened lug nuts that one of them striped almost to the end and the wheel began to wobble.

He managed to get the truck stopped sitting broad side on the road and knew that something had happened to the wheel but he didn't know what. He thought about getting out to look at it but knew that it wouldn't make any difference. He should have let the Samaritan take them ... no, that was impossible. The fewer who knew, the better. He checked the form wrapped in the blanket to his right, opening the fold and feeling her forehead. Hot and damp – hotter than before. The fever was getting worse. He had to get help.

Despite its age, the truck had continued running because instinctively he had never removed his foot from the clutch. He oriented himself the best he could, backed the truck up a few feet, turned the wheel and slowly started forward. The knowledge that she needed help – more than he could give – urged him on and once the truck was moving, he started increasing the speed. He could feel the wobble in the rear wheel and knew for certain what had happened. Something bad but there was nothing he could do about it. There was no choice but to continue on his way – she need help, help that he couldn't give her.

He knew that he was coming up to Comrock's Point and its infamous S-curve, called Dead Man's Turn by many of the locals. It had taken several lives over the years. The most recent, two earlier that year when a couple of young men heading home from a night at one of the local bars, had misjudged the turn in the snow and flown thirty or forty feet, smashing into a huge oak that now had two white crosses at its base.

He knew the road even in the whiteout having lived in the area all his life – except for those three years in that godforsaken jungle hell hole. He was getting close and would have to ... what was that? Something in the road! Something big! His right foot moved from accelerator to brake as his left foot moved to the clutch. The truck immediately started to skid to the left. Ice! He turned the wheel to the left but no – the skid stopped as he felt the tires get traction and he released the clutch and spun the wheel to the right. Immediately, once again under power, the tires spun, the wobbly one gripping for traction but finding only ice. The truck swung to the right in another skid, he released the brake, cursing himself for his foolish response. Even as he turned the wheel the right rear tire caught another pothole, the poorly fastened lug nuts gave, and the right wheel buckled. The remaining lug nuts stripped and the wheel came off, falling and catching the brake housing and turning into a sled. The skid turned into a sidewise slide taking the truck off the road, across the shoulder – into the nothingness at the south end of Comstock's Curve. The right rear wheel spun, catching only air and swirling show. The truck seemed to teeter momentarily, then disappeared from view.

The sixteen-point stag hadn't moved from its position in the middle of the road since it was first caught in the glare of the truck's headlights. Even the sounds of the final crash as the truck came to its resting place at the bottom of the fifty-foot embankment hadn't bothered it.

Stillness pervaded the air. The snow whipped wildly about the stag as he slowly continued his journey across the road and into the shelter of the woods. Within minutes the winds and snow of the late winter storm had obliterated all signs of the stag and the truck. Nature was in control.

*****

Muddy Waters

Chapter 1

To anyone watching, the cloud of dust on the gravel and dirt road would have announced the arrival of some vehicle. Or if someone wasn't watching but listening, the crunch of heavy tires on gravel and the squeal of brakes covered with road dust would have made known that something big had stopped. Through the haze of light dust, one could see the vintage yellow school bus with its red lights flashing and stop signs sticking out from its sides. As the dust settled, the door to the bus opened with an audible swoosh and, after a brief moment, a tow-headed thirteen year old boy wearing a yellow tee shirt, cut-off jeans and flip-flops jumped from the last step. He stumbled as he landed, as he often did, and his backpack went flying into the drainage ditch, narrowly missing the mailbox post that would have retarded its progress. Fortunately two weeks with no rain had left the drainage ditch dry and no harm came to the backpack. Recovering from his near fall, the boy turned to the bus and waved.

"Bye, Lucy," he said to the driver. "Have a good summer."

"You too, Chris. And be more careful."

Lucy, the driver, was a matronly woman in her mid-fifties who drove the bus more to get out of the house then to earn money. She mothered the kids on her routes mainly because some of them, like Chris, were on the bus for almost an hour. This year Chris, whom his friends called by his nickname of "Muddy," had been first on the bus in the morning and last off the bus in the afternoon. Lucy grabbed the handle to close the door, pausing a moment to watch Chris clamber into the ditch to retrieve his bag. Satisfied that all was well, Lucy pulled the handle closing the door and checked her rear view mirror. Seeing that no one was coming from either direction, she turned off the flashers, retracted the stop signs, turned on her left-turn indicator, shifted from neutral into first and stepped on the gas. The old bus seemed to groan expressing discomfort at the request to get moving again at its age and slowly moved away from the dirt road leading to the farmhouse set back from the road. Situated about a quarter mile from a wood copse by the road, the old house was surrounded by fields, which were already beginning to show the green of summer crops. Lucy shifted into second glancing in the right-side rearview mirror to see Chris opening the mailbox, backpack at his feet. *Kids these days*, she thought shaking her head, *wearing flip-flops to school instead of something sensible for foot support*. However, to her knowledge that was the only fault Chris Waters had and she knew him pretty well, as it was fifteen minutes to or from her next pickup on this route this year. The routes changed every year depending on who was going to school and this had been her first time on this particular route. The kids were well behaved for the most part although unduly rowdy today but with it being the last day of school, and a half-day at that, it was to be expected. She would miss them during the summer and she made a mental note to ask for this particular route again or whatever route Chris was on.

Muddy sorted through the mail as he always did hoping that he would get something but he never did. Of course, he never wrote a letter to anyone or at least not a hard copy letter, preferring email or texting communication as most young people did. The mail was catalogs, which his mother enjoyed, a bill or two he supposed, and some advertising circulars. He stuffed the mail into his backpack, slung it over his left shoulder and was about to start his walk home when the distant squeal of brakes announced the fact that Lucy and Alcona County School bus number 14 had reached the end of Creek Waters Road. He looked and saw the bus sitting at a stop, right turn indicator flashing. Lucy would turn onto Black River Road and follow it several miles to F41 where she would turn south and follow the road into Lincoln, proceeding south on Barlow Road to the school bus garage across the street from the high school and middle school building. There she would leave it, sign out the last time until fall and then go home to … Muddy didn't know where home was or what it was. Lucy was closed mouthed about that but pretty much open about everything else.

Muddy waved and, to his surprise, heard the distant sound of the bus's horn and saw the yellow warning lights flashing. Then the lights were shut off, the bus turned onto Black River Road and soon disappeared. Turning toward home, Muddy started his walk to the farmhouse he shared with his parents and younger sister Katie who was only five, eight years his junior. His parents never talked about why the age difference and he hadn't asked because, he felt, some things are private. Maybe someday when he was older he would. The road was gravel, well packed down with the many years of travel by farm vehicles, but the sand and dirt still accumulated and as he shuffled along so that he wouldn't lose the flip-flops, he grinned at the warmth of the dirt that settled briefly between his toes. There was the occasional stone but those he easily shook out, hardly breaking his stride. After about a hundred feet, he turned off into the woods, stopping near the stump of an oak that had blown down several years before and been used to heat the house the following winter. Reaching behind the stump Muddy retrieved a two-gallon zip lock freezer storage bag in which he stashed his sneakers while at school. He exchanged the flip-flops for sneakers and socks and started to put the bag back behind the oak stump. Then his brain, already on summer holiday, kicked in and he put the bag with the flip-flops in his backpack. He really didn't like wearing flip-flops to school but it was the "in" thing. Not wanting to be totally ostracized, he had chosen to change before boarding the bus knowing that his mother would have objected stringently to that choice of foot apparel. He could hear her, "I don't care what other kids wear to school; no son of mine is wearing flip-flops. Now go change to sensible shoes."

"Hi, Dad," Muddy shouted entering the house as he knew that his mother was still at work and his sister in daycare. There was no answer to his shout and Muddy hurried up the stairs to his room. Removing the storage bag from his back pack, he put the flip-flops under the bed with two other pairs, folded the bag and put it in a pocket of the back pack, which he then put on the shelf of his closet. Now to get down to the business of summer vacation – first on his list was fishing at Hibbard Pond.

The Body Under the Ice

PROLOGUE

A light autumn wind blew dry leaves across the vacant parking lot as a pickup truck rolled quietly into the lot and, with its lights off, coasted beside a six-foot tall wooden fence on the far side. A man wearing night vision goggles standing in the pickup's bed was able to look over the fence and rapped once on the roof when the truck came alongside what looked like several stacks of large packing crates. The truck stopped and the Spotter hopped out of the pickup's bed carrying a portable drill. He quickly removed screws from both ends of a section of the fence and was joined by the driver who was also wearing night vision goggles. With the screws removed, the Spotter put the drill into the bed of the truck. Then he and the Driver moved the fence section from its spot and carried it down the fence until the opening was clear and they leaned the section against the fence. Both men were big and could easily have been mistaken for NFL defensive linemen but neither of them was or had been.

Moving through the opening, the men surveyed the stacks. What seemed to be large packing crates were boxes of slats about eight feet long by three feet by three feet. They were stacked in four rows, each three boxes high and each row four deep. The last was actually five wide with the last row only two high making a total of fifty boxes. The men moved purposely to the next-to-last row and, grabbing the top box at each end, they moved it and set it out of the way. They did the same with the preceding row and then reached over the first row of crates, all of which had open tops. Securing the second crate in next to the last row, they pulled it out to the edge. Then they picked up the second crate they had re-moved and put it back. From the ground you couldn't tell there was a missing crate. They picked up the first crate they had taken out and carried it outside the fenced area and set it behind the pickup. The Spotter lowered the tailgate of the pickup and the two of them picked up the crate and slid it into the extended bed of the truck. The men moved the fence sec-tion back into place and the Driver held it while the Spotter got the drill from the truck and proceeded to put the screws back in. Then the two men climbed into the truck and covered the crate with a tarp and secured it with bungee cords. They got out of the bed, closed the lift gate and got into the truck's cab. Both men removed their night vision goggles and the driver started the truck and drove quietly out of the parking lot.

Twenty minutes later the truck turned off West Hibbard Pond Path onto a private paved road and passed under an en-try sign that read Timber Point. They turned off the main road onto a dirt road and drove until it ended at the lake where a pontoon boat was sitting nudged into the shore. The two men got out of the truck, lowered the lift gate and the Spotter got into the pickup's bed, removed the tarp and then slid the crate out onto the lift gate where the Driver could grab it and help pull. Joining him on the ground the Spotter helped pull the crate out of the pickup's bed and set it on the ground. Each grabbing the crate in the middle of a side, they carried the crate to the pontoon, lifted it up and over the rail and, guided by the pontoon's Helmsman, slid it into the pontoon on an inclined ramp made of two by fours.

The Helmsman, who was virtually indistinguishable from the other two, size-wise, started the pontoon's engines while the Driver and the Spotter lifted the front end of the pontoon and slid it off the shore before hopping aboard with an agility that their sizes belied. The Helmsman turned the pontoon around and headed out into the lake while the two men removed wooden slats from inside the crate. Then they removed a tarp covering a naked body lying on one of the pontoon's bench seats, picked the body up and unceremoniously dumped it into the crate. Picking up a six-foot fir that was lying on the deck, the two shoved it into the crate on top of the body. Then they added eight concrete blocks weighing sixty pounds that had been sitting along the sides of the pontoon, four to a side, handling them as though they were papier-mâché. Each grabbed a handful of nails from a coffee can and put them in a pocket of their jackets. The slats that had been removed from the crate earlier were set on the crate's top. Picking up hammers and getting a few nails from their pockets, each moved to a side of the crate where the Spotter positioned one of the slats and they each fastened it into position with two nails. They worked quickly and effortlessly and soon the top of the crate was covered with slats about two inches apart. Extra nails from their pockets went back into the coffee can and it and the hammers were put out of the way. The two took positions on either side of the crate and stood silently looking ahead of the boat as though on lookout but seeing only the blackness of the dark fall night.

About ten minutes later the Helmsman, who had been watching his depth finder, took the engines out of gear and the pontoon started gliding on a virtually glasslike surface. He walked to the inboard end of the crate and started pushing it up the ramp with the aid of the Driver and the Spotter until about a third of it stuck over the bow. Waiting until the pontoon had virtually stopped the Helmsman grunted and the three pushed the crate up the ramp with relative ease until gravity took over and the crate tilted, wavered, and then with a final shove slid over the side into Hibbard Pond. That final push changed the manner in which the crate went down. It was hard enough that the crate tilted forward and when it hit the bottom, it kept moving and settled on what had been the top before it was pushed off the pontoon boat. That was the second and most consequential mistake the Helmsman had made. The Helmsman went back to the con, slid the throttle from neutral to forward and turned the pontoon back the way it had come, not moving fast so as to minimize noise but this late in the season the lake was empty.

The Driver and the Spotter sat on the bench seat where the body had been and after a few minutes the Spotter broke the silence that had ensued from the time the truck entered the parking lot, "What did he do to deserve this?"

The Driver shrugged and said, "It doesn't pay to take the Boss's money or product."

~*~*~*

About our Author

Douglas Ewan Cameron

Douglas Ewan Cameron is a retired professor of Mathematics from The University of Akron, Akron Ohio. He grew up in Oak Ridge, Tennessee, attended Miami University (Oxford Ohio) and The University of Akron and received his Ph.D. from Virginia Polytechnic Institute and State University (Blacksburg, Virginia). Upon retirement, he and his wife Nancy spend their summers on the shore of Hubbard Lake in the part of Michigan's lower peninsula known as "Up North" and winters in Copley, Ohio. Douglas loves to fish and spends many summer days out on the lake fishing for walleye and smallmouth bass. Retirement has also afforded him and his wife time to travel and they have visited all seven continents. When not traveling or fishing he has been able to return to his writing, something that he was not able to do while working. The stories he writes are those that have occurred to him while either fishing or traveling.

Visit the author's website: http://books.dragonweir.com.